Read what everyone's saying about

NEVER ENOUGH

"Denise Jaden positively *nails* the love-hate relationship between two polar opposite sisters who share a single quest: the desire to be perfect, regardless of the cost. A compelling, often gut-wrenching coming-of-age novel, *Never Enough* will haunt you long after the last page."

—Jeannine Garsee, author of
Before, After, and Somebody In Between

"Denise Jaden's *Never Enough* is honest, gut-wrenching, and oh so beautiful. It's a book you can't wait to share."

—Eileen Cook, author of *Unraveling Isobel* and
The Education of Hailey Kendrick

"A poignant, important book, *Never Enough* tackles self-esteem and body image issues while always remaining true to its three-dimensional characters. Denise Jaden has created a cliché-free zone filled with hurt, heart, and personal strength. Jaden's tender sympathy for her characters and dedication to honest storytelling shine through every page."

—C. K. Kelly Martin, author of *I Know It's Over*

"Raw and unforgettable, *Never Enough* is an authentic portrait of a teen girl faced with an impossible situation. Loann's relationship with her sister is beautifully drawn and heartbreaking."

—Tara Kelly, author of *Amplified*

"A poignant look at sisterly devotion and heartache woven into a sweet tale of first love and a girl coming into her own."

—Holly Cupala, author of *Tell Me a Secret*

ALSO BY
denise jaden

Losing Faith

NEVER ENOUGH

denise jaden

Simon Pulse

New York   London   Toronto   Sydney   New Delhi

Amala Harrison

SIMON PULSE
An imprint of Simon & Schuster Children's Publishing Division
1230 Avenue of the Americas, New York, NY 10020
First Simon Pulse paperback edition July 2012
Copyright © 2012 by Denise Jaden
All rights reserved, including the right of reproduction
in whole or in part in any form.
SIMON PULSE and colophon are registered
trademarks of Simon & Schuster, Inc.
For information about special discounts for bulk purchases,
please contact Simon & Schuster Special Sales at
1-866-506-1949 or business@simonandschuster.com.
The Simon & Schuster Speakers Bureau can bring authors to
your live event. For more information or to book an event contact the
Simon & Schuster Speakers Bureau at 1-866-248-3049
or visit our website at www.simonspeakers.com.
Designed by Karina Granda
The text of this book was set in Berling.
Manufactured in the United States of America
2 4 6 8 10 9 7 5 3 1
Library of Congress Cataloging-in-Publication Data
Jaden, Denise.
Never enough / Denise Jaden. — 1st Simon Pulse paperback ed.
p. cm.
Summary: Sixteen-year-old Loann admires and envies her older sister Claire's
strength, popularity, and beauty, but as Loann begins to open up to new possibilities
in herself, she discovers that Claire's all-consuming quest for perfection comes at a
dangerous price.
ISBN 978-1-4424-2907-9
[1. Sisters—Fiction. 2. Popularity—Fiction. 3. Eating disorders—Fiction. 4.
Photography—Fiction. 5. Family problems—Fiction. 6. Self-realization—Fiction.] I. Title.
PZ7.J153184Nev 2012
[Fic]—dc23
2011033407

ISBN 978-1-4424-2908-6 (eBook)

For J. R.
because I never knew what else to do

CHAPTER ONE

They say you shouldn't try to be someone you're not. But what about someone you almost are? Or how about someone you used to be?

My sister, Claire, walked into the Alder Grove High cafeteria, and on impulse, I sat up a little straighter. As kids, people used to tell us that we were like two peas in a pod with our perfect posture. "What little ladies!" they'd always say.

We're far from twins, but I hoped others still might notice some small similarity. Our perfect posture could be the one reminder that Claire's not the secret love child of Gwyneth Paltrow and Ashton Kutcher. And I'm not the true offspring of Danny DeVito and an ungroomed poodle.

"You trying to make them look like double Ds?" my friend Shayleen blurted at me from across the table.

You know those moments when you say something embarrassing and everyone around you stops talking at that exact second?

Yeah.

Even Claire looked over to see what everyone was gawking at, and in that second, I realized how stupid I probably looked. As if I could morph my potato-like body into the skinny French fry it used to be. Claire still wore her long, lean—and erect—body as naturally as her white capri pants and strappy sandals.

I collapsed back into a slouch, wrapping my arms across my chest. Thankfully, before Claire could register another of my attempts to emulate her, Josh raced up to give her a hug, stealing her attention away.

She leaned in and whispered something in his ear. Heat circulated like lava in my veins. Josh.

As in, Josh Garrison. *The* Josh Garrison. Not the quarterback, but certainly the cutest guy on the football team. I gripped my arms tighter, wondering if she was whispering about me.

This was Josh, the guy I'd been silently swooning over since middle school.

Josh, my sister's boyfriend of three weeks, two days—I checked my watch—and about twenty-two hours.

Claire looked over again, but this time, the second my eyes met hers, her mouth broke into a huge smile, like her face wasn't big enough to contain it. My embarrassment calmed with her excitement. Whatever she might have been saying about me didn't look to be bad. She leaned in to say something else to Josh and then pointed in my direction. I resisted the urge to touch my chest. *Who, me?*

I was sitting with my friends Shayleen and Deirdre at our usual table, close to the cash register. Shayleen had her attention where it usually was: on her pocket mirror and eyeliner. I had to wonder, wasn't she already wearing enough? She'd overemphasized her already large eyes and lips, making her look a little like Betty Boop. She was my reason for going easy on the makeup. Well, that and my lack of skill at applying it.

Shayleen and Deirdre looked up just as the rest of the most popular group of seniors turned our way. Other juniors probably didn't have the same kind of senior envy we did. I think it stemmed from the fact that all three of us fit better with the freshman crowd than with our own class. Deirdre looked about twelve with her freckles and pixie cut, Shayleen had a habit of throwing juvenile temper tantrums about breaking a nail or something equally catastrophic, and I could pretty much walk upright through a doggie door. Not only was I the shortest person in the entire junior class, I was also the youngest. My parents registered me for kindergarten at the tender age of four, thinking I'd be some kind of prodigy like my sister.

It was only natural that the three of us "youngsters" had bonded, but Shayleen was the only one who seemed determined to break out of our mold. She had a broader circle of friends than either Deirdre or I, but always wanted to make more—especially of the senior boy variety. She practically frothed at the mouth toward my sister's friends. Deirdre just gaped at the group of them.

"Hey," I said, trying my best to act normally. Hopefully, if I broke my friends' stunned gazes, we wouldn't look like the starstruck nerds that we were. "What's for lunch?"

"What *is* for lunch," Shayleen stated, looking Josh up and down. He'd gone back to ordering his food, and thankfully the rest of the group also quickly lost interest in our little envy fest.

Shayleen knew I'd had a crush on Josh for forever, and she said things like that to egg me on, even if he was way out of my league. But still, when she continued to eye him, it irked me. I motioned to a wrapped gift sitting on the table beside her.

"What's that?" I cringed inwardly at my question. I'd always been annoyed by people who made a big deal of their own birthday.

Shayleen turned her attention back to our table. "For you, of course!" She passed it over. "It's from both of us." Deirdre started to interrupt with a "But . . ." when Shayleen cut her off, asking me what I got from my parents.

I rolled my eyes. "You know what my mom's like. She gave me these clothes that I'll *never* wear." I pulled open the pink shimmery wrapping of Shayleen's gift. A few people glanced over at the flashy paper.

I barely had the back of the present open when I recognized it. More pink. Which was *not* my favorite color. But it wasn't just the color. Shayleen's gift was the exact same shade and texture as the tank top I'd gotten from Mom last night.

We'd had an early family birthday party because Mom and Dad both had to work late today. When I first saw the outfit Mom had gotten me, I figured there had to have been some mistake. She must have bought it for Claire and forgotten to give it to her for Christmas. Pink made my sister look like a fairy princess. Mom must've missed my sweats-abounding wardrobe and my acreage of boobage.

I swallowed, turning over the gift from Shayleen. Sure enough, the same dainty white flower shone up at me like a beacon of femininity.

The beacon had the *wrong* girl.

I'd never liked the term "tomboy." I felt instead like I simply brought balance to the force of Claire's flowery life. I could understand my mother wanting me to be more like Claire. But Shayleen and Deirdre?

"Uh, thanks. Wow," I said, trying to sound happy and dazzled and all those other positive emotions I wasn't feeling.

Shayleen pulled the tank fully from the wrapping, letting it fall open. "I hope I got the right size. Here, hold it up."

I did as she said, purposely keeping it a foot away from me, as though the distance would hide the discrepancy between the size of the tank and the size of my breasts. In that second, I realized what seemed really strange about the tank top: it would perfectly suit Shayleen, especially with her dark skin and hair. Part of me wanted to push it back and hold it up to *her*.

"I hope it'll fit." Shayleen gave me a sideways look, scrunching her mouth a little in decision. I glanced at Deirdre for help. It wouldn't seem so rude if *she* told Shayleen it would look much better on her.

But Deirdre's dilated eyes looked like she'd been hypnotized. I followed them a few feet away.

Claire. Coming straight for me. With Josh Garrison on her heels, carrying a tray full of food.

Claire let out this lighthearted laugh before she'd even reached us.

"Look what Shayleen gave me," I said, at the exact same time that Claire said, "Why'd you bring *that* thing to school?" She glanced behind her, laughing again, and that's when I noticed how many people had followed Claire to our table. At least six, but it felt like a hundred. I sat there stunned, unable to speak, while Claire's best friend, Jasmine, went on.

"Your mom always gets the most unsuitable clothes, Loann. I mean, can you see her in that tank top?" Jasmine said to Claire. Jasmine had been over for my birthday dinner last night. Claire had asked me if it was okay to invite her, and I figured, why not? Now I knew why not.

Shayleen's face went from its normal flawless bronze to a deep tomato red. "What did you say?" she demanded.

Jasmine didn't seem to notice the edge in Shayleen's tone or me motioning toward the wrapping paper. "Did you bring the miniskirt, too?" she asked me. I shook my head, silently praying that Jasmine wasn't about to make any kind of judgments on miniskirts. Shayleen was wearing one.

There was an awkward pause while everyone digested what had just been said. Recognition eclipsed Claire's face first. She looked down at the discarded wrapping paper, then at Shayleen. She nudged Jasmine.

"Oh, you got this for Loann?" Jasmine's words tapered off until they were almost a whisper, which made the whole episode seem even more humiliating for Shayleen. As if that wasn't bad enough, now that the seniors had joined our little discussion I could feel stares from all over the cafeteria.

"Look, it was a stupid idea," Shayleen seethed, "and it's the last time I'll ever get you a gift." She pushed herself to a standing position.

"Wait," I said, reaching for her hand, but she brushed it

out of reach, spun, and marched for the cafeteria doors. The doors smacked shut behind her.

I turned to Claire for help. She always knew how to deal with people, how to solve problems that required charisma and diplomacy.

"You should let her cool off," Claire said, reading my mind. "That Shayleen has quite a temper on her."

I jerked my head in what might look like a nod, barely being able to function with Josh in such close proximity. I would just have to stay as still as possible until they made their way to their usual table near the window. Then I could calm down and talk over Shayleen's hostility with Deirdre.

"It's Loann's birthday," Claire announced, picking up the gift wrap and folding it. "Do you mind if we sit with her?"

Her friends surrounded our table like the Northern Lights, bright and brilliant in all their glory. I cowered in my seat. I wasn't sure who Claire was asking, but if it was anyone at *my* table, I doubted it would be taken as anything but rhetorical.

Claire knew how much the upset with Shayleen would eat away at me and was trying to make me feel better. My sister wouldn't want my birthday ruined if she could help it.

I thought Claire would squeeze in beside me, but instead she took the seat across the table. Deirdre shifted to make room for her. A few other seniors sat at the far end of the benches on either side. Jasmine and Lazarus—aka Jaz and

Laz, a nickname Jasmine had come up with before they were even dating—stood staring down at Deirdre.

This was a problem. Jasmine obviously wanted to sit beside her best friend, Claire, and I wondered if in Deirdre's awed state she'd be able to figure that out.

"Hey, Deirdre, could you . . ." I nudged my head to the side.

Suddenly Deirdre looked like she'd been woken up by electrical currents. "Oh! Of course!" She grabbed her bag lunch and cleared out of their way. Only I guess she'd taken my suggestion more drastically than I'd intended, and moved to the next table. She sat down and picked at the bottom of her short hair like she always did when she was embarrassed.

Great. Now I've alienated both of my friends. I opened my mouth to call her back, but when I glanced at the empty seat still beside me, my mouth went dry. Josh stepped over the bench and his leg brushed mine as he sat down.

Sure, he was sitting across from his girlfriend, my sister. But I had never, ever been this close to him. Close enough to smell his musky boy scent. Even though I'd crushed on him for years, it's not like I ever expected to do anything about it. It was more like a celebrity crush, and I felt as nervous as I would sitting three inches away from Zac Efron. I was certain my heartbeat was as loud and erratic as a pinball machine.

Claire slapped one of her schoolbooks on the table in front

of her, interrupting my cardiac arrest. It was kind of bitter-sweet, Claire dating Josh. It irritated me and yet gave me these beautiful opportunities to be near him I'd otherwise never have.

"Happy birthday, Loann," Josh said quietly, like it was a shared secret. I met his eyes and his adorable, slightly off-center smile made my lips tremble.

I cleared my throat for some composure. *He's my sister's boyfriend*, I reminded myself, though I was as likely to score an Olympic gold in men's pole-vaulting as I was to have a chance with someone like Josh Garrison.

"I hope you like my gift," Josh half-whispered in my direction.

Suddenly I had no feeling in my hands. Or the rest of my body, for that matter. *Josh got me a gift? He must be joking.* But he was so absorbed in his lunch, it was impossible to tell. His hand brushed my leg as he shifted on the bench and my heart stopped dead for a few seconds.

Get a grip, Loann.

Claire and her other friends chattered about classes and teachers and after-school plans. I could barely keep up. Deirdre watched from a few feet away with a huge grin on her face, like she couldn't believe her luck getting to hang out with these people. Or at least *near* them.

Even though all the conversation at our table centered on

my sister and her friends, it was way more entertaining than any normal day for me at Alder Grove High. I wondered how my sister handled living with this kind of adrenaline.

Purely out of nerves, I opened my sandwich and scarfed it down as though I was watching a really good movie. But I couldn't get what Josh had said out of my mind. He had a gift for me. *Seriously?*

Claire scrunched her nose at me and I realized how rude my gorging probably looked. A couple of the other girls at the end of the bench were also raising their eyebrows.

"Did you forget your lunch again?" I asked Claire, to divert the attention from me. Claire forgot her lunch on the kitchen counter so often I'd started counting on it for my after-school snack.

"No." She concentrated on the paper she'd pulled out to doodle on. I could dazedly daydream for hours, but Claire couldn't let thirty seconds go by without doing something with her hands. "I have a big history test after lunch. Nerves," she said.

As the girls started talking again, I felt a nudge to my arm.

"I love a good sandwich with lots of protein," Josh said, as if to make me feel better. "Makes me strong and fast." The football player in him clapped his hands together and rubbed them like even lunchtime was a competitive sport.

I was tempted to push the rest of my turkey sandwich in

his direction so he could enjoy it, or inspect it for protein levels, but thankfully caught myself. He had a full plate of shepherd's pie in front of him. And besides, passing a half-eaten sandwich to someone you barely know is just weird. "It's good, too!" I said, cringing inwardly at my overenthusiasm.

Claire slid her golden-brown hair behind her ear as she doodled. It wasn't a picture, just her name in big, embellished letters. Her full name first: Claire Isabella Rochester. Then just her middle name with a loop from the last *a* all the way around to the *I*. Then just "Claire" in letters so ornate I decided someone should name an opera after her.

My name wasn't nearly as pretty. Loann Rochester. No middle.

Lo, as in low—the story of my life. Low man on the family totem pole, low grades in school, and a full six inches shorter than Claire. Then there's the second half: Ann—aka ordinary. Take everything flashy in the world: metallic eye shadow, sparkly clothes, red sports cars—Claire—and wipe it all off the face of the earth. Basically, I'd be what's left. I've always wondered if people grow into their names or if it's just one big coincidence when someone like me ends up with a name like Loann.

As if Josh could sense my insecurity, I swear his foot touched the top of my sneaker. Nibbling at my crust, I waited a second to see if he'd do it again.

A little blond Superman curl fell onto his forehead and I had the urge to reach up and twirl it in my fingers.

He caught me looking and, pulled on the curl, letting it spring back up again, like he was teasing me with it.

Then. He winked.

I breathed in through my nose slowly and convinced myself I'd misread it or it was nothing or maybe he was just being nice because it was my birthday or sandwiches and shepherd's pie gave him a homey feeling and I reminded him of his sister. Or maybe, oh, I don't know, maybe he was just way too nice, and why couldn't I stop thinking about my sister's boyfriend?

My stomach started to bulge with a turkey sandwich and about a million acrobatic, caffeine-overdosing butterflies. The girls at the table all laughed at some joke I missed. I took one deep breath after another, trying to bring my body temperature down from a boiling point.

Laz stood, saying something about wrestling practice and a coach and something else I didn't hear. Jasmine gathered her things and said she'd go with him. *To wrestling practice? Whatever. They were pretty much Siamese twins.*

But Laz obviously had the same thought. "You can't come into the locker room, hon. You know that."

She gave him a pouty look, so he leaned in to wipe it off with his lips. Josh got up too, and seemed to have a silent, nodding conversation with my sister.

"I'll be right back," he said, as he followed Laz out of the cafeteria. As sad as I was that he'd left, I was glad he'd be back. And that I'd have a chance to catch my breath.

"So, I wasn't going to say anything yet," Jasmine said, watching the boys walk away, "but I'm just way too excited! I got into the U!"

This grabbed the attention of the entire table. There was a pause while no one reacted. I admit, I felt a little stunned. Jasmine could barely think her way through a traffic light and it was hard to picture her walking the grounds of the University of Wisconsin.

"Seriously," she added.

This seemed to kick everyone into excited banter. The girls at the end of the table let out squeals of excitement. Comments flew so fast I couldn't place any of them. "No way!" "I got in, too!" "When did you find out?"

Claire smiled with her own congratulations. But even though she had gotten early acceptance to the same university, I could see something else in the way her eyes drooped slightly and didn't light up with the rest of her face.

Was this one area in which Claire thought she'd trumped Jasmine, and now she was sad because Jasmine had caught up? Or did Claire, for some strange reason, not want to go to college with her bestie?

Claire met my eyes, blinked a few times, and then her

whole face brightened. I had the feeling she wasn't *that* happy to see me. She just didn't want me to read her right now.

And that was one thing we had always been good at. She'd succeeded in distracting me from Shayleen's outburst, the same way she'd realized I needed help talking to our parents when I got a D in math last year. I didn't save her the way she did with me, but I at least understood.

And right now I understood she didn't want to talk about this.

"Josh's back," I blurted, and then gave an inconspicuous slap to my chest to kick-start my heart again.

He walked toward us—toward me!—a gold-wrapped, toaster-size box with flouncing purple ribbons in his hands.

Josh placed it in front of me, then sat down again, leaning in even closer.

I hesitated, a little afraid to get fingerprints on the wrapping.

"I came up with the idea myself." Claire beamed.

So the gift was from both of them? Even though another twinge of jealousy hit at the idea of them doing "couple things" like this, my foot bounced under the table. I'd never even dreamed that Josh would give *me* a gift.

I dug a blunt fingernail along the tape and yanked at the ribbons. All eyes at the table stayed on me and my shaky hands. Eventually the wrapping came free and I pried open the cardboard box inside.

At first I couldn't tell what was inside, and I had to pull the heavy object all the way out of the box to see it.

"It's a camera," Claire confirmed, clapping her hands.

A camera? Okay. But this wasn't the miniature digital kind of camera Mom had. It was a gargantuan fossil of a thing with a large, round lens sticking off of it like the cannon on a tank.

"Do you . . ." Claire ducked her head down to try to meet my eyes and I realized I was grimacing. I forced a quick smile.

"So cool!" I said, looking between Claire and almost at Josh.

"It's used," Josh said with a shrug. "But Claire saw it at my place and thought it might be your kind of thing."

It was *his!* My cheeks warmed. I rotated the camera, staring at the zillions of buttons and sliders and gizmos to adjust. When I held it up and pressed the button on top, the mechanics inside sprang to life, surprising me and making me nearly drop it.

"You've always been so artistic," Claire said, scratching her nail into a dent in the table. "Those paintings you brought home last year, and with drama."

Okay, true, I've always taken art and drama, but only in an attempt to make up for my waning academics. Still, my face felt like it was about to catch fire with all this attention and compliments.

"Here's some instructions from the Internet," Claire went on. "But I don't know, they seem pretty complicated."

"I might be able to help you figure them out, if you need." Josh nudged me with his elbow again, and in three seconds I pictured our entire lives together: taking pictures in our yard, hanging them in our house, inviting our couple friends over to see.

The others at the table had lost interest quickly after I'd opened the gift, and I could tell by the way Claire kept picking at the table that she felt unsure of whether to keep focusing on me or turn her attention to them.

I gave her a nod to let her know it was okay if she ignored me now, but instead she said, "I know you don't like being in front of the camera, or onstage . . ." She flipped her hair and that garnered the attention of the girls at the table. "But you're the perfect person to meld into the background and capture everything around you."

My hand slipped on the edge of the camera box and I gave myself a paper cut. Sucking on my finger, I tried to process her words. *Did she really just say I might as well just fade into the background? In front of everyone? Okay, I knew I was no match for her talent and grace and beauty, but was I that unimportant?*

I looked over at Josh and he was nodding, but I couldn't tell if it was at me or at Claire or at the story Jasmine had just started telling.

The bell rang, and I swallowed my embarrassment. I didn't want Claire's words to end my birthday lunch. "Thanks for the camera!" I said, forcing some volume as they all stood and the din in the cafeteria rose. "And for saying I was creative," I added, practically shouting, but I don't think a single one of them heard me.

Before I could think of another way to get their attention, they were gone.

CHAPTER TWO

When I arrived at my locker, the quiet guy assigned the one next to mine was hunched over, struggling with his lock. I knew of him from my drama class, but he was one of those quiet nonparticipators who always sat at the back.

It seemed he'd slipped his padlock on backward and was having an awful time with it. Something about his tall, lanky frame bent over, his tongue wedged out to the side, and his big hands fumbling over the small lock made me smile. He looked like a little kid trying to untangle the chain on his first two-wheeler. An exceptionally *tall* little kid.

"Here, let me try," I said, placing my camera box at my feet. "I'm short. I can probably get right underneath it."

He laughed, but at five feet nothing, it wasn't much of an

exaggeration. He gave me the combination one number at a time, and it occurred to me as I dialed to the last number that he was putting a fair amount of trust in a stranger. I was the opposite. I kept things private, never even giving Shayleen or Deirdre my combination, and we'd been friends for years.

I popped off the lock and passed it to him.

"Thanks." He took it and met my eyes, but only for a second.

"No problem." When he slung the lock through the open latch, I saw the 1492 stamped above it. I sang the little Columbus rhyme I'd learned in elementary school in my head. "You must be Christopher," I said playfully.

He hesitated, looking lost. "Uh, no. Marcus."

"Mmm. I think I'll call you Christopher."

Marcus studied my poker face, furrowing his brow slightly, then nodded.

"I'm Loann." I slid the camera into the bottom of my locker and reached for my books for next class.

I didn't expect a reply, so his voice surprised me. "Yeah, I think I'll call you . . . Curly Fries."

I suppressed a cringe. My übercurly (read: frizzball) hair was the most noticeable thing about me. Shayleen avoided talking about my hair but she often glanced up like there was something really wrong with it. Marcus's blunt recognition of the state of my hair—I didn't quite know what to do with that. But I shot him a grin anyway. He seemed nice, and I wondered why I'd never talked to him before. Well, besides the fact that I rarely talked to boys.

"So is that yours?" He motioned to the pink tank top draped over the camera box.

"Um, it was a gift." Even though it was folded and he couldn't see the Kleenex size of the thing, my face flushed.

He scrunched up his face, looking between me and the tank. "Hmmm. Pink? Really?"

A small part of me loved the fact that this total stranger could figure out this one thing about me: *No, pastel pink is not my color—thanks, Mom. And Shayleen. Maybe you should take lessons from Marcus here.*

He finished with his things and shut his locker. "See ya, Curly."

As he fed his lock through its hole in the proper direction, I replied, "Going to sail the ocean blue, Chris?"

I tapped his locker number, and suddenly the 1492 registered. He coughed out a laugh and walked away.

Art class was next, and since I didn't want to run into Shayleen quite yet, I cut through the cafeteria to the electives wing. I hoped to ask Mr. Dewdney if he'd marked my portfolio before class started.

Eagerness to check my grade may give the impression that I'm Artiste Extraordinaire. I'm not. I mean, I try. I've always loved the way the slightest change in shadow and light can give drastically different effects, but I only seem to recognize this in other people's projects. I can't accomplish it myself. Besides, a few of Mr. Dewdney's tightly structured projects this year have killed my creativity.

Still, I worked really hard on the portfolio. It wasn't like I expected a college scholarship from it, but maybe an A.

When I rounded the corner into his room, Mr. Dewdney emerged from a supply closet at the back.

"I was wondering if you've marked any of the portfolios," I said, breathless.

He waltzed toward his desk at the front, his eyebrows knit together. "Yes, I've marked a few, but I haven't seen yours. Are you sure you handed it in?"

Am I sure I handed it in? No, I just spent five hundred hours making it perfect and then left it at home. I cleared my throat and held back the sarcastic comment that was practically nose-diving off of my tongue about how mine was the very *first* portfolio handed in, well ahead of the due date.

"Positive," I told him, keeping my face straight.

He flipped through a pile of portfolios on the table behind him. When he uncovered my bright-red folder, I yelled, "That's it!" as if he had just found my missing arm. He flipped through it, and as he did, I could see sticky notes throughout with red-pen scratchings. His comments.

Finally, he shut it. "Um, no. I haven't had a chance to give it a final grade yet, I'm afraid." He glanced up to the clock. "I'm working my way through the pile and will have to go back over some of them again." The way he motioned toward the pile, you'd swear it reached the ceiling.

I swallowed, and walked to my seat, suddenly noticing the room was full. I was too stunned to say "Thanks for checking," or anything at all to anyone.

It's not like I needed to be a natural performer or good with boys, like Shayleen. Or multi-talented and popular like my sister. All I've ever wanted was to be kind of good at *one* thing. Worth a second look. Maybe a compliment.

But not only was my work not good enough for an A, it wasn't good enough to *remember*.

CHAPTER THREE

At home after school, I had only my nagging mind to keep me company. I questioned whether Claire was right about me. If she thought I should just fade into the background, is that what everyone thought? Was I just a vase or knickknack on the shelf of the rest of humanity?

It wasn't like I needed to be in the spotlight. I'd never be the star of a ballet recital or step-dance captain like Claire, and that was okay. So why did I feel the need to keep trying to compete at that level?

I didn't, I decided. Who needed that superstar stuff? Not me. I could be happy in the background if I didn't always see it as such a bad place to be. I set the brown cardboard box with my new camera on my bed and flipped through the instructions.

Mom and Dad wouldn't be home for hours. After some water damage to our house three years ago, my parents had had to put the whole repair amount on their credit cards. Mom increased her hours to full-time at the nursing home and Dad started working overtime at least a couple of days per week to keep up with the bills. Even if it was my birthday, I knew it was just what they had to do.

But I *did* take offense that Claire had after-school plans that she thought were much more important than me. It had been only a couple of years ago when she'd rushed home to pin up balloons and hide my gifts.

But she was busy and popular now, and I knew I should be happy for her. I *was* happy for her. Except that sometimes I wasn't.

I flipped ahead a few pages in the camera manual until I found the instructions for loading the film. They seemed easy enough to understand. Following step by step, I inserted a roll of film.

When I picked up the loaded camera, its weight made it feel important. As I ran my hand over the buttons at the top, my brain surged on how intricate and stimulating and inventive photography could be.

In the instructions I found a layout of how to adjust the amount of light that came through the lens, and thought back to a picture Mr. Dewdney had drawn in art class of a big house with an eerie shaded quality. At the time, I'd done my best to copy it, but my drawing had turned into a muted mess of colors. It was completely unrecognizable.

A photograph. Now *that* you could recognize without even trying.

Even though I heard Claire come in sometime after dinner, I was absorbed and didn't bother opening my door. I fell asleep with the camera on my chest, the instructions spread across my bed like a treasure map. There was so much more to play around with than on Mom's little digital point-and-shoot model.

The next morning my birthday disappointments had vanished and I woke up with a smile on my face, thinking:

I have a cool new camera.

The camera was a gift from my sister and *Josh*.

Josh sat with me, smiled at me, and winked at me during my birthday lunch.

Why did I always have to focus on the negative, on all the ways that my life wasn't good enough?

Two jocks stood right inside the school's front entrance when I walked in. They laughed and said something I couldn't hear as I walked past. Normally I would have wanted to be swallowed up by my hoodie, but today their reaction made me pull my shoulders back and walk a little taller.

When Marcus arrived at his locker, he focused on his books, not even saying hello. I tried not to take it as a snub. It probably had nothing to do with me. Maybe he was just incredibly shy and I'd have to work a little harder at getting him to talk to me each day.

The idea made me smile. That could be kinda fun.

I turned, about to open my mouth, when he said, "Did your highlighter explode?" He gestured to my shirt—a gray tee with a big orange blob that said *SPLAT* across it. "That happened to me once, only mine was green and went all over my hands."

He said it with such a straight face, it took me a second—and a twitch at the side of his mouth—to realize he was joking. He wasn't *that* shy, it just took him a little while to start a conversation. We were similar that way—not quick-mouthed like Shayleen.

I nibbled the inside of my cheek, holding back a smile. "Or maybe you just *told* people it was your highlighter after a really big sneeze."

His stoicism was no match for *my* dry humor. He reached up like he was wiping his mouth, but I caught the edges of a smile there first. I liked how he didn't hand his smiles over easily. How he was making me earn them.

"Later," I said, waving a hand over my head as I spun and headed off to class.

All through English I noticed weird looks shooting my way from people I had never spoken to before. Jocks. Cheerleaders.

A folded turquoise paper was making its way around the room and I wondered if that had something to do with it, since the note conveniently bypassed me.

Seriously, what were we, in sixth grade? I had more important things to think about than if people were sending around notes saying "Loann has a fat ass" or whatever. I still had to tweak the last paragraph of my essay before handing it in. *Grow up, people.*

Thankfully our teacher quickly took over, and I didn't think about the strange looks again until drama.

A lot of students take Mr. Benson's drama class because it's nonthreatening. He rarely calls on students who want to fly under his radar, and likes to work with those who participate. The kids who love to get involved sit in the front, people like Shayleen, who's about as shy as a tornado.

And I'd always sat with her. But today she leaned in, murmuring with Deirdre and two other guys. Maybe my insecurity had risen because of the weird looks in English class, but I immediately wondered if it was about me. Shayleen had had temper tantrums, yes, but I'd always let her cool off. She was obviously no longer the object of anyone's scorn after yesterday's lunch episode, judging by all of the people huddled around her. So the whispering probably had nothing to do with me, I reasoned silently. I was overreacting.

I sucked in a breath and marched for my usual seat beside Shayleen. She didn't look my way, but with the giggling going on between her and her crew, I didn't really know if she'd noticed me.

Turning to the back of the room, I found Marcus and gave him a little wave. He returned it, along with a few scrunches of his nose—like he was going to let go of a really big sneeze—and then checked out his shirt and his hands to see if anything had exploded on them. I laughed quietly.

I'd never considered myself one of the nonparticipators like him—I'd *always* sat in the front—but now that I thought about it, when *was* the last time I'd volunteered for one of the drama games? The most I ever did was call out prompt suggestions when Mr. Benson asked for them.

Maybe I was more like Marcus than I realized.

The group around Shayleen dispersed to their seats when Mr. Benson started class with a long spiel about this year's play. Shayleen watched our teacher intently, nodding her head at regular intervals. She looked consumed with thoughts of getting a good part in the play, and I was glad that she'd forgotten yesterday's outburst.

Except she leaned in her seat to angle toward Deirdre and away from me. I heard whispering from behind me, from the guys she'd been talking to. Something wasn't right. I could feel it.

By the time the bell rang at the end of class, Shayleen had not looked in my direction once. I tried to keep talking myself down about it, but when she stood and turned for the door, I decided I needed to know if she was still mad.

"Hey, Shay . . ." I said.

She stood with her back to me for several seconds so I couldn't read her.

"I'm, um, sorry about yesterday," I said. Because I was. Even though there was nothing I could have done about it, I did feel bad that Claire and Jasmine had embarrassed her in front of everyone. "My sister and her friends . . . they can be like that," I added.

Shayleen turned around slowly, her eyes narrowing. "So now everything's your sister's fault?"

"That's not what I meant. I—"

She cut me off, slapping a turquoise paper down on the desk in front of me. Then, with a smirk, she spun toward the door and marched away.

I flipped over the paper and my eyes widened at the lines of text. This *was* the sixth grade! Literally.

Shayleen had printed off a quiz—a private quiz—I'd done at least five years ago when we emailed each other almost every day. She'd obviously copied it on bright paper so it wouldn't be missed. I gripped the edge of my desk and stared down at the list.

Most of them were lame questions about favorite movies and books, and there was nothing too embarrassing. Except for the last three:

Have you kissed a boy? NO! But *WANT* to!

Have you ever had a boyfriend? Sadly, no.

If you could kiss a boy, who would it be?

JOSH GARRISON

The asterisks were mine, along with a Google Image of a pair of pursed lips I'd included at the bottom. If the header of my email address wasn't enough to identify me, Shayleen had scribbled the words YOUR SISTER'S BOYFRIEND, LOANN? right underneath. Of course it didn't mention that Claire didn't even *know* Josh when I'd answered this.

My face burned. How many people had seen the paper this morning?

For the rest of the day, my main agenda was this: Avoid Shayleen, avoid Claire, and hopefully—please, God—avoid Josh. *It will blow over in a few days*, I told myself again and again and again under my breath. I avoided people's eyes in the hallways and ignored their whispers in my classes.

The only person I came face-to-face with was Marcus.

He gave me a playful nudge with his elbow at our lockers. Because I was off in another world, I lost my balance.

"Ha, ha," I said, righting myself, but truthfully, after holding in my frustration and embarrassment all day, it almost brought tears to my eyes. "Don't tell me *you* don't know your own strength," I said with as much sarcasm as I could muster to cover up my fragile emotional state. As soon as it left my mouth, though, I wondered if it might have sounded pretty mean. The guy wasn't exactly oozing muscle.

But he came back quickly with, "Is that an invitation for an arm-wrestle?" He lifted his eyebrows a couple of times in quick succession.

I licked my finger and striped it in the air, giving him one point, mostly for distracting me and bringing a smile back to my face. He closed his locker with a bump of his hip. "Later," he said on his way to his next class.

At least he hadn't said anything about the turquoise paper. But the more I thought about it, he'd have to know someone who was passing around a copy to actually see it.

I spent the lunch hour alone on the grass outside the back of the school, and after last class I left the building before the bell finished ringing, my book bag already packed for home.

I sulked quietly in my room for about an hour before a faint tap sounded from the bathroom that joined my room on one side and Claire's on the other.

I swallowed. I hadn't heard Claire downstairs and I'd assumed—hoped—she had after-school plans.

"Come in," I murmured.

Claire pushed through the door with a mug in her hand. Her head tilted to the side in concern, and in a second I knew she'd seen the turquoise paper. And worse, she wasn't mad. Not at all. She pitied me.

I chafed a finger back and forth over the edge of my thumbnail. I didn't want Claire and her perfect world anywhere near me right now.

"I heard about what happened," she said, in this caring voice that reminded me of when we were younger. It was nothing like her strong and confident school voice, the voice she'd used at the lunch table yesterday. I don't know how she pulled off a dual personality like that.

She held the mug out toward me and I noticed a few magazines in her other hand. "That Shayleen really doesn't know when to stop."

After a long second, I took the mug from her, smelling the sweet chocolate steam, and placed it on my nightstand without taking a sip. "Thanks," I said.

She sat beside me on my bed. Years ago, Claire laid on my

bed daily, flipping through fashion magazines, going through quizzes, or asking my opinion on things, even though it was obvious way back then that she had better taste.

Silence fell between us. I think we both knew we wouldn't be able to bond over stupid magazines anymore. But sitting with her did make me feel a little bit better.

Claire put her hand on my knee. "It'll be okay, Loey. It will."

The moment was sweet, like we'd gone back in time together. She wasn't this popular, perfect person. She was just my sister. My sister who would make things better with Shayleen if I asked her to. Heck, she'd probably even break up with Josh if that's what would make me happy.

There's something peaceful about knowing that someone cares more about you than anything else in the world.

Even if it is only for a moment.

CHAPTER FOUR

I had never been so glad for a weekend.

I didn't have to put up with stares—or glares, in Shayleen's case—from anyone at school. With all my homework done early on Saturday, I stared at the camera sitting on my desk. Every time I came back to it, it seemed intimidating all over again.

I skimmed through the instructions to where I'd left off. There was a lot to learn—about aperture, shutter speed and lens care, how to adjust the focus on different distances, ideas for placing my subjects—and this was just the basics!

I tried a few test shots around the house. Claire held a hand out like a stop sign whenever I came near her, but Mom was happy to be my first real subject.

My mother stood halfway between Claire and me in all respects: five-three, with hips like mine, yet lean like Claire. She had dull coffee-colored hair with more wave than Claire's silk tresses and still miles from my frizzy coils. She had the ability to say all the right things, but could cackle in the middle of a library.

Mom waltzed through the house, saying, "Here, Loann, get a shot of me by the banister." She moved with a flourish, like she was sure she'd missed her calling as a supermodel. Too bad her oversized Saturday work shirt and mussed-up hair didn't complete the image. By the glint in her eye, though, I think she knew we were both out of our element and just having fun. "See, this is the kind of natural, spur-of-the-moment thing that makes a great photo, Loann," she said, opening the oven door. We both burst out in laughter.

When Mom got bored with parading around and showcasing the household appliances, I focused my energy on nature. I photographed the oak tree in our backyard: tall, covered in new leaves, looming over our house like a bushy guardian. It was the perfect perch for sparrows, blue jays, and other small birds, but unfortunately there were none around today for me to capture on film. Focusing on the tree at different angles became my second choice.

The more photos I took, the more I wanted to search out and capture something deeper—better—from the world around me. I explored for hours in our backyard. When I found something—a blade of grass from inches away, or a spider building its web—my heart sped up and I fumbled my fingers over the intricate adjustments of my new camera to frame it.

Click.

I headed into the house for a drink and found Claire stretched out on the living room floor, flipping through a beauty magazine. I'm sure she went through about a hundred of them a day, with grad coming up. She was constantly trying to figure out the perfect hair or makeup or shoes, and with her intense focus she must not have heard me. Before she could say no, I pulled the camera to my eye to adjust the zoom.

Claire must have felt me there. She stared up at my camera, then gave me the strangest look. Her eyes pulled together and her jaw tensed. I tried to read her face, but her hair fell in front of it as she looked back at her magazine.

The moment was gone. I'd missed it. I lowered my camera in disappointment. It would have been a great shot. Skipping my drink, I pushed my way back out the front door and snapped pictures until I'd used all of my film.

I didn't have to ask Mom to develop my first rolls, probably because she knew she was on them. She took them off my dresser when she picked up my laundry, and returned the photos later that day.

I sighed as I started to skim through them. The lack of vibrancy and spontaneity showed just an album's worth of ordinary. My heart sank. I thought some of them might actually be good.

Then I came to a photo of the oak tree. I'd taken this one looking up the trunk. The sunlight shone between the leaves in trickles, and the shadows gave the tree an almost unearthly largeness. This was exactly what Mr. Dewdney had meant about getting the shadows right.

There was another photo with a luminous glow surrounding the tree. I'd probably missed it with the aperture, but it looked kind of cool, like a glimpse of heaven. I leaned the photos against the mirror of my dresser and flipped through the rest, thinking: *Not bad for my first time.*

CHAPTER FIVE

I had completely forgotten about Shayleen and Deirdre until they walked down the school hall toward me on Monday morning.

Before they saw me, I ducked my head and rounded the corner away from them. I didn't start to relax until I saw Marcus with his back to me at his locker.

I quickened my pace, but stopped when two guys decked out in their sports jerseys passed behind him. One of them gave Marcus a shove practically right into his locker.

"Fag," the bigger one said, and then laughed to his friend. Next to lanky Marcus, the guys looked to be at least three times his breadth.

Marcus kept his hands braced on either side of his locker so he wouldn't end up inside. The moment the jocks released him, he straightened up but kept his head down and away from them. The two jocks chortled all the way down the hall. I looked both ways and it didn't seem like anyone had noticed. No one except me.

"Hey," I said tentatively, keeping my eyes on my lock as I dialed my combination.

"Hey, Curly." His humor-infused tone surprised me, like the bullying hadn't affected him at all. He grabbed a binder and flipped it open to check its contents. "Guess I'll see you in the green room," he said, reaching over and tugging lightly on a tendril of my hair before he shut his locker and walked away.

In drama, Shayleen and Deirdre sat in their usual seats, chattering like parakeets with the rest of the overanxious front-row students. They ignored me. I stood near the door and scanned the classroom, but I already knew where I planned to sit. Sure enough, there was an open spot beside Marcus at the back.

"Curly," he said, when I sat down in the empty chair.

"Hi, Chris."

"That's Mr. Columbus to you."

I laughed, probably too loudly, and Shayleen turned to glare at me. I focused on Marcus. "Truce. Marcus, all right? I'll call you Marcus."

"Okay, Curly." He smirked and then even laughed a little. "Okay, Loann."

Marcus was nice, and funny. I couldn't figure out why he was such a loner.

"You want to get a coffee after school, Lo-Ann?" He pronounced my name like it was two very long and separate names.

"Coffee?" was all I could get out, and seemed to be my entire vocabulary at the moment. I said it again. "Coffee?"

"Yes, coffee. Ever heard of it?"

Was this a date? No, he didn't say "movies" or "dinner" or any normal date stuff. He just meant coffee.

"Um . . . okay."

Just then, Mr. Benson interrupted our conversation. "As you know, I was planning to do *Hometown Heroes* for our year-end production." Shayleen and Deirdre immediately started whispering. Deirdre had obviously picked her side against me. I tried not to be offended. I wouldn't want to go up against loud and domineering Shayleen either, if it were me. But still, it made me sad.

"The play has a large cast," Mr. Benson went on, "and so I'm asking all of my junior and senior drama students to audition." He scanned the room slowly, as if to reiterate that he meant every single one of us. I sighed inwardly. It would have been one thing to audition with Shayleen and Deirdre. In years past, we'd spent afternoons running lines with one another, anxiously awaiting our turn on the stage. I'd gotten a bit part one year, but usually I just helped backstage. As I glanced toward Shayleen, she turned to me with an obvious sneer. "Unfortunately, we didn't have enough interest for a stagecraft class this year," Mr. Benson rambled on, "and without much money in the budget . . ."

Out of my peripheral vision, I saw Marcus's arm go up. When Mr. Benson nodded in his direction, Marcus said, "Loann and I don't mind working on the set. During drama block, I mean."

Mr. Benson stared at Marcus for a few seconds, which gave me a chance to process this statement. Okay, he obviously didn't want to audition either. But besides that, I wouldn't mind not having to face Shayleen every day in class. Another thought hit me: *Was Marcus trying to find a way to be alone with me?* I swallowed a lump in my throat. Sure, I'd swooned over Josh for years, but with Marcus, I don't know, it seemed realistic for there to be a mutual attraction. Possible.

Mr. Benson cleared his throat. "Uh-huh. Well, I don't know about the *two* of you—"

My face warmed as I wondered if Mr. Benson could read my mind.

"Oh, come on, Mr. B." Everyone stared at Marcus as he said this. "I can't do it alone. You'd normally have a full crew, and we'll get the job done, I promise."

Mr. Benson looked back and forth between us. I nodded

in agreement for good measure. A guy across the room made a catcall in our direction, but Marcus and I ignored him, staring down the teacher.

Finally Mr. Benson sighed. "All right. See me after class."

For the next forty minutes, Marcus and I snuck looks at each other, and by the way his fingers thrummed on the side of his chair, I knew he was excited about this. Which made my excitement bubble up too.

When Mr. Benson showed us backstage, my face fell. It was cluttered with what looked like decade-old debris. I didn't know a thing about set construction, even if we did have the proper supplies, which clearly we did not. But my stomach still did a flip at the thought of hanging out alone in the dimly lit area with Marcus. *That* part still seemed exciting.

"Looks great," Marcus said.

I had no idea what he was thinking, but I nodded anyway.

Mr. Benson looked us both over. "Now I can . . . trust you two alone together, right?"

My face instantly heated about four hundred degrees, but Marcus laughed, louder than I'd ever heard him. He gave a little push to my shoulder. "Of course, Mr. Benson," he said. "Loann's like my sister."

I swallowed. Really, Marcus and I hardly knew each other, but was it such a ridiculous notion that we could be more

43

than friends? I tried to keep an even smile for Mr. Benson's benefit, but I could feel my lip trembling.

"All right, then. You kids can come here for drama block, and keep me informed each week on your progress. You'll find old props and costumes in the cupboards in the wings, as well as up on the platform." He pointed to an overhead storage area stacked with boxes about halfway up to the lighting catwalk. "And I'll print you both a copy of the script. You'll be graded accordingly."

After Mr. Benson left, I turned to Marcus, waiting for him to fill me in on his plan. Because he must have some kind of plan, right? I felt a little irked about the "sister" comment, and I crossed my arms. "So. Where do we start?" I demanded.

He surveyed the junk. "Huh. Not much here to work with," he said. "You ever used one of those?" He motioned to some big tool in the corner that I didn't even recognize.

I shook my head, thinking it wasn't a great sign that he called the contraption "one of those" and was looking for *my* expertise here.

He met my eyes and, for just a second, I felt like he didn't want to look away. Like he was trying to convey something serious, but I was horrible at reading those looks. I blinked and that seemed to bring him back to the task.

"Well, I guess we'll think of something," he said, and led the way to the school doors.

* * *

I stressed out all through my afternoon classes about my drama grade. I always counted on that B to pull up my average, but now Marcus and I had to build an entire set, which seemed to carry a lot more responsibility and room for error. Just after the last bell of the day, I stood at my locker, trying to look occupied, while students swarmed past me toward the exits. If my nervousness about our stagecraft assignment wasn't enough, now I also had to think about going for coffee with Marcus. We hadn't made any detailed plans. Were we supposed to meet here?

"Hi!" Claire suddenly said from behind me.

I clutched at my chest. "You scared the crap out of me."

She giggled. "I'm off to watch Josh's football practice." She looked down at her nails. "Jaz is busy with Laz. Hey, do you want to come with me?" She said it like she'd just thought it up on the spot, but I could tell by her quick words this was the reason she'd come to find me. "Their practice starts in fifteen minutes."

Sure, I was second choice, but she wanted to watch a football practice with me? *Josh's* football practice? I nibbled my lip. What if he'd seen the turquoise paper?

As if she could read my mind, Claire said, "Josh told me he thought you were so cute the way you got all embarrassed over the birthday fuss."

Cute? Had he really said that about me? If he had seen the quiz, he obviously wasn't disturbed by it.

"Come on, Loey. We have to hurry."

"Shh. Don't call me that here." "Loey" was a nickname Claire had given me when I was a baby and she was just learning to talk. I didn't mind it at home, but at school it made me feel childish.

"Oh, right. Hey, Josh wanted to know if you liked the camera."

My palms moistened. They'd had an actual conversation about me? I hadn't seen him in the halls since my birthday. The truth was, it would be much easier to face Josh now, with Claire, than it would be if I saw him with his friends while I was all alone.

She looked at me seriously, with her eyebrows raised, and I could tell she was anxious to go. But Marcus . . . I'd never actually been invited out for coffee before and even though I was nervous, I guess part of me had really been looking forward to it. I glanced down the hall. "I kind of have plans with someone," I said finally.

She threw me a doubting glance and stuttered a little when she said, "I-I thought we could, you know, hang out."

I didn't quite know what to do with the sudden sisterly interest. Or *her* nervousness. Claire didn't get nervous around anybody, least of all me. My heart sped up at the thought of watching Josh from the sidelines. Or of him coming over to talk to us. Maybe I could chat him up about all I was learning about photography. Maybe he didn't mind that I'd had an all-consuming crush on him in sixth grade.

Not to mention now.

Marcus appeared from out of nowhere and sidled up to his locker, interrupting my thoughts. I wondered if he could do coffee tomorrow instead.

"Hey," he said quietly, like he was trying to get away with talking in class.

I knew I should probably introduce him to Claire, but part of me didn't want to. What if I did, and Marcus liked Claire more than me?

"Whoever it is will understand, I'm sure," Claire said. "Come on, we have to go."

Marcus kept his eyes down and started rearranging his books in his locker. His shoulders slumped and he already looked rejected. How would I introduce these two, anyway? Loner Marcus and my gabbing, popular sister? It didn't compute.

"Don't you have ballet?" I blurted.

"No, it's Tuesday." She rolled her eyes like I should have known that. And yeah, if my brain hadn't been on autopilot, I would have. I'm that girl that knows her whole family's schedule because I don't have enough going on in my own life.

"Come on, you know you want to." She grabbed my books and slid them into my locker.

I *did* want to. But I also wanted to hang out with Marcus. I just couldn't explain that to Claire. Her eyes bore into me. She hadn't even glanced in Marcus's direction, which was quite a feat, considering his proximity.

I stared straight into the cavern of my locker and said, "I don't think I can go." But even as the words came out of my mouth, I couldn't figure out who I was saying them to.

CHAPTER SIX

Marcus closed his locker, then turned and walked away without another word.

Claire tapped her foot. "Oh, come on, Loey. We have to hurry. I want to say hi to Josh before it starts."

Marcus was almost at the exit. *Why was she doing this? Why now?*

She took a step in the other direction and pulled at my hand. "Come on. Let's go."

I couldn't do it. Suddenly I didn't want to go to the game.

"Marcus!" I yelled, just before the door clacked shut behind him. He paused on the other side of the threshold. "Sorry," I said to Claire. "Can we do it another day?" I gave her hand a squeeze and plunked on my lock. Avoiding her eyes, I ran for the door and didn't look back.

When I caught up to Marcus, he kept his face straight ahead. "Let's go," he said, and started walking.

I followed him through the parking lot without a word. Not a *Glad you decided to come* or *Thanks for choosing me*. Nothing.

Which made me wonder . . . did I make the wrong choice?

My sister was my *sister*. We'd always looked out for each other, and the more I thought about it, maybe she really needed me today. Maybe all her other friends were busy too and she really didn't want to go to the game alone.

By the speed of Marcus's march, he clearly had no idea I was still wavering. I felt like I should apologize for almost jilting him, but really, if I needed to apologize to anyone, shouldn't it be Claire? It was pretty nice that she wanted to include me when she knows I'm not exactly popular.

But the more I battled it over in my mind, the clearer it became. Claire didn't *need* me. She'd probably already forgotten she'd ever invited me.

I was lost in my thoughts as Marcus and I plodded over the backfield and cut through someone's yard to reach Main Street. Even though I'd grown up in Alder Grove, I hadn't realized how close downtown really was. I'd always thought I needed rides to get anywhere besides school.

Marcus had a long stride and I could barely keep up. His loose black T-shirt and jeans would likely still fit him twenty pounds from now. We made an odd pair, me being a foot shorter and not nearly as skinny. My face warmed at the thought of us as a pair, especially now, off alone together. Practically a date, even if he hadn't called it one.

He rounded a corner off of Main Street and headed for an unmarked door. I'd never noticed or been in the building, so a rush of nervousness hit me. *Where is he taking me?*

Marcus pushed the thick wooden door open, and the colors inside hit me like a palpable sunrise, calming my anxiety. I stepped into what appeared to be another world.

The strong coffee aroma overtook me as the door closed behind us. The bright yellows and oranges and reds on the walls were unlike colors I'd seen in any kind of business establishment. Artwork, large and small, covered every wall, crammed next to one another like cars on a busy street during rush hour.

There were tables here and there, brown and distressed, not at all matching the atmosphere of the walls. Two old men played checkers at a corner table, but we were otherwise alone. Marcus led me to the counter and one of the old men stopped his checkers game to meet us on the other side.

"You got money?" Marcus asked me. I blinked a couple of times and then fumbled in my pocket for my last few dollars. We both shifted to get our money and our arms touched. It gave me goose bumps. Marcus cleared his throat, ordered us two large dark-roast coffees with cream and sugar, and put our money in a pile to pay for them. The old man puttered behind the counter, working on our order.

While we waited in silence, I wondered who Marcus had brought here before. It didn't seem like he had many friends, and I couldn't really picture him on a date. Did he actually like me, and he was too shy to say it, or was this just a friendship thing? It was hard to tell with him.

Finally the old man put two tall mugs on the counter, and without another word, toddled back to his game. Marcus took one mug, left mine on the counter, and headed to a table near the front window. I waited for a second, to see if he'd turn back for me. Finally, I followed, trying not to spill the hot drink on myself.

Okay, definitely not a date.

We sat and looked at our coffees. Said nothing. Looked out the window at a small walkway and the side of another brick building. Shadows moved across the brick wall as people walked along the main street at the end of the alley. Real exciting stuff. I wondered what Claire was doing now. Was she still at football practice? Was she clapping and shouting to Josh from the sidelines? I waited until Marcus started to drink and followed suit.

I cringed at the burn of the liquid on my tongue and put it down with a scowl.

Marcus snickered. "Sip," he said. "Coffee is for sipping."

I was sixteen, not four. And I knew how to drink a hot drink, thank you very much. But I guess I was distracted and nervous. We sat and stared out the window some more.

"I'm not gay, you know," Marcus said, breaking the silence.

My eyes popped open. He must have seen me in the hall this morning when the jocks were picking on him. Still, I was so surprised that he brought it up that I got tongue-tied. How could he be so casual about it? "I—I know," I said finally.

More silence. I took another drink to fill the space, this time just a sip.

"I like to come here." He glanced around. "You see that?" He pointed to a large painting across the room. I nodded. "That's Michelangelo's painting of Daniel the prophet. It's not real, but it's a good reproduction. At least Armando says so."

I stared across at the painting, displayed in an old wooden frame. "Who's Armando?"

Marcus motioned toward the checkers game, to the guy who had made our coffee. "He knows all the art. Which one do you like?"

I studied the walls, recognizing several pieces, but my eyes skimmed over those. I wanted to find something differ-ent. Something unusual. At last I settled on a frame behind Marcus.

"The one with the sailboat is cool."

Marcus turned and studied it for a minute. Nodded. "Looks scary," he said, turning back.

It did. That's why I liked it. The tiny wooden boat was weathered, with its sail torn almost in two. It didn't look like it could survive the swelling wave headed for it. But somehow I knew it could. It just had to stay strong. I always liked rooting for the underdog, the ugly duckling. I guess I felt a kinship with them.

"Yeah," I answered.

When I brought up the drama set, Marcus gave me the same vague response about figuring something out together. I liked the sound of "together," but at the same time, "Loann's like my sister" kept ringing in my head.

I changed the subject and told him about my family to remind him we *weren't* related.

"Remember the girl who was at my locker?" I asked. "She's my sister. Claire."

He nodded in a show of recognition. I braced my hands on the edge of my chair. When other students found out that Claire and I were siblings, a myriad of things followed: wanting to be introduced, needing to know every last detail about her, grasping for some explanation of how I'd come from the same gene pool.

"You don't look much alike," he said, eyeing the checkers game again, clearly bored with this topic.

I couldn't quite think of a response. "Duh," would have worked, I guess, but somehow Marcus seemed genuine in his response. I wasn't sure if I'd ever really met anyone so genuine in my life. I kept quiet and waited for him to share something about himself. But apparently he needed some prodding.

"So what about your family?"

Marcus looked out the window and nibbled at his lip. *Had I asked something wrong?* Maybe his parents had split up. Maybe one of them had died. Or maybe I was way off and he just didn't like to talk about his boring home life.

But then he gestured to the checkers game and said, "Armando, he's my uncle," so fast I barely caught it.

I glanced over at the old man and smiled. Armando was focused on his game and didn't look up. I turned my smile back to Marcus. "Do you live with him?"

Marcus tilted his head a little and pulled his eyebrows together like my question didn't make sense. "Um. No," he said slowly, but there was an edge to his voice.

I squinted. "So that's why you like to come here?" I asked.

His hands fumbled over one another on the table, and the motion made *me* nervous. "That's . . . one reason," he said. There was clearly more to the story. But it felt like an invisible barrier had gone up between us. This subject was off-limits.

We sat for a little more than an hour before I decided to head out. Mom would be home anytime after five, and it seemed easier to be there, like normal, than to answer a bunch of questions.

Marcus didn't offer to walk me home. He told me to take my cup to the counter before I left. "Armando's old," he added. Then Marcus reached over and squeezed my hand as I stood to deliver my mug.

It was only a light touch, and he didn't try to hold it or anything. But my heart skipped all the way to the counter.

When I turned back toward the door, I looked over at Marcus, expecting a smile or a nod or . . . something. But he just stared out the window, lost in thought.

CHAPTER SEVEN

"You want to go to the Arts Club Café again?" Marcus asked first thing the next day. I thought it was odd that the place had a name, since there didn't seem to be a sign.

"I don't have any money," I told him.

"I'll get it this time."

I smiled. It might not be a date, but it felt good to have someone want to hang out with me.

"You can pay me back," he added, taking a little notch out of my grin.

After school, Marcus and I headed straight to the café, where we talked more about the art on the walls. He used words like "existentialism," which I planned to Wiki when I got home.

An hour later, we ran out of things to say and I left. I'd told Claire I wouldn't be home after school, but when I turned the corner toward our house, I nearly swallowed my tongue. Josh Garrison's blue Civic sat in our driveway.

To anyone else it might have looked like an average car—a decade old with a dent in the back fender. My heart raced with excitement. To me it looked like the pearly gates of heaven welcoming me in, and as I walked toward it, I waited to hear a chorus of "Hallelujah."

I strode through the front door with a permagrin, expecting to see them on the couch, but there was total silence. I checked the kitchen, but found only a mess of crumbs on the counter. Maybe Claire made him a sandwich and then they went out to the backyard? But the only movement back there was the wind in the trees.

Mom and Dad had sat Claire and me down and talked about dating (not allowed until we're sixteen) and boys in our rooms (not allowed *ever.*)

So much for that.

I opened the front door again, but this time I slammed it, nice and loud.

A moment later, as expected, Claire's voice trilled from the upstairs hallway. "Yeah, so that's the grand tour. Not that exciting. Let's go watch some TV now, like we planned."

Claire can be a great liar, but her false words wavered. She came into view with a slightly exaggerated bounce in her step. Josh followed, looking less enthused.

"Oh, you're home!" I said, feeling like such a fraud. "Hi, Josh," I added in little more than a whisper.

Josh smiled and I couldn't help smiling back. His bright blue eyes were like the pictures of water in travel brochures that make everyone want to go on vacation. I blinked and forced myself to stop staring. The whole exchange, *in my very own house*, was making my stomach do jumping jacks toward my throat.

"I'm hungry. Want anything?" I strode for the kitchen, forcing one foot in front of the other.

"I could go for another sandwich," Josh said, dropping onto the couch beside Claire.

"My mom will be home with pizza soon." Claire patted him twice on the knee and gave a little head-shake in my direction.

I slipped into the kitchen, letting out a long-held breath.

I wasn't actually hungry, more like ready to toss my lunch from the idea of Josh being here, but I pulled cupboards open anyway, just to calm myself. It helped, and a few minutes later I walked back into the living room with a plate of crackers and a few cheese slices. I wasn't *really* disregarding Claire's instructions. And who cared if I was?

I set it down in front of Josh. "Just a little snack. You know, until dinner."

I'm pretty sure he smiled at me again, but I focused on the TV to keep my raging anxiety levels in check. In my peripheral vision, Josh leaned forward and helped himself. I inched away and sat on a chair in the corner.

Claire and Josh murmured between themselves, things I couldn't hear. Then, I couldn't believe it—Claire leaned forward and helped herself to a cracker and some cheese! It was all I could do to hold back from making a comment about ruining *her* dinner.

Not long after, Claire excused herself to the bathroom upstairs. She was funny about using the main one when guests were over. I kept my eyes drilled into the TV—it would be all I would need to have Josh catch me staring at him—but when I took a quick microglance his way, *he* was staring at *me*! The room suddenly felt warmer. And smaller.

"What?" I blurted, in all my eloquence.

He smiled, and there was something so delectable about those upturned lips. "I was just wondering if it was true? What that paper at school said?"

I coughed, nearly choking on my saliva. "I-I . . . It was from sixth grade," I said, wanting to find a bucket of ice water to submerge my head into.

"Oh." He nodded, his grin still in place but faltering just a little.

I glanced toward the stairs, and suddenly Claire was there. A rush of guilt ran hot through my veins.

I concentrated on breathing in and out, and pretended to watch TV again.

When Mom got home, I bolted out of my chair and went to meet her. She had two large boxes with a clear plastic container of salad on top. "Hi, Mom! Let me get the pizza for you. Claire's boyfriend, Josh, is over," I said at around three hundred decibels and then mentally kicked myself for it. As if that wasn't totally obvious. As if Claire shouldn't be the one to make that statement. *Shut up already, Loann!*

Minutes later we were all seated around the table, Josh right between Claire and me. It reminded me so much of our cafeteria lunch that I felt myself flush at the thought of how Josh's leg had brushed mine.

"So, Josh," Mom launched in. "It's nice that Claire could finally bring you home for dinner. You go to Alder Grove High with the girls, right?"

"Yes, Mrs. Rochester," he said, sitting up a little straighter. "I'm a junior, and on the football team. I'm hoping to get a sports scholarship next year."

I'd almost forgotten that Josh was in *my* grade and not

Claire's. We didn't have any classes together and I usually saw him with other seniors like my sister. Whether he knew it or not, though, he'd just scored major points with Mom by mentioning a scholarship.

Claire scrunched her nose when Mom passed a plate with a slice of pizza toward her, and instead asked for one of the clean plates and reached for the salad. Claire liked pizza, and Mom had ordered her favorite—vegetarian with no onions and extra peppers. The act must be because Josh was around. Though the way he was shoveling back his third piece, I doubted he cared.

"Don't hog it all, Claire," Mom said about the salad. In the last couple of years, a power struggle had cropped up between the two of them—who ate better, who dressed better, you name it. I was glad I wasn't in that particular race.

Claire had only taken one small scoop of salad, but she closed the lid and passed it back to Mom. "Don't worry," she said pointedly. "I'm really not that hungry."

After dinner, I cleared the plates, but kept one eye on Claire and Josh in the living room. Even though they were both smart in school, they sure seemed stupid sometimes. Claire gabbed nonstop in her regular blossomy way about her hair, which I'm sure bored Josh, and he talked about new football plays as though she was an aspiring coach. It was entertaining to watch—them staring into each other's starry eyes, not hearing a single word out of each other's mouths.

After cleaning up, I set my homework on the dining room table and settled in, glancing in their direction every few minutes. They didn't leave the TV.

At nine o'clock, Mom announced the time. Which meant, *Say good-bye to your friend, please, Claire* in Mom-language. Claire took the hint while Mom headed back to the kitchen with her empty wineglass. I watched Claire through my eyelashes as she walked Josh to the door. Neither of them acknowledged me, but I knew I had faded into the background over the last couple of hours, so I wasn't offended. But then Claire turned and caught me watching.

I darted my eyes back to my homework, but I guess it was too late. The door opened and they took their good-bye outside.

I was interested to see exactly how their good-night kiss worked: Would he just kiss her right away, or stroke her cheek or something so she knew it was coming? Would they both shut their eyes like they do in the movies, or do people always have to shut their eyes when they kiss? I had so many questions. Peeking out the living room window, I didn't see any sign of them near Josh's car so I raced upstairs to my window that overlooked the side yard.

I'd missed the beginning. Josh and Claire were already kissing out beside the oak tree and the streetlight gave just enough glow to see them. The jealous irk in my gut soon gave way. It was mesmerizing to see two such beautiful people kissing in real life. After the weekend I'd spent photographing our yard, *this* new addition made me want to tilt my head to try to frame it. It *would* make a great photo.

I reached across my desk to grab my camera, then pulled it up to my face, bringing Josh and Claire quickly into focus.

Seconds later, I had the shot. And it was perfect.

I placed my camera on the desk gently, then looked up in time to see Josh walking to his car. As Claire headed for the front door, Josh backed his car out of our driveway. When he pulled into the street, he looked up to my bedroom window. I stayed perfectly still, hoping the dark would conceal me. But I knew by the way his eyes lingered, my room wasn't quite dark enough.

CHAPTER EIGHT

By the next day, I was so psyched at not having to go to drama class that I'd actually picked up some of Marcus's confidence about our ability with the set.

"Come on," I said, grabbing him by the arm and dragging him through the hallway. "It's our first day of stagecraft."

His eyebrows rose, but I suspected he was holding back a smile. "What's got you so excited all of a sudden? Been taking your caffeine intravenously today? Or got some brilliant construction ideas?" When I let go of his arm, he shoved his hands deep into his pockets.

"Well, no. But I've been looking over the script and I took a book out of the library on set design. I don't know, I thought it might spark something."

Marcus didn't agree or disagree with this, but when we

walked into the backstage area and I remembered just how haphazard the whole place was, my enthusiasm faltered.

Marcus headed over to a pile of what looked like garbage and started pulling off pieces of drywall and wood. "Why don't we see if there is anything usable here first?"

Okay. *What was a usable-sized piece?* I moved over to the pile and followed his lead. I held up pieces and asked him if he thought this or that would work for anything, but his answer was always no.

"What are we going to do?" I asked under my breath for probably the hundredth time.

Marcus must have heard me, because this time he replied. "We'll figure it out," he said. "Just don't give up hope."

When the bell rang fifty minutes later, we left the place in more of a mess than we'd found it, and even though we'd flipped through my book, the elaborate designs only depressed me more.

Hope. How was I supposed to have hope?

The next couple of days were much the same, except we tidied up a bit and took the odd break to walk the stage in a vain attempt to find inspiration. We headed to the Arts Club after school each day, and I became more and more comfortable being with him, even when neither of us had anything to say. In fact, the quieter it grew, the more comfortable I became. Normally I worried about saying the right thing, but

I didn't have to worry about the way I acted or what did—or didn't—come out of my mouth with Marcus.

"Hey, drama queen," Marcus said when I showed up at our lockers Monday morning. "Can't wait to get back to our kingdom." He nodded toward the theatre.

Did that make him my king? I didn't care if it was a joke. It still warmed my insides.

I gave him an eye roll to combat my giddy smile. Just then Shayleen and Deirdre rounded the corner. Deirdre looked away like she hadn't seen me, but Shayleen stared straight at me.

As she passed by, she let out a breathy laugh.

Good. Laugh all you want. He's a real *friend*, I felt like saying. But I bit my lip.

"What do you have now?" Marcus asked, distracting me.

"Art," I gulped out. I wished I had Marcus's ability to not let things affect me.

I'd finally gotten my drawing portfolio back from Mr. Dewdney with a B at the top. The plethora of notes about different ways I should try looking at my subjects made me feel like he was being nice with the B. But I had a good eye, I knew I did. It was getting it from my head to my paper that screwed me up. If only I'd been able to submit a photography portfolio.

Mr. Dewdney chattered on about the mediums he wanted us to explore during the last month of classes. I didn't pay much attention until he said, "You'll find some interesting paper supplies in the darkroom at the back."

"The what?" I blurted. Everyone stared at me, so I sheepishly raised my hand.

Mr. Dewdney furrowed his brow and nodded in my direction. His beard looked like he hadn't bothered to trim it since the beginning of the year, and I wondered if there were rules about stuff like that.

"Um, did you say 'darkroom,' Mr. Dewdney?" With all twenty-nine other students' eyes on me, I muttered, "I was just . . ." My eyes moved to my desk in front of me. "Curious."

"Yes. Of course, with the popularity of digital cameras these days, our room is used predominantly for storage now." Mr. Dewdney cleared his throat. "It was originally designed as a small room to develop film prints," he said slowly, as though we'd all have trouble understanding the concept.

"All right, then." Mr. Dewdney clapped his hands.

My hand shot up again.

Mr. Dewdney stroked his scruffy face and looked back at me. Thankfully, the other students seemed to be losing interest.

"Can I use it?"

Mr. Dewdney's eyebrows pulled together.

"The darkroom," I said.

He pursed his lips like he was thinking about it. "Talk to me after class."

* * *

After the rest of the students filed out of the room, I stopped next to the giant metal teacher's desk. Mr. Dewdney looked up at me with a blank expression.

"The darkroom?" I offered.

"Mmm, yes." He took a sip from his coffee mug. "Now why do you want to use it, Miss . . . ?"

"Rochester. Loann Rochester." He still didn't remember my last name after an entire year of art with him. *Why do you think I would want to use it?* I felt like saying. "Um, to develop my film?"

"Oh. You don't have a digital camera?"

I shook my head, suddenly embarrassed. Up until now I'd thought myself lucky to have the camera I'd been given. But his tone, it made me feel so . . . incomplete.

"Have you ever developed your own film?" Mr. Dewdney asked.

"Mm-hmm," I lied. Surely I could figure it out.

"Well . . . I can't leave a student here alone, and I'm only here a few afternoons per week."

"So I can use it?" I bounced a little off my heels. "Thanks, Mr. Dewdney!" I held myself back from giving him a hug and practically skipped for the hallway. I didn't have any film with me, but I'd bring some tomorrow.

How hard could it be?

CHAPTER NINE

All Marcus usually wanted to do was go for coffee, and soon I developed a taste for it. But he'd paid so many times that I'd lost track of how much I owed him. I didn't exactly have allowance money sprouting from my pockets. I decided before he could offer up his invite today, I would offer my own.

"Why don't you come to my place?" I said from my side of a pile of scrap metal we were sifting through out behind the metalwork shop.

He tossed a rod he'd been studying back into the pile with a bit too much force. His eyes glazed over. I kept watching him, but he just kept pulling hunks of metal off and chucking them back without a reply.

"No one's there after school," I added. "We can make coffee if you want."

"I guess," he muttered as the bell rang. There was more to this, but I wasn't sure what, and so I wasn't sure if I should ask.

Inside our front door, Marcus stood glued to the mat while I threw my jacket and shoes in the direction of the closet.

"Come on. It's okay. And no one's home, anyway." He still didn't move, even as I headed for the kitchen. "Seriously."

Slowly he pulled at the back of his sneakers to get them off.

"Do you want coffee?" I asked, even though I had no idea how to start up Mom's ancient brewer.

"Nah, it's okay." He still sounded anything but comfortable, and I felt bad for bringing him here. This seemed like a whole new level of weirdness.

"Have a seat." I motioned to the couch. "I'll get us some cookies." I headed for the pantry without waiting for a response. Was Marcus worried that I was going to jump him, or what? That didn't make sense. We'd been alone plenty of times backstage and at the Arts Club. When I returned, he sat on one end of the couch, straight and tall, like he was waiting to jump up and say "Bingo!" I sat at the other end, leaving enough width for a set of major appliances between us, and placed the open bag of cookies on the table. There were only four left in the package, though I was sure Mom had just bought it a couple days ago.

Marcus helped himself to a cookie.

I flicked on the TV, and after five minutes of sitcom fun, I could feel him start to relax. He even laughed. An actual laugh out of Marcus. I watched his face jiggle in my peripheral vision.

When one of the characters used the word "footling" Marcus twisted his mouth to one side.

"You don't know what it means either?" I asked.

When he shook his head, I ran upstairs and grabbed my dictionary from beside my desk. I traipsed back down with it already open.

"'Footling: Adjective . . .'" I read out. "Means trivial or silly."

"So 'footling' and 'Loann' are, like, synonyms," he said.

"Ha, ha." I forced my eyes together in a glare, even though his joking made me feel suddenly bubbly.

"I like to learn new words," he said.

I tried to think of a good word to get back at him. But it had to be something really smart. One he didn't know.

I thumbed through my dictionary. One of my photos I'd used as a bookmark slid out and landed on the floor between us. It was one from the backyard, a squirrel with its tiny paws reaching out toward the camera. The sky was dull behind the little rust-colored guy, and it made him stand out like a shot of color in a black-and-white movie.

Marcus picked it up. "Cool," he said, looking at it for almost a full minute. "You have anything else like this?"

I nodded, swallowing hard. He kept staring at me, waiting for me to elaborate, so I raced back up to my room and returned with the pictures of the oak tree.

He studied these even longer. My knee bounced against the coffee table. I'd never seen anyone so taken with anything I had done before. Looking at Marcus's face, I wanted to cry from joy or take his picture, I wasn't sure which.

He held the photo a few feet away from him and squinted.

My armpits moistened. "You're going to start snoring any second, right?" I said with a forced laugh. Now that he was analyzing them, they probably weren't that good after all and I felt the need to intercept him from saying so.

"You know," he said at last, "this might be perfect for that outdoor scene."

I crinkled my brow. "I have no idea what you're talking about."

"For the play." He tilted his head. "I wonder . . ." He clucked his tongue a couple of times, keeping me in suspense. "If we could blow this up on the screen somehow. You know, at the back of the stage."

And that's how we came up with our brilliant idea: To create a photo-set.

By the time Claire and Mom ambled through the door,

Marcus and I had written down nearly a hundred different photo possibilities for me to track down. Marcus said he could help with the computer projection part of things, which was great because I had no idea where to start with that. I casually called out, "Hi," to Mom and Claire, while Marcus kept writing down new ideas.

Mom's mouth dropped open and she quickly snapped it shut.

I laughed under my breath, trying not to acknowledge her weirdness. *Holy heart attack, Batman, Loann has a boy in the house!*

"Mom, this is Marcus. My friend from school." I expected a similar scene to when Josh had been here the other night. Marcus standing and shaking her hand. My mom asking if we had any classes together.

But Marcus looked at the floor as Mom gritted out, "Nice to meet you," her head flicking between him and me. Then she continued on her path for the kitchen. "Come on, Claire. Help me with dinner."

I knew Marcus wasn't her ideal idea of a BFF, but did she really have to act so pissed off?

Of course, Marcus wasn't exactly the ambassador of friendliness either, but that was different. He wasn't outgoing with anyone. Well, except for me.

The nanosecond they were out of the room, Marcus jumped up to leave. I followed him to the door.

"Sorry my mom was so rude," I said.

Marcus didn't even unlace his shoes, just slid them on, crunched down on the heels, and turned for the door. "See you tomorrow," he muttered.

I barely had the door open for him when he pushed his way through it. I thought about watching him walk down the street, but he seemed to want some privacy. Besides, I was too mad at Mom to just stand there.

I shut the door and marched for the kitchen. How could she do that? It's not like I had friends to spare, or anything. I was ready to give her a piece of my mind, but before I reached the door Claire's voice trilled through from the other side.

"I wouldn't worry about them, Mom. Loey just had a fight with her friends and she's using him to hang out with in the meantime."

Um, *what*?!

I stopped in place and stared at the door. I figured Claire would be able to see what a great guy Marcus is. How he's so much better of a friend for me than Shayleen. Then again, Claire had a "popular" brain, and probably thought the same way as the guys who teased Marcus and pushed him up against his locker.

I couldn't believe how much my opinion of Claire was changing. I'd always looked up to my sister. Always.

But for the first time, I thought of Claire as not only different from me, but as one of *them*—the enemy of *us*.

CHAPTER TEN

I checked out the darkroom briefly after art class the next day and found a cupboard full of solutions and supplies. Who knew how old they were, but they would at least give me a start. Now all I had to do was get Marcus to help me with the research on how to use them.

"I swear, my parents are working until, like, ten tonight," I told him after last period. "My sister's almost never there either, but even if she is, trust me, she won't want anything to do with us."

Marcus shrugged like he didn't really want to, so I said, "Or we could go to your place."

"Your place is fine," he said quickly. He must have felt my

surprise, because he added, "It's just—parents don't usually like me."

"My mom doesn't like anyone, including me, after arguing with old people all day. It's totally not you," I told him as we headed down the hall for the outside doors. It was partially a lie. If Marcus was friendly and outgoing like Josh, Mom would no doubt be a little warmer.

To change the subject, I explained my idea to Marcus. "It won't cost anything for developing if we do it ourselves," I said, after telling him about the darkroom. "So we wouldn't have to talk about our plans with Mr. Benson until we have something to show him."

Marcus's brow crinkled. "We're talking about a lot of pictures, Loann. And it's not like either of us have done this before."

Seeing how unsure Marcus was, my confidence wavered. But we talked it over, and finally decided to research it before we made a decision.

Marcus's shoulders tensed when we got to my front door. We climbed the stairs toward the computer room. Before hitting the top landing, I heard Claire pecking away at the keyboard.

I looked at my watch. "What day is it?"

"Tuesday," Marcus said, in an uncomfortable whisper. He took a step back down the stairs.

Great. The one day my sister had free from her many activities. But I didn't want Marcus rushing off. "No biggie," I told him. "We'll just ask Claire if we can use the computer for a few minutes."

I took the rest of the stairs two at a time.

"Can we get on there for a bit?" I asked.

Claire grabbed a paper bag from beside her and crumpled it up, then turned back to the computer and chewed something before she cleared her throat. "I'm busy. Can't you use it later?"

"Oh, come on, Claire. You're just on G-chat. We both know you'll be on there for hours."

"And you won't?" She tilted her head until her hair fell like a barrier between us. Like she was trying to get her hair to have the last word in this conversation.

"We just need it for a bit of . . . homework." I put my books down, accidentally knocking her brown crumpled bag to the floor.

"Fine." She hit the X at the top of the screen, grabbed her trash so quickly I was sure the bag must be on fire, and marched out of the room, not even looking at Marcus as she went.

I wondered what she needed to hide in the bag. Did she think I would take it from her? Marcus pulled up a chair beside me, seemingly much more relaxed, which brought me back to the moment.

I stared at the screen, not knowing where to start, but I knew I had to put up a confident front. I Googled "darkroom," which garnered more than a million entries, everything from electrical advice to children's slumber parties. Marcus reached past me and added the word "photography." I felt the heat of his arm hovering in front of me until he pulled back. Our search results were slightly more manageable at twenty thousand.

Marcus pointed to one called "Darkroom Basics."

I clicked on it and a splash screen for Kettleton College in Chicago appeared. The screen morphed into one of black text, an article with the heading "Introduction to the Darkroom." Underneath that, a few lines advertised the college's photography program. I skimmed over the ad and went straight for the information I needed. Scrolling down, I read about chemical mixing, light, temperature, and resin-coated and fiber-based papers. More than anything, I was starting to grasp how much there was to learn.

Since Marcus seemed like the computer whiz out of the two of us, we switched spots. He printed off some pages, and I leafed through them, circling things I thought were important while he continued searching. I figured if I could make the amount we had to learn appear smaller somehow, that could only be good.

The next thing I knew, Claire tapped her foot in the doorway. "I thought you weren't going to be long, Loey. It's been more than an hour. I need to get back on there, and you know you're not supposed to have boys upstairs."

I couldn't believe my ears. Did she really just say that?

"Oh, like *you've* never had boys upstairs," I snapped back. Her face went beet-red, and I wondered exactly how many of Mom and Dad's "boys rules" she had broken. The idea made me more angry than giddy or jealous. "Don't worry. *We'll* go downstairs and work, since *we* have nothing to hide."

I knew it was a bitchy thing to say, but she'd really embarrassed me. She glared, but didn't say anything back, and she was in my warm chair with her G-chat screen open before Marcus and I reached the door.

A couple of students sat at a side table working on art projects when we arrived after school the following day. Thankfully Mr. Dewdney remembered why I was there.

He opened the door at the back of his classroom for us. "Now I expect you both to keep this room clean."

I scanned the messy storage area. "Um, of course."

"Obviously you know what to use for light and temperature. The controls are here." He motioned to some dials on the wall.

I nodded, trying to don my most confident face.

I thanked him and let Marcus into the small room first,

surprised when Mr. Dewdney didn't made a big deal about me being alone with Marcus the way Mr. Benson had.

The door had rubber trim around the edges, so I had to give it a good pull to get it to shut behind me. There were only a couple of feet for either of us to move between a small sink near the door and two counters, one in front of us and one behind. Colorful construction paper, old, rusted tubes of paint, felts, brushes, and broken pencil crayons covered the surfaces. The room felt claustrophobic—but in a good way, because Marcus was here. I could smell him in the small space. Different from Josh. Still boy, but more outdoorsy, like fresh-cut grass.

Marcus and I spent the next half an hour cleaning and then checking all the solutions. The small space made it diffi-cult to move without bumping each other and touching hips.

I wiped my sweaty palms on my jeans, and gave the basin a quick rinse. Then I flicked off the fluorescents and turned on the red light.

"Cool," Marcus said.

It took our eyes a few seconds to adjust, and in the dim-ness, Marcus suddenly felt even closer. I kept my eyes on the supplies in front of me as I jostled my film out of its case.

Marcus poured the package of developer powder into a brown gallon jug as though he'd done this a million times. I squinted at him, wondering how much he'd studied the darkroom notes. Even though I'd read the directions more than twenty times last night and again during classes today, I still felt so unsure. I ran the water in the sink, trying to gauge with my fingers what seventy-two degrees might feel like, but with my body playing weird temperature games in here being so close to Marcus, it was hard to tell. I'd need to bring a thermometer next time for sure.

My arm brushed across Marcus's, but he didn't shift back the way most people would. My little arm hairs stood up, like they were just waiting for me to do it again. I swallowed, wanting to, but knowing that with my grace, it might come across more like I was pushing him out of the way.

I needed to concentrate on the task. After adding the lukewarm water to the jug, I screwed the lid back on and shook.

"Two to three minutes of shaking," the directions had said, but my arms gave out after thirty seconds.

"Here." Marcus took the brown jug, reading my mind.

I watched the clock and thought about that picture of Claire and Josh kissing. If Marcus saw it, would he think I was some kind of weirdo stalker?

And more important, *was* I some kind of weirdo stalker?

When the shaking time was done, I memorized where each of the items I needed was, then switched off the safe light and fumbled to find my roll of film. Trying to wind the film onto the reel, I got quickly flustered. "I can't get this stupid thing!"

Marcus's arm brushed me again as he slid his hands over mine, holding the edges of the film and helping me guide it onto the reel. His hands seemed so warm and calm compared to my clammy, spastic ones. The film didn't go on at first, and I almost made a crack about keeping our day jobs but my mouth was too dry to talk, with him leaned right up against me like that. After a few tries, the film fell into place like a key in a perfectly fitted lock. Marcus's breath echoed in the darkness beside me, close enough that I could feel the warmth of it.

"Thanks," I whispered, liking the way my hushed voice made it feel even more intimate.

He pulled his hand away and cleared his throat. "What's next?"

How embarrassing. I was glad for the first time that the lights were off. I put the reel into the canister, and once the lid was closed, I took a big breath and then turned on the safe light. At least the red light wouldn't give away the flare in my cheeks.

"Now we wait," I said. Marcus had the strangest smile. "What?"

He shook his head and stared at the canister. I couldn't help but let my mind try to figure him out. Maybe he *was* as excited as I was about waiting in the dark together.

I inched my fingers along the counter toward him, but then lost my nerve and picked up the canister. Every twenty seconds, I rotated the can, glad to have something to do.

"So, you and Claire . . ." Marcus's deep voice surprised me, sounding louder than normal in the small space. "You love each other? You hate each other? What?"

I let out a breathy laugh. "Yeah. Pretty much. We're sisters," I said, as if that should explain everything. But by the silence that followed, I wondered if it did. "It can be hard sometimes."

"I always wanted an older brother," he said. I wondered if that meant he had a younger brother. Or maybe he was an only child. Before I could ask, he leaned past me, so his chest practically touched my arm, and angled the timer so he could see it. He pulled away slowly, then focused on his pile of papers with the directions. The guy was hard to read. One second I felt like he was trying to get closer, the next like I was invading his space. I thought girls were supposed to be the complicated ones, though I admit, hanging out with Marcus was a lot more fun than hanging out with Shayleen had ever been. Marcus and I talked about more than just crushes and fashion. We weren't afraid to try new things like this together.

When the time was up, I popped open the drainage spout and dumped it down the sink with some running water.

Did we do it right? I looked at Marcus, but his eyes stayed on the instructions. I poured in my tray of stop bath solution.

Few things can kill a romantic moment—or what *might* have been a romantic moment—like a bad smell. This one smelled like vinegar.

After emptying that solution thirty seconds later, I ran plenty of cold water to try to get rid of the fumes. Then I poured in the final solution and shook gently, trying not to create bubbles.

"Who knows if it'll work or if it'll turn out like little black blobs of nothingness?" I babbled, not knowing if I was nervous about seeing the pictures or about being alone with Marcus, or both. "First time for everything, right?"

Marcus didn't respond, and his silence made me feel the need to talk some more.

"I think it'll work, but even if it doesn't, we can try again. It's not the end of the world. It's not like this cost us anything, and my mom brought home another multipack of film for me the other day so I can try again." Even though my confidence was waning by the second, I was still glad to have this new hobby, and I wanted so badly for it to be something I was good at—maybe even good at the first time.

Finally the timer dinged. I drained the solution and took the negatives out, running them under some lukewarm water.

They felt slimy in my hands. In the dim light, I could

see that there were actual shapes on each little square. They may not have been perfect, but I'd actually done it properly. *We'd* done it properly. A grin spread across my face. Marcus grinned back at me.

After hanging the negatives on a string, I put the solutions away while Marcus rinsed the containers. "I think that's it for today," I said. "They'll take a few hours to dry."

Marcus followed me out of the small room, and it wasn't until we were back in the light of day that he looked at me and uttered his first word in what seemed like forever.

"Coffee?"

CHAPTER ELEVEN

The next day in the darkroom was full of experimentation. I took out the enlarger—an overhead projector on steroids—and attempted to make prints. Marcus had all sorts of suggestions for adjusting temperatures and distances, but didn't talk about anything else. Today he stood farther away, and it looked uncomfortable being squished up against the far wall like that. We weren't going to be "accidentally" brushing against each other today.

I clipped prints to our drying line, trying not to take his distance personally, and had completely forgotten about the picture of Claire and Josh kissing until Marcus handed it to me.

I sucked in a breath, then opened my mouth to say something, but just blubbered out an "Uh" followed by a few more unintelligible syllables. Marcus met my eyes. I felt like he could see right through me, not only about why I'd taken the picture but also my feelings for Josh. A rush of shame washed over me.

"It's almost five o'clock," sounded suddenly through the door, making me jump in place. It was Mr. Dewdney. I looked both ways, then down at the print I was still holding.

"We'd better clean up," Marcus said. He must've realized exactly what kind of a person I am and was rethinking the whole friendship, I just knew it.

After an uncomfortably quiet good-bye, I jogged all the way home to work off my anxious energy. When I reached our street, I came to a dead stop, surprised to see Josh's Civic in the driveway again. I caught my breath, then walked through the front door and slammed it. Sure enough, murmuring and footsteps emanated from the upstairs hallway.

I was halfway up the stairs when Claire's door opened and Josh whisked by me with his eyebrows pulled together and an angry look on his face. He must've been in a hurry, because he was several steps past me when he muttered an "Oh, hey, Loann" back in my direction. I'd barely turned when our front door opened and shut behind him.

Claire was just inside her bedroom door, her hair all mussed. I suppressed an embarrassed smile, as if it had been *me* doing whatever they had just been doing.

"Oh." Claire looked around dazedly. "Is Mom home?"

I shook my head. Claire backed into her room.

"She's going to catch you if you keep it up, though, you know."

Claire crinkled her brow. "I'm not—I won't . . . It's not . . ." she trailed off, closing her door between us midsentence.

Sheesh. She didn't need to be so private. Not with me. Okay, I'd been a bitch about Josh being upstairs the other day, but only because of how she'd treated Marcus. Still, we used to tell each other stuff. She told me about her first kiss with Brett Watson in seventh grade. In fact, she'd told me way more than I'd wanted to know, back then.

Things had definitely changed between us lately, but I wasn't sure I really wanted them to go back. Sure, it would be exciting to hear what was happening with Josh, but I kind of liked that I didn't feel as hidden in her shadow. I was finding my own source of light. I still hadn't discovered it completely, but I liked seeing things that other people couldn't, like how I could envision from the moment I framed an object how a photo would look once it was developed. How I could see beauty where other people couldn't. I thought, for the first time in my life, that maybe I was the special one.

I was feeling especially confident on Monday when the jocks paraded by our lockers and pushed Marcus again. Hard. One of them called Marcus his bitch.

I shot back, "Shut up! He's straight, okay? Leave him

alone." The second it left my lips, I wished I could've come up with something a little more quick-witted. Laz stood behind the other two guys. He averted his eyes, but certainty washed over me that this would get back to Jasmine, and probably Claire. The other two guys laughed and made faces at me as they all took off down the hall.

I gave Marcus an understanding pat on the shoulder. His jaw went rigid and he turned the opposite direction and walked away.

Marcus didn't say a word backstage during drama later that day, either. Not one word, and it took me a minute to realize why. He hadn't just been embarrassed about being teased earlier. He was mad. At me.

"Sorry about this morning," I said lightly. He still didn't even glance in my direction. "So where should we start today?" I had been excited about the few pictures I had developed and was ready to start talking about how they would work with the play.

Without turning toward me, he said, "We haven't checked that upper storage platform yet. I'm going to the front office to see if there's any budget at all for lumber." He was already walking away, and by his tone, this didn't seem up for discussion.

Disappointment dug at me. Did he not want to do the photo-set anymore? I definitely couldn't do it without his help. And, okay, what I had said to the jocks this morning was lame, I'll admit it, but I was trying to stick up for him! How could he be mad at me about that?

I couldn't even look through my photos, so depressed that the unique set we'd been planning might not happen. I spent the class up in the storage area, too sad to try to visualize using any of the small knickknacks up there for set pieces and instead just leafed aimlessly through smelly costumes.

I was sure I had somehow made things worse for Marcus. He could see it, and I just couldn't. Maybe tomorrow the jocks would lock him right *inside* his locker. Or push him out of the locker room without his clothes—I'd heard about that happening to a guy last year.

Marcus didn't show at our lockers after school, and the whole way home I couldn't stop thinking of what I could do to make this better. What I could do that wouldn't involve my big mouth.

My mind ricocheted to Claire. Maybe I shouldn't have let my frustration toward her take over just because I'd found myself another friend. Maybe if I made an effort with Claire we *could* be friends again.

But the more I thought about it, the more we just seemed like not only two branches on a tree that had grown apart but two entirely different species.

* * *

That evening, Mom and I sat across the table from each other, slurping stew. Dad hadn't made it home for dinner again, even though he'd told us he probably would. Claire had dropped by my locker between classes to ask me to tell Mom that she and Jasmine were going for sushi. Even though I'd sooner eat my own flesh than raw fish, I'd scrounged for an invitation from Claire. But she had just looked past me like she hadn't heard a thing I said.

Mom barely acknowledged me at the dinner table, which made me feel even more insignificant. There was a new floor-to-ceiling shrub in the corner of our living room, and it seemed to be all she wanted to look at. It occurred to me how many new plants Mom had been collecting lately. Our house was starting to look like a greenhouse.

"Why don't we put up some art?" I asked. And then, because I wanted to broach the subject again, and maybe even sway Mom a little into liking Marcus, I added, "I could ask Marcus. I'm sure he could tell us where to get something nice. He's really great with stuff like that." Even saying his name, I wondered if he'd ever talk to me again, about art or anything else. But hanging out at the Arts Club, I'd been more inspired with photography, and I could only imagine how much having something expressive at home might help.

"You need to get some nice girlfriends, Loann," Mom said

matter-of-factly. "Look at Claire, she has Jasmine and Julia and Katie . . ."

Look at Claire, the first three words I'd learned as a toddler.

"Whatever happened with you and Shayleen?"

I obviously wasn't going to tell Mom the whole story of the pink tank top. But I did have a few choice memories I could share if she pushed the issue. Like when Shayleen had told us all about her first time, right after the big seventh-grade sex talk. She had explained how we should all be jealous because she had already done it, and it was the most gentle and natural thing that could happen to a *woman*.

"You want me to be friends with Shayleen again?" I asked.

"Well, I don't know, honey, but Marcus . . ." She shook her head.

The more I thought about Shayleen, the better Marcus seemed. Even though Mom didn't know about how he'd been ignoring me, she was making me more determined than ever to patch things up with him. I tilted my bowl and slurped the last of my stew. I had to come up with a plan to solve things tomorrow.

I pushed my bowl away. "I've got homework. I'm going upstairs."

"The kitchen, please, Loann."

"Aw, Mom. It's Claire's turn. It's been Claire's turn for, like, a week now."

She put her head in her hands on the table. "Oh, Loann, why do you fight me? Can you just be helpful for once?"

I snatched her bowl, grabbed my own, and headed through the door into the kitchen. As I loaded the dishwasher, I muttered away to myself, "Yeah, I'm the problem. I'm the one who doesn't bother to show up for dinner, or invite her sister out, let alone do the dishes. Yeah, it's all me." I knew I was just jealous of Claire, who did no wrong. My sister, who never seemed to screw up with her friends. I didn't care. Gripping the dish sponge tightly in my hand, I wanted to let my jealousy swallow me up.

Ten minutes later, I'd almost calmed down when I overheard arguing from the dining room. I left the soup pot mid-scrub to lean in to the door and listen.

"Young lady, that's the third time this week you haven't been home for dinner. The least you could do is call."

"I told Loann to tell you," Claire said. "Besides, Mom, you would *love* this new sushi pla—"

"That's not the point, Claire. You have a family, and we *will* eat dinner together."

Oh, just like Dad does was my first thought. But right at that second he traipsed through the front door, making a racket with his briefcase and shoes.

"You cook so much meat and potatoes, Mom. Or bring home *take-out*." She said the words as though they were one step below garbage. "I can't eat that stuff. I swear, I put on five pounds every time I eat at home."

"Are you insulting my meals?" I could picture Mom folding her arms across her chest.

"I'm sorry, Mom, but look at me, I'll gain from even looking at a slab of meat, and I have to stay fit for dance. You know that. I think I'm going to go vegetarian for a while."

"Oh, Claire." Mom let out a huge sigh.

With the sudden burst of an idea, I pushed through the door. "Actually, Mom, I've noticed you have been cooking a lot of beef lately. More vegetables might be a healthy choice for all of us."

Claire and Mom both looked at me, stunned for a second, but then Claire's mouth turned up just a little on the edges. Perfect. Why hadn't I thought of this earlier? There was an easy way to renew my friendship with Claire: show her I'm still an ally.

Of course, Mom's mouth turned down. Way down.

"I mean, I really love your chicken casserole," I added, trying to intercept her rant. That was the one thing about ganging up on Mom. Sure, it got me in Claire's good graces, but it turned Mom into one big throbbing vein of anger.

"How's everybody today?" Dad asked, clapping his hands together like he expected a chorus of *Just dandy, Daddy!* He hadn't been home this early since before my birthday, and

I suspected he had been looking forward to a few hours of relaxing family time.

"I better get to my homework," Claire said.

"You *will* be home for dinner tomorrow night, young lady," Mom said.

Claire took mouselike footsteps toward the stairs, giving Dad a kiss hello on her way. She didn't even acknowledge Mom.

"You need to talk to her, Darren," Mom said to Dad, shaking her head. "She won't listen to me, and you're always home so late, you practically never see the girls."

Great. The blame game. And as I could predict, Dad made for his escape route—the kitchen—before she even finished her thought. Since I didn't want to be her target either, I bolted to my bedroom.

So much for relaxing family time.

CHAPTER TWELVE

I had a plan for fixing things with Marcus.

I cut out of English the second the bell rang the next day and raced straight for the auditorium. No sign of Marcus yet. Perfect. I climbed the rickety metal ladder.

By the time I heard him, I was ready.

At first he just marched for our box of photography supplies and flipped through my photos without even bothering to see if I was around. I was happy that he was looking through the photos again, though. At least he wasn't giving up on that idea. And he'd shown up for class, so he couldn't be *that* mad at me.

"Hey, Marcus, I need some help up here." I squished myself back away from the edge of the storage platform so he wouldn't be able to see me.

"Where are you?" he asked after a long pause. His voice didn't sound as annoyed as yesterday. It didn't exactly sound pleasant, either.

"Up here. I just can't"—I added a grunt for good measure—"get this box down."

Seconds later, I heard him on the ladder. He stepped onto the platform before he looked in my direction. The storage area was small, a few feet at most, with boxes piled up along one edge. Even in the dim light, my eyes adjusted quickly and I suspected his would too.

He stared first at my baggy blue pants. Then at my shiny gold vest. And finally at the white turban balanced carefully on my head. But I knew this wouldn't be enough to cheer him up.

I stroked a small lamp, and then said in some sort of accent that even I couldn't place, "Poof! Congratulations! The genie grants you three wishes for finding her, kind sir."

I caught just the slightest twitch to his lip. He was trying to hide his amusement. Or at least, I hoped so.

"There is only one condition," I told him. "One condition, I say. You can have three wishes, any wishes in the world." I moved my hands in a big circle. "But first you must forgive all your friends with big mouths."

Now he couldn't hold back a smile.

"And not just the tall ones," I babbled in my silly accent. "The short ones, too!"

He took a step toward me. "Hmmm. What should I wish for?"

I waggled my finger back and forth in his face. "No, no, no. There must be forgiveness first."

He took another step toward me, so he was close enough to take the lamp from my hands. I felt strangely defenseless without it. "My friends," he said in barely a whisper, "all one of them, are forgiven." His low voice made me shiver.

He stroked the lamp a little and my heart galloped. I didn't know what *he* was wishing for, but *I* was wishing he'd come a little closer.

And then he did. My gold vest almost touched his shirt.

"So, three wishes, huh?" He set the lamp in an open box beside him. Now we were both defenseless. He looked at me with serious eyes, but not the kind that made me wonder what I'd done wrong. The kind that made me wonder what I'd done right.

Is Marcus going to kiss me? I wondered. *And why, oh why, do I have to be wearing a turban for it?*

He reached over and touched a curl that had popped out from beneath the turban and pushed it back. Of course it didn't stay, but he held his hand there like he wasn't sure where to put it.

I wanted to tell him—put it on my face, on my shoulder, on my hair, I didn't care at this point. Just put it somewhere!

But a loud bang made us both jump and he pulled his hand away fast.

Someone had opened the stage door too wide on their way in. Voices echoed from down below, but Shayleen's carried above the rest.

"It's about time Mr. B let us use class time to figure out our blocking."

Marcus took a step away from me. My heart sank. As the sounds of other students got louder, my adrenaline kicked in and I started to unfasten the complicated buttons on my vest.

Shayleen led several other members of our drama class onto the stage and ordered them to stand in different places. One guy nearest the curtains on our side whispered loudly, "Who died and made her director?"

A couple more students came through the door below us. I recognized Deirdre's short hair. Even though I slid my vest off silently, I guess the shiny gold caught the light. Deirdre looked up at us, shading her eyes so she could see past the glare of stage lights.

I wasn't sure what to expect. Deirdre and I hadn't talked since things went sour with Shayleen. I held my breath, but seconds later, she let out a little giggle.

If there was one thing I knew about Deirdre, it was this: she didn't know how to pull off a mocking giggle—the kind

Shayleen had perfected. Deirdre genuinely thought my outfit was funny. And if she thought that, maybe she didn't hate me as much as Shayleen did.

I brought a finger to my lips, hoping I had it right. She nodded, but before she turned for the stage, Shayleen came barreling toward her.

"We're waiting for you!" she said in an angry tone. "What are you laughing—" she looked up. I took a step back toward the boxes and eyed the ladder that went further up to the lighting catwalk. But it was too late.

"What on *earth* is she doing?" Shayleen said, loud enough that everyone onstage looked up at Marcus and me.

I tried to quickly remove the turban, but it caught in my hair—stupid curls—and I ended up leaving it tilted on my head while Shayleen marched for the side door.

I could hear her calling Mr. Benson even after the door slammed behind her.

Marcus and I were just climbing down the ladder—with a whole audience of Shayleen's cronies watching us—by the time Mr. Benson came backstage.

"I'm sorry, Mr. Benson," I said. "We were just checking through the costumes to see if any props were buried in them. I guess we got carried away."

Shayleen spoke over me. "Obviously that costume is completely inappropriate for the performance. They think this show is some kind of a joke! Some excuse to stay back here and play dress-up without doing any *real* work." She huffed and crossed her arms. "And we all know Loann would do just about anything to be alone with a guy."

"Is this true?" Mr. Benson asked, turning to me. I wasn't quite sure what his question was, and even if I did, I doubted I could form anything other than a gurgle.

But before I had a chance to embarrass myself further, Marcus appeared beside me holding a box. Our photography box.

"We've been working really hard," Marcus said, setting the box down and pulling out the envelope of my favorite photos from the top. He passed them to Mr. Benson, who opened it and looked inside.

Marcus continued. "Since there's not much in the way of usable supplies—"

"And since these pictures go so well with the theme—" I interjected.

"We're going to try to do a photo-set, on the back scrim there," Marcus finished. I pointed to the back wall of white. The class turned to look as we waited for Mr. Benson to say something.

"Ptff, as if that'll work," Shayleen murmured behind me. "And leave the stage totally empty? Yeah, that'll look *great*."

Sarcasm dripped from her tongue and I was sure if I looked down I'd see a pool of it on the floor.

All the other students looked between my pictures and our teacher, waiting to see how he would react. Should they take Shayleen's side and start mocking Marcus and me, or go on ignoring us as usual?

"Brilliant!" Mr. Benson finally said. "I can't wait to see it!"

While everyone else stared up at the white scrim, trying to picture it, Marcus reached over and squeezed my hand.

CHAPTER THIRTEEN

The backstage area swarmed with students until the end of class. I kept looking at Marcus. I wanted so much to have another moment with him, at least an unspoken understanding, but he didn't meet my eyes. I hated Shayleen for ruining things.

I didn't see Marcus again until after school at our lockers.

"Arts Club?" he asked, without looking at me.

I tilted my head to try to see more of his face, to figure out what he was thinking. Did he wish we hadn't been interrupted on that upper platform as much as I did?

"Actually, I can't today," I said, trying to get a reaction from him. "I have a dentist appointment at three." It was true, and I should've been headed to the front doors to meet Mom so we wouldn't be late.

His mouth turned down slightly. Was that . . . disappointment?

"I *wish* I could stay today," I said, hoping he'd catch my genie innuendo. "I really *wish* I could."

He pursed his lips. Then he shook a finger back and forth in front of me. "Uh, uh, uh. You can't get me to waste one of my wishes on a silly dentist appointment."

A wave of relief hit me and a loud laugh escaped.

"I guess we'll save those wishes for another day then, hmm?" he said with raised eyebrows.

My skin tickled with goose bumps. I stood there in a daze, staring at him until he said, "It's ten to three. Don't you have to go?"

"I, uh, oh yeah. Or I could just stand here staring all day." After shutting my locker, I backed away, I guess to make my embarrassing moment last a little bit longer. But he held up a hand to wave, just held it in the air like he was almost as dumbfounded as I was.

I practically skipped from the school to Mom's car. Then even into the dentist's office, of all horrible places. But it was the best dentist appointment ever. I lay there on the chair, closed my eyes, and relived our time in that upper storage area.

The only problem was, my dentist had to keep telling me to open my mouth wider, because I was grinning from ear to ear.

* * *

That night at dinner, true to her word, Claire helped herself to only the vegetables on the table.

"Here," Mom said, passing her a big casserole dish. "I made it meatless, just for you." Mom forced a smile in Claire's direction, as if to say: *Just try to say no after I made this especially for you!*

It took Claire a second, but she reached for the dish. We both knew Mom could be like a drill sergeant, the way she never let up on anything.

Claire helped herself to a small half-spoonful, and then eyed Dad, who had actually made it home for dinner. Claire took a fuller spoonful and cleared her throat. I was sure she was trying to come up with an argument about being scared her grad dress wouldn't fit, or another reason she didn't want Mom's casserole, but then she said, "Hey, Dad, I've been looking through housing brochures for college, and they have some great single rooms on campus."

I wasn't sure why she was using her suck-up voice until Dad balked. "A single room? They're three times the price. We talked about this. I thought you said Jasmine was going."

"Yeah, she is." Claire didn't say anything else, so it left me to wonder: Why *wasn't* Claire eager to share a room with Jasmine? Was Jaz already set to share a place with Laz? But why wouldn't Claire just say that, if that was the case?

The conversation died quickly and Claire just stabbed at

her food, taking a bite every ten or twenty jabs, like she was angry at the casserole.

When I finished, I went straight for my room, glad to not be on dish-duty. I glanced at the homework on my desk halfheartedly, then plunked down on my bed and stared up at the ceiling, thinking more about what Marcus's first wish might be.

My stomach made noises while digesting and I looked down at it. The only time it flattened out was when I lay on my back.

Vegetarian, huh? But who was I kidding? I couldn't live off of vegetables. My stomach let out an extra growl at even the thought of it.

But still, after my day with Marcus, I wondered if I should start watching what I ate. And maybe dressing a little nicer.

The next morning I spent more than half an hour picking out my clothes for school. I didn't end up choosing anything *that* mind-blowing, but I wore the jeans that made my butt look the best and a green tee that complemented my dark hair.

Eager to get to my locker—to mine and Marcus's—I wove through the hallways, which were scattered with members of the grad committee putting up banners and posters.

Instead of finding him there, though, Deirdre stood by my locker. She let out a quiet sigh when I reached her. I usually diverted my path when Shayleen and Deirdre were together—who needed to deal with whatever they were dishing out?—but Deirdre on her own? I bit back a smile. Maybe we could get past things.

"Hi," she said, still sounding somber. I spun my lock and popped it off.

"Um . . . hi." I gave her an awkward smile.

"Great picture." She pointed to a recent portrait of our neighbor's dog I'd taped inside my locker door.

"Thanks." I paused, wondering if I should ask. "Where's Shayleen?"

"I don't know," Deirdre replied quietly, picking at her thumbnail. "Listen, I'm sorry about yesterday. I didn't mean to, you know, get you into trouble."

She was just as nice as I remembered, and I couldn't believe I'd actually thought she was a bitch like Shayleen. Still, I was sure she didn't want to go head-to-head with Queen Tantrum for talking to me.

When I thought I heard Shayleen's voice, I blurted, "Oh, no problem. Don't worry, I don't blame you." I shut the door, gave her a half-wave, and walked away.

By drama period I knew Marcus wasn't in school. He hadn't looked sick yesterday, and I personally wouldn't have missed seeing *him* today if I'd had pneumonia. But I tried not to be offended. I tried not to let depression take over as I sat alone at lunch, headed home alone after school, and realized how unevenly yoked our friendship probably was.

Marcus had likely always been a loner and could deal with it. But I found it really hard to get used to. It wasn't like I'd had the largest circle of friends, but still, having someone to sit with at lunch meant a lot to me.

As I fed my books into my locker the next day, my mind stayed on Marcus. Would he miss another whole day of school? I was just shutting my locker when Deirdre came up and just started talking.

"So we had a fight. Shayleen and me," she clarified. "It's not . . . she's not the type of person I want to be friends with. So, it's cool." She motioned between us.

It was weird. I'd never really spent much time around Deirdre without Shayleen. They'd always been better friends than Deirdre and me. But I wasn't complaining. "What was the fight about?" I asked.

She nibbled her lip and stared at the floor. "Oh, nothing. You know, just one of those things."

"She's not going to hear you, you know." I looked up and down the hall. No one paid us the least bit of attention.

After a moment, she shrugged. "I, uh . . . I told Ben Kroeker something I shouldn't have."

"Something *she said* you shouldn't have?" I didn't look away, hoping Deirdre would see she could trust me.

"Well, yeah." A small smile crossed her face.

By her quiet voice, it didn't seem like she wanted to talk about any of it. "Whatever. It's none of my business."

Later that day, without so much as a hello, she said, "All I told him was that she was a tease. The truth is, she's also a liar. I should've told him that part too."

That's it? I just assumed it had been a fight over me— I'd imagined Shayleen had gone on about finding me in the genie costume with Marcus; about how our photo-set would probably ruin the whole play. To which Deirdre would have defended me.

But no. It had nothing to do with me. "Hmm," I replied, letting this new information settle in.

Deirdre didn't have many other friends now that Shayleen wasn't on her side, and I knew what that felt like. People seemed to follow loudmouths like Shayleen, probably afraid to get trampled by them. But I knew Deirdre would attract new friends soon enough and surely would not turn into an outcast like me.

Over dinner that night, I interrupted Mom and Claire gabbing about Claire getting her makeup professionally done for prom, and brought up my renewed friendship with Deirdre. I suspected Claire would be glad. And if she wasn't, Mom sure would be.

"We've been talking quite a bit," I said.

"Hmm. I don't remember which one she is." Claire flipped a page in her magazine and ignored the salad in front of her.

Figured. I knew every single one of Claire's friends, who they were friends with, who their siblings were, what kind of cars they drove. But Claire, she didn't know the very small trio of people I'd shared my entire school life with. I took a deep breath and resigned myself that I wasn't going to impress her anyway.

"You should try the yams," I said, passing them over to Claire to change the subject. "What did you put on them, Mom?"

Mom started to answer—just butter, salt, and sugar—when Claire interrupted, not even glancing at the bowl in my hands.

"Is she one of the ones who made that big scene yesterday?" Claire asked.

I crinkled my eyebrows. "Who?"

"Deirdre. Your friend."

Deirdre? A scene? "I don't think so."

"Didn't you see that big fight in the cafeteria?" Claire flipped through her cell phone, even though she wasn't supposed to have it at the dinner table. She had yet to take a bite of her plate full of salad, and I wondered why Mom wasn't on her about it.

"I haven't been eating in the cafeteria, but I'm sure it wasn't her." Marcus and I usually ate our lunches in the backstage area, since it was always deserted and it gave us a chance to brainstorm more set ideas, but I'd been on my own there since he'd been absent.

"Yeah, I was wondering about that. Where do you eat, Loey?"

"Here and there." I wanted information. "Tell me about the fight."

Claire moved a tomato from side to side, not answering right away. Mom had also made pasta, but Claire refused it, saying she still felt bloated from lunch. It was obvious that Claire's diet was getting crazy deficient. Was Mom just going to let her eat—or not eat—whatever she wanted until prom?

"Well, it was so funny"—Claire leaned in toward me conspiratorially—"they walk in, giggling together, and all of a sudden Shayleen slams down her tray and starts yelling that Deirdre's sleeping around with, like, five guys. The teachers broke it up right away, of course, but not before Shayleen started naming all these guys and saying only a skank would sleep around like that!"

"Claire, that's enough. Those aren't nice things to say." Mom stood up from the table and started to clear the dishes. I was still trying to process Claire's story. She must have had it backward. Deirdre had hardly dated since I'd known her. Though I couldn't exactly picture Deirdre using the word "skank" about Shayleen, either. Even if she was mad.

"I didn't say them, Mom. I'm just relaying the story. Loey deserves to know. These are her friends."

Mom shot me an accusing look.

"They are not!" I scowled, wishing I could take back the whole conversation.

"Oh yeah, right," Claire added. "Marcus is your friend." She looked down at her salad with a smug smile. I didn't have a clue what I'd done to her. I mean, every time Josh had been in her room, I'd kept quiet. I hadn't pried into her secrets. We'd *always* defended each other to our parents.

My fists clenched beneath the table as I fumed, ready to say something to get back at her. But as mad as I was, I'd never done that before, and it just felt wrong. Thankfully Dad tromped through the door, interrupting my rage.

"Hey, honey, I wanted to send a check to the university for your deposit," he said to Claire. "Is your housing application all filled out?"

Claire had just looked at her phone two seconds ago, but she pulled it out again.

"Claire?" he repeated.

"Oh, yeah. I kind of wanted to talk to you about that, Dad." Claire switched to her magazine and flipped another page. *Was she nervous about something?* My anger was edged out by curiosity.

"What's there to talk about? I thought you said it was due by the fifteenth."

Claire nodded into her magazine. "Yeah, it is. For this year," she added after a second.

Dad started to say something, but stopped with half of an unintelligible word out of his mouth. Mom came back from the kitchen and seemed to catch on faster than the rest of us.

"For this year? What are you talking about, Claire?" Her tone was that patronizing, all-business one she usually used on me. "You're *going* to college this year."

"Wait. What?" Dad looked between Claire and Mom. My invisibility cloak seemed to be working. "You're thinking of deferring? Now?"

"No way." Mom said. "Not a chance."

"It's not that I don't want to go," Claire said, now looking up at them. "I do. And I will," she pleaded. She watched Dad until he met her eyes. "It's just that the University of Wisconsin is so generic, and I don't even know what I would major in yet. Mrs. Avery thinks I might be able to get into a performing arts school with my grades and experience, and if I work really hard at ballet this year—"

"Mrs. Avery is suggesting that you skip college?" Mom sounded like she was ready to send Claire's poor ballet teacher to prison. For life. On another night, I might have come to Claire's rescue. But not after the whole Deirdre/Marcus conversation. It didn't matter, Dad took my place.

"I'm sure that's not what Mrs. Avery meant, Beth," Dad said. It came so naturally for him to take an opposing side against Mom that I wondered if he'd even thought about what he was agreeing to.

"It's not," Claire confirmed, and I could suddenly see it as though the words were painted on a scoreboard above them: Team A = Dad and Claire; Team B = Mom, all on her own.

As expected, Mom put up a fight, but Claire fought her right to the end. Dad cited all sorts of excuses about how another year would give them something to pay on the Visa.

It was settled. Claire would take the year off college to practice her *pliés*. And Mom couldn't do a thing about it.

CHAPTER FOURTEEN

On my way to my room that night, I knocked on Claire's door. She'd been pretty argumentative with Mom at the table, and I knew from experience that could drain a good chunk of emotional energy. I thought Claire might want to come to my room to talk.

She didn't answer at first, so I knocked again. Seconds later, our toilet flushed, and I heard the door open from the bathroom into her room.

I knocked again.

"What?" She sounded exasperated, like she'd heard the first two knocks and ignored them.

"It's just me," I said.

I waited, but she didn't tell me to come in or anything. After a few long seconds, she said. "I'm not in the mood, Loann."

I stood there, stunned. At first I felt hurt—why would she talk to *me* that way? I hadn't even been part of the whole postponing-college conversation. But then I grew angry. She was getting her way, not to mention, if I was lucky enough to get early acceptance into college, I sure wouldn't throw it away like it was nothing. Besides that, I was trying to be nice, and Claire thought I was a nuisance?

I stomped to my room and shut my door behind me. We usually leave both bathroom doors open a crack so we each know when it's not occupied, but Claire had obviously forgotten to crack mine.

The simple mistake made me even angrier.

I marched over and yanked it open, but a weird stench made me push it shut again. Okay, so maybe her stomach was intolerant to this vegetarian thing. Maybe she wasn't feeling well and her bad attitude had nothing to do with me. I guess she was entitled to have a bad night.

The next day, Marcus returned to school. I couldn't help grinning like a Cheshire cat when I saw him at our lockers. He smiled weakly back. I picked at my fingernail, immediately feeling insecure. He wasn't as happy to see me as I was to see him. Not even close.

"I've got to get to class early to find out what I missed," he said without inflection. "But I thought we could meet at the computer lab at lunchtime to work on our photo-set. Sound good?"

I nodded, trying not to let my disappointment show. I thought we'd have time to catch up and talk about more personal stuff during lunch backstage. So much for that. So much for any private time.

When I arrived at the computer lab two minutes after the lunch bell, Marcus was already at work behind one of the terminals near the teacher's desk. I sighed. Two other students worked at the back of the room, and didn't even lift their heads when I arrived.

"Hey." I plopped down in the chair beside him and splayed the photos out on the desk.

His mouth turned down. I wondered if he really had to rush off this morning. Was he trying to avoid me, or had I inadvertently done something wrong again?

Marcus pointed to a contraption on the other side of him. "Put one facedown in the scanner. I'm going to see what kind of quality I can get."

I did as he instructed and watched as he scanned the photo, then resized it, and added all sorts of effects. My eyes widened as Marcus's fingers flew over the keyboard.

"Yeah, I don't think the caricature look is going to work for *this* play," I said, forcing a laugh at something he was trying on the screen.

"Hmm, I guess not." Marcus smiled a little now, and I hoped my laugh had broken the tension. "What about sepia tones on the house photo for the beginning of the play?"

I handed him the picture and he nodded, slipping it into the scanner. When he adjusted the color and then enlarged it, my mouth opened in awe. All this time I'd been thinking a photoset could be okay, passable. But now . . . I really thought it could be great. My heart thumped with excitement. And from the way Marcus's fingers paused typing, I suspected his did too.

When I opened my locker after last class, caught in the crack between my door and Marcus's was a blown up vignette of my squirrel picture. I caught it just before it hit the ground. I'd left all my pictures with Marcus for the afternoon, since he had computer class after lunch. He'd obviously fiddled around with it. The background was now muted tones, with the bright brown squirrel standing out in the middle. I loved it.

I studied it with wide eyes, marveling at not only his talent but also at mine. How could two different people with opposite abilities come up with something so beautiful?

Suddenly Deirdre appeared beside me.

"Hey, Loann. A few of us are going swimming this afternoon. Want to come?"

I blinked. Well, I wasn't wrong about her finding a new set of friends quickly, but she seriously still wanted to hang out with me?

"Uh, I can't today," I said. Even though Marcus and I hadn't made official plans, I figured now that he was back, we'd for sure go to the Arts Club today. "But thanks," I added.

"Well, maybe next time." She fiddled with the edge of her binder. "Hey, cool picture!" She pointed to the squirrel in my hands.

I nodded. She jabbered on. Something about the swimming pool and her new friends, but all I could hear was *Cool picture* resonating again and again in my ears.

I waited around, but Marcus didn't show at our lockers. He wasn't at the computer lab, either. Not that I'd have gone swimming with Deirdre and her friends, whom I didn't know, anyway, but I tried hard to swallow my frustration.

Was Marcus trying to give me a hint—he would work with me on the set, but that's all he wanted?

I nibbled at my lip, looking around one more time for him.

Shayleen came tromping down the hallway right then. I hated to admit it, but the jeans and short cardigan she wore made her look really good. She was having a great hair day, too. I suddenly felt frumpy.

"Where's your boyfriend?" Shayleen scoffed. "Get stood up for another guy?"

"I'm not—" I stopped myself. I didn't owe her any explanation, and I knew she was just trying to rile me up. She used to do it in a good way, like when we had sleepovers at Deirdre's and Shayleen had us both thinking we'd be marrying the guys we were crushing on.

It's not like I was scared of Shayleen—well, not in any physical way. But she knew a lot about me. Not just that I'd wanted to kiss Josh Garrison, but lots of things about how insecure I was about boys. I didn't want to give her any more reason to try to hurt me.

Turning back to my locker, I grabbed my history notebook and shoved it into my backpack, even though I didn't have history homework.

I didn't turn around again until her footsteps echoed down the hall.

CHAPTER FIFTEEN

I came home to find Josh, with his head down, walking for his car.

"Hey," I said, forcing some volume so he'd be sure to hear me.

He looked up and his face broke into a smile. "Hey, yourself."

"Leaving already?" I wasn't sure where the words were coming from. My mouth seemed to be spewing them without the help of my brain.

He glanced to the upper floor of our house and pursed his lips like he wasn't sure what to say. Then he just looked back at me and nodded. I wondered if he and Claire had a fight. Josh didn't make a move for his car, but I had no idea what else to say. I really needed to take a class in Small Talk with Boys.

"Not out with your boyfriend today?" he asked.

I looked at him blankly. Did he mean Marcus? How would he even know about him? Did he and Claire talk about us—about me? "Marcus? He's not . . . my boyfriend," I said finally, looking down at my feet with a twinge of regret. I'd always known I didn't have a chance with someone like Josh, but I guess I had let myself get my hopes up with Marcus. Now it didn't look like that was going anywhere either.

"Huh." Josh reached for his door handle. "Too bad for him."

I stood in my driveway with my mouth hanging open, unable to form a good-bye, until Josh had driven down our street and turned the corner.

When I could finally prod myself in the front door, I smelled his lingering cologne. And the aroma lasted all the way up the stairs.

Claire's door was shut, so I suspected she was putting her prim appearance back together after a quickie. A strong pang of jealousy hit and I headed back downstairs to grab some food to distract myself. Claire's uneaten lunch wasn't on the counter. Even though I knew I shouldn't be angry about that—it was *her* lunch, after all—I was. But also, when I opened the fridge, the pan of leftover lasagna had disappeared. Had Claire fed it, and all of its protein, to Josh? Lasagna was my *favorite*. I checked the sink, the cupboards, even the garbage, but the pan wasn't anywhere.

I didn't see it until I walked past Claire's empty bedroom

to go down for dinner later. I nudged open her door with my foot—just trying to see her room through Josh's eyes for a second—and there on her dresser sat the empty pan.

Even if he had a huge appetite, I found it hard to believe Josh could have eaten all of it. So Claire would only eat vegetables at the table with our parents, but she'd feast on meat and pasta all afternoon with sweet, wonderful Josh? Was her dinner-table eating all an act to one-up Mom? I don't know why it got to me. Honestly, I wasn't mad about missing out on a delicious after-school snack. I could probably use the calorie curb, but my whole body still heated up in a jealous rage.

Why did Claire always get exactly what she wanted, and I couldn't even seem to get the scraps?

"Where's the lasagna?" I said pointedly to Mom across the dinner table. I looked over at Claire, too, but she kept her face in her cell phone.

"Eat what I made you first, Loann," Mom said, her eyes in the newspaper as she chewed a bite of potatoes. It used to be an unwritten rule that we spent dinnertimes focused on one another. Now I felt like I needed to bring a book to the table just to fit in.

"Yeah, I know, but there's none left."

She sighed. "Is it gone already?" She said it like *Ho-hum, another thing to buy.*

"There was half a pan yesterday," I added.

"Hmm?" Mom said, without looking up. She was no help at all.

Claire had stopped studying her cell to look at me. She mouthed the word, *"Sorry."*

At first, I thought she was sorry because she understood that she got everything and I got nothing. But after a second I realized it was just about the lasagna. Still, she flashed me a smile, and my grudge softened.

She did deserve Josh. She did. I was just feeling insecure about Marcus.

And when Marcus was cold to me again Monday, only talking about our set, my normal playful comments took a turn for the worse. "Let me guess—you want to spend lunch staring at a computer again." With all the times Marcus had jilted me lately, my tone came out more sarcastic than I meant it. On the upside, in my free time I'd been taking some excellent photographs around town. Mr. Dewdney had also started letting me use class time to develop photos when I told him about our drama project.

Our check-ins with Mr. Benson were going extremely well. The more he saw of our photo-display backdrop, the more he appreciated our ingenuity. Aside from the need to go back and resize a few things, they looked even more impressive on the scrim at the back of the stage than I had expected. A forest of trees appeared on the right of the scrim, with my cute little squirrel blown up on the left. Mr. Benson hovered over us in the sound booth of the auditorium, but I barely noticed him.

"That looks so . . . amazing," I said as Marcus flipped his PowerPoint onto the next image, a house that Marcus had doctored up to look like a cabin in the woods.

He nudged his leg against mine under the computer desk. "Yeah, it does."

We hadn't been close since that day up in the costume storage—we'd barely made eye contact—and the sudden touch felt shockingly friendly.

Mr. Benson jabbered on about how each photo would work with the play, not noticing our silent connection. I hadn't even been planning on going to the play, since Shayleen had been bragging through the hallways for weeks about her part in it. But now, seeing our art up there on the big screen . . . how could I miss it?

"So do we get complimentary tickets or something?" Marcus asked, reading my mind.

"Oh, I think that's the least we can do," Mr. Benson said. And I could tell by his tone that Marcus and I could expect something better than a B this term.

But as excited as I was, I felt sad, too. Now that the set was pretty much done, Marcus and I would no longer get to spend drama block alone. We wouldn't be working toward something together. And with summer looming, I started to fear that we might lose touch completely.

Through the next weeks, life whizzed by, though, and I didn't end up having much time to think about it. My exam schedule was heavy and I studied most afternoons. Marcus and I still sat together in drama class and he flashed me the occasional smirk. The class was small; only a handful of us weren't off rehearsing for the play. At least I only had to see Shayleen's daily glare for the first few minutes of each class.

Mr. Benson had bragged about our photo-set during our first class back in the drama room, and Shayleen hadn't wasted any time telling him she hoped someone "professional" would be running the computer for rehearsals.

She obviously didn't want us around, which was just fine with me. Things started to feel more relaxed between Marcus and me, and I started to wonder if this was better: being back in a classroom, where things were less threatening.

Coming up to opening night of the play, I didn't bother to tell my parents about the photo-set we'd done, since Claire's grad, and all of the many events surrounding it, obviously took priority. When they were home, Mom and Dad bantered constantly about which nights each of them would have to take off work to drive Claire and her friends around. I sure didn't want to be an extra obligation on their schedule.

I met Marcus outside the school on opening night.

It hadn't occurred to me to change out of the jeans and T-shirt I'd worn to school that day—I mean, it *was* a school event—but it surprised me that Marcus now wore khaki pants with a navy button-down shirt. I felt embarrassed at my inability to be a normal girl who knew when to dress up for things. And because I was so embarrassed, it took me way too long to choke out some words.

"You look really nice," I said.

He let out a breathy laugh, like he either didn't believe me or was equally embarrassed by my comment. He led the way to the door and handed the ushers our tickets. They directed us toward the front of the auditorium.

"Wow," I whispered as we sat down. "First row?"

"You don't know how good your pictures are, Loann."

My face warmed. Now it felt like we were on a date. I stared straight ahead at the sepia cabin picture, the one that would fill the scrim until the play started, and gripped my armrests. "It wouldn't have worked at all without your expertise," I said, barely able to get out the words.

Silence fell between us, but it wasn't the comfortable silence from the Arts Club. No, this was different. I fidgeted with the side of my armrest and turned over my ticket stub again and again in my hands. Marcus sat totally still. Rigid. It was a relief when the lights finally dimmed.

Fifteen minutes into the play, Marcus leaned in and whispered, "The backdrop is the best part." His warm breath tickled my neck and his arm rested against mine on the armrest. I nibbled at the inside of my lip.

The people beside me murmured about the set, and oohs and ahhs sounded each time the picture faded into a new one, which made me flush even more. It wasn't until right before the intermission that I realized I hadn't seen Shayleen yet. I knew some of the parts had been trimmed due to time, because Mr. Benson had talked about it during drama class, and most of the lead parts had been given to seniors. But still, where was she? I was about to ask Marcus when all of a sudden, there she was: stage right.

"Wow," she said in an overprojected voice. "I think I like it out here!" Ironically, she made a motion to the back of the stage, to our photo-set with a picture of an open expanse of overgrown grass and wildflowers, when she said it. She swept across the stage like a windstorm, distracting the audience from all the other actors until finally she exited off of stage left. And *that* . . . was the last we saw of her.

Even though I really wanted to gloat, at least inwardly, part of me felt bad for Shayleen. I'd seen many of her outrageous attempts at being noticed over the years. But I don't know, her trying to make her one line into something it wasn't just seemed so public and embarrassing. Even though she could be mean, I've always known that it was because she just didn't feel good enough.

On our way out of the theater after the show, Mr. Benson called Marcus and me over to where he stood in the lobby. "I'd like you to meet our set designers. A couple of my most creative students," he exclaimed to his friends, some faculty members from his old college. "They came up with the setting for the play all on their own."

Nods of approval came at us from every direction. I stood there, soaking up their compliments, until I felt Marcus's tight grip on my arm. My overactive sweat glands reappeared, even more so when he leaned in and whispered, "Can we go now?"

I made a big deal of thanking the teachers, telling them we didn't want to keep them, and then nudged our way out of the circle and toward the front doors.

When we were almost there, Shayleen came into view, surrounded by her mom, who I recognized, and a few other vaguely familiar family members. They all chatted among themselves, ignoring Shayleen. Over the years I'd been to plenty of Claire's dance performances, and afterward all the dancers could be found in the lobby with their families. But the focus was always on them. I suddenly felt worse for Shayleen. No matter how small of a part, your family should be there for you, congratulating you after the show. Shayleen shifted from side to side, like she couldn't wait to get out of there.

Since we were close enough, I veered slightly toward her and tapped her on the side of the arm.

She looked at me with surprise. Before she registered why I was tapping her, I rushed on with my words. "Good job up there, Shayleen."

Her eyes scanned my face and her forehead crinkled.

"That's all I wanted to say," I told her, and headed for the door. It wasn't like I was trying to repair our friendship. At all. I didn't want to be her friend. Tonight, I don't know, I just couldn't leave her feeling that way.

When we were outside, Marcus walked slower than usual, keeping pace with me instead of rushing on ahead like he usually did. The way he kept glancing over, I could tell he wanted to say something, and I'll admit, my hopes rose that it might be about us. The two of us. Together. I tried to give him a meaningful look that said, *Whatever it is, you can tell me.*

We walked in silence for a while. Then he said, "That was pretty cool, what you said to Shayleen."

Even though Shayleen was *not* the subject I wanted to be on, I loved that he understood how hard it was for me to compliment her. But at the same time, I wasn't trying to get her back on my side or anything. He understood it all without me having to say it. "Thanks."

He nodded, and didn't say anything else for at least a block. "I've never had a friend like you, Loann." He looked up at the cloudless, darkening sky. "Someone who just accepts me for who I am. Someone who understands things and doesn't ask questions all the time."

Even though I really wanted to know how he felt about me, I decided right then that I would do my best to keep my mouth shut.

Maybe all my questions didn't need answers.

At least, not quite yet.

CHAPTER SIXTEEN

With most of my exams, the play, and all the set work over, I didn't know what to do with myself. I hated going home after school because Jasmine and Claire were always there, talking nonstop about grad dresses and nails and hairstyles. I was eager for Marcus to ask me to do something, anything, with him.

He didn't.

Since I wondered if going to the Arts Club felt too much like dating to him, I came up with another idea.

"Hey, it's pretty warm out today," I said at our lockers after last period. "There's an old bridge down by the river. It's where I got the picture for the closing scene of the play."

Marcus nodded like he was remembering.

"You want to go?"

He agreed, and twenty minutes later we were dangling our legs from the bridge over the water. Nobody had been here when I'd photographed it, and the place appeared deserted again.

"So I don't have your phone number," I said casually, picking at a rock that was wedged between the bridge planks. My voice betrayed me, as usual, and I was sure the insecurity I felt came through.

Marcus scribbled something on a piece of paper from his pocket and passed it over. "Here's my e-mail, but I don't always get to check it."

He didn't say why he didn't want to give me a phone number, or if he even had a cell. I'd never seen him use one, but then I hardly used mine, so that didn't necessarily mean anything. Marcus had always been so private, and I remembered how much he liked the fact that I didn't pry. With things already on shaky ground, I decided not to ask.

Instead I told him, "My mom asked me if I'd do some photos of Claire for grad. She didn't like the ones from the school."

He pulled himself up to lean on the upper rail of the bridge. "You'd be good at that."

I looked down at my lap. "Well, to be honest, I'm kind of nervous about it. I'm sure she'd rather hire a *real* photographer. I haven't shot many people before."

Marcus scoffed. "Photography is one thing you don't have to be nervous about, Loey."

He'd never called me Loey before. I liked it. "Will you help me?"

He ran a hand through his hair. "You don't need me there."

"But I do." I stood and leaned against the railing beside him. "You keep me calm. I couldn't have done the photo-set without all your ideas and your help learning how to develop them." I didn't know how to explain how much his confidence in me had helped.

The way he rubbed at his hands, I could tell he didn't want to do it. He was probably waiting for me to let him off the hook, but I really, *really* wanted him there.

Finally, without even giving me an answer, he said, "We should probably head back."

We walked all the way to the main road before he said, "You know you'll owe me one, right?"

The last week of classes zoomed by. Shayleen didn't pay much attention to me in drama, but seemed to have flanked herself with a few new male friends who all sat at the front of the class with her. Deirdre started sitting with me and Marcus, and we talked more, but mostly about school stuff.

I figured I could ask Deirdre if she wanted to hang out in the summer. But I really wanted to hang out with Marcus.

Even though he'd given me his e-mail address, it hadn't felt like much of an invitation. With him, I felt like I had to wait around for him to ask.

Finally, at the end of our last drama class, I turned to Deirdre and said, "Hey, maybe we can hang out sometime."

She smiled. "Sure."

So easy.

I glanced toward Marcus's steady frontward gaze.

The bell rang and Deirdre called "See ya," on her way out. I waited for Marcus to get up to leave, too, but he didn't right away.

"You could . . . meet me at the Arts Club sometime." He paused and then finally turned to me. "If you want to hang out, I mean."

I grinned with what was probably way too much enthusiasm. "I would," I said. "I really would like that."

I felt cheery the whole rest of the day, and even into the weekend. Marcus clicked OFF on the TV remote and dropped it on our coffee table when we heard voices from outside my house on Saturday afternoon. I'd brought him back here early, trying to get him more comfortable before the photo shoot, and I think it had worked. I told Marcus to grab our shoes while I organized my camera equipment.

But Claire was quick with the door, and suddenly there stood Marcus, a pair of shoes in each hand, staring a foot away from not only Claire, but also Jasmine, Laz, and Josh Garrison.

Claire, Jasmine, and Laz held their grad gowns draped over their arms.

"Hey, Loey," Claire said, nonchalantly leading the way. She pointed toward her room and asked Jasmine to go plug in her flat iron.

"Hi, Loann," Jasmine said in a nicer-than-usual tone on her way up the stairs.

"H-hi," I forced out. Why were they *all* here? No one had said anything about *this*.

"Oh! Hi, Marcus." Claire looked at me when she said it. I was quite sure she was waiting for me to tell her why he was here. But I was waiting for an explanation too. "You know Josh and Laz, right?" she asked, turning to Marcus.

Marcus took a step back and nodded. As if it wasn't bad enough that Josh and Laz's jock friends had been hassling Marcus at school for several months, now he had to face them at my house, too? Why hadn't I known they would all be here?

To my horror, Claire continued the introduction. "This is my sister's friend, Marcus."

Josh turned toward Marcus. "Uh, yeah," he said. "How ya doin'?" Laz gave Marcus a single nod.

Marcus let out a barely audible, "Hey." After a lengthy pause, where apparently none of us knew what to do, Marcus said, "I . . . better go get things set up," and headed for the back door.

Claire showed the boys to the TV and headed upstairs to primp. I hiked my camera bag over my shoulder and walked toward the backyard, hoping Marcus was serious about staying to help and hadn't just taken off. I'd barely wrapped my head around doing this just for Claire. I really couldn't do *this* whole production on my own.

Marcus stood by the trampoline, and I immediately let out a huge sigh of relief.

"I'm not exactly sure why you need me," he said.

My adrenaline rushed with hope that I could convince him to stay. "I had no idea it would be *four* of them," I said quickly. I decided to keep quiet about the fact that my parents were planning to get home early to be in some of the pictures. "Now I *really* need your help in setting up the shots." Before he could jump in with excuses, I rushed into photographer mode. "What do you think for the backdrop? The rosebushes, maybe?" I walked toward them, tilting my head like I was considering angles, even though I knew this would not make a good background for any full body shots, with the broken lattice jutting out from behind.

But I was baiting him.

Soon Marcus came up behind me and reached forward, touching the lattice. "Over by the oak tree has a nice feel."

Exactly my thought. "You think?"

He nodded, backing away to another part of our yard. "Or actually, with the four of them, you could try in front of the fence." He reached out his hands sideways, as if measuring it. "What if we draped something on it?"

"That's so perfect! You're a genius."

I rushed into the house and riffled through our linen closet for something I could use. I found a large cream-colored bed sheet, and when I came back out, Marcus had moved the lawn furniture out of the way. He helped me drape the fabric so it hung nicely over the fence. Then I ran inside to grab the tripod my mom had found at a garage sale.

As I set it up, I swallowed hard. It felt like I was a real photographer, doing this for a living. This was beginning to feel way out of my league.

Even more so when the foursome strode out the back door in all their grad-gown glory. Jasmine's chest looked even bigger in her gown, and Claire looked even skinnier in hers. I didn't look forward to seeing what one of those did to *my* frame, come next year.

"Where do you want us?" Laz clapped his hands together. The boys really were swoon-worthy. Josh wore dress pants and a white button-down shirt that made him look extra tan. He winked at me, and I realized I'd been dazedly staring at him for way too long.

"You got it set up okay?" Josh asked, motioning to my camera. The camera that *used to belong to him!*

I nodded and cleared my throat, then motioned everyone over toward the fence. Jasmine and Claire murmured about how nice the fabric backdrop looked. Part of me wanted to give Marcus the credit. But the greater part of me knew that wouldn't be smart.

I took my time focusing my camera as Claire and her friends hung out and chatted. Marcus stood beside me and whispered ideas about how to frame them, as if he knew how panicked I felt about it. While I made final adjustments behind my Nikon, though, I noticed the twitchy movements of the foursome. *They were nervous about this too?* That made me feel a little more at ease.

I walked toward them, clearing my throat again.

"So let's start with you over here," I said to Laz. "And Jasmine can stand in front of you." I flashed Marcus a quick smile of *Thanks for the idea.* Then I waved my hand at Claire and Josh. "You two mirror them on this side."

I had never thought much about the fact that Claire was dating a younger guy, when she could probably get any guy her age or even older. But today, with Josh in different clothes, their age difference suddenly looked shockingly obvious.

Claire nodded to me with a permagrin plastered on her face. Josh patted her butt, but she swatted his hand away, looking annoyed. My sister was certainly not one for PDAs, even if Jaz and Laz so obviously were, always kissing or groping each other in the hallways at school.

I had to ask all of them to shift their angles until it looked right. When I looked through my lens, I could make better sense of what would work best, and I called out directions without taking my eye from the camera. The four became strangely quiet and obedient. You'd swear I was threatening them with a weapon.

It felt bizarre to have power over these people.

I thought I'd have trouble concentrating with both Josh and Marcus so close, but surprisingly, through my camera I wasn't distracted at all.

I ended up having to move Jasmine and Claire a little farther apart. Jasmine was proof-positive that beauty and popularity could be bought, but even though her parents had paid for her perfect nose and eyebrows, and I suspected her boobs, every time I saw her beside my sister, she just wasn't as naturally beautiful.

After a few shots in that position, I organized them in several different combinations and displays, all with Marcus's help. I sat them in chairs and made them wear sunglasses. Some of the pictures would be bizarre, but I was having a great time watching them run around like puppy dogs after my every command.

After I'd shot all the poses I could think of, I led Claire over by the oak tree. "No, just Claire," I said when the others started to follow. I used almost a whole roll of film as I directed her. She was so photogenic, I didn't want to stop. It was like photographing someone for a magazine cover.

Besides that, all my life, I'd wanted to impress Claire. To have her think I was worthwhile. And I could tell by the way she listened to my direction that this was my moment.

Halfway through my roll, I went over to Claire, pretending to adjust her cap for the shot.

"I think it's time to take a break so you can fix your hair," I whispered.

She went running off, saying she had to use the bathroom. When she came back, it didn't look any better.

"It still looks a little frizzy," I said, adjusting the cap again.

She took off again, this time with Jasmine in tow, and came back ten minutes later looking exactly the same. But now she patted her hair self-consciously every two seconds. Claire's hair had always been shiny and thick and flawless. But now that I thought about it, hadn't it been looking a little dull lately?

I decided not to say another word about it, not wanting to kill her confidence. I got back to work and finished the roll.

Shortly after, my parents arrived home. I avoided Marcus's eyes at first, hoping he wouldn't be mad at me. I knew he wasn't crazy about being here when Mom was around, and I suspected it might be even worse with Dad here too. But surprisingly Marcus stayed right by my side and even said hi to them when they came over.

Mom didn't seem to hear him, consumed with the backdrop and her oldest daughter, decked out in her grad gown. But Dad extended his hand toward Marcus.

Marcus looked down at it for a second, then he lifted his hand to shake it. Dad was pretty good with pleasant introductions. Much better than Mom, anyway.

Marcus's shoulders relaxed when Dad finally left him alone to go shake the other boys' hands. When the introductions were over, I said, "I'm ready for you all over by the fence."

I took the shots quickly. With such a large group, I didn't move them around much, so I could be sure to keep them all in the frame.

"Maybe Marcus could take a shot so you could be in a picture, Loey," Claire said when I was just ready to wrap it up.

I looked down at my T-shirt and shorts. "I'm not dressed for it at all."

"But we need at least one family shot," Mom said. She was already taking over organizing this one for me, nudging Jaz and Laz to the outside and leaving a space for me between Claire and my parents.

Great, right in the middle. I glanced over at Marcus. Mom

had still made absolutely no effort to say hello to him. She certainly hadn't welcomed him into "the family shot" the way she had with Josh.

Suddenly that made me angry.

"Hey, Marcus," I whispered. "Help me figure out how to set the timer."

I've never been good when it came to electronics, but Marcus seemed to have a knack for it. As soon as he confirmed it was set, I grabbed him by the wrist and pulled him toward the cream backdrop. He stiffened, but he stood back against the fence with me in front of him.

"Wait, wha—" Mom started, but I could tell she was fumbling for words that wouldn't sound too bitchy.

"Smile, everybody," I said. And hopefully they all did, because the flash went off only a second later.

After finishing the group shots, I claimed exhaustion. And really, I probably was, though it was hard to tell, with my pumping adrenaline.

"This was amazing, with the backdrop and the tree," Claire said in front of her three friends and our parents. "I have no idea when my little sister became Ansel Adams." Claire met my eyes, and there was something so close to admiration in hers, I wanted to cry. "You're the best, Loey." Everyone nodded in agreement, and for that second, I almost believed that I was.

CHAPTER SEVENTEEN

On the first Friday after school let out for the summer, I headed to the Arts Club. I bit my lip when I saw Marcus sitting at "our" table, waiting for me. We had coffee, and he paid without even asking me if I had cash.

"Thanks again for helping me with the grad photo shoot," I said. "The pictures turned out great." I passed him a copy of the one family picture that had both of us in it. His neck went a little pink. Surprisingly, Mom hadn't gotten on my case about inviting Marcus into the shot. Hopefully she was softening toward him.

After looking at the photo for a few seconds, Marcus slid it into the front of a car magazine he'd been reading.

"It was weird, feeling like I was the one in charge of the photo shoot," I said.

"You *were* in charge," he said with an arched eyebrow, like I was being silly.

"Well, yeah, I know, but . . ." I had to think of how to explain it to him. "You know how geese always fly in that *V* kind of formation? I just always thought of Claire as the front goose, you know, breaking the wind for little misfit birds like me."

He laughed. "You know that the front bird has to switch out, though, right? And another bird has to switch in. The front bird is always changing."

Hmm. He was right. Maybe that wasn't a good example. Then again, maybe it was a good example after all. Maybe sometimes I *did* need to switch in and become more of the leader.

When it was time for dinner, I stood to head out. Marcus and I didn't talk about seeing each other again, so I assumed I would come back to find him there next week. I still had his e-mail address, but for some reason I felt weird about using it.

I stayed around the house the next few days and watched TV whenever Claire's soap operas weren't on, or hung out in my room, listening to her rattle away on the computer down the hall. I thought a lot about Marcus. How often would be too much to drop by the Arts Club? If I went every day, would that seem clingy? And would he be there every day?

Claire interrupted my thoughts from my bedroom doorway.

"Wanna come to the movies with me and Jasmine?" she asked.

"Sure," I said, trying not to register my shock. "What are we seeing?"

"That new one with Miley Cyrus."

Even though it wasn't my thing, I followed her out the door without complaining. It wasn't often that Claire invited me to do "friend" things with her anymore, so who cared if it was a little perky for my taste?

"We should get inside," I said when I noticed Jasmine looking me up and down outside the theater. The way she kept scrutinizing me, you'd swear I'd worn my bra on top of my shirt today. I didn't actually care what Jasmine thought, but I hoped her embarrassment wouldn't rub off on Claire.

Jasmine flipped her enhanced blond hair over her shoulder and led the way, like she couldn't get in there fast enough.

During the previews, Claire kept whispering to Jasmine about Josh.

"It *was* a big deal," she said. "Trust me, he was mad."

I leaned in to try to hear more. Even though I couldn't make out many of their words, I got the gist. Josh and Claire *had* had a fight.

"Don't worry, he still totally likes you," Jasmine said with a sigh, like this was barely worth talking about.

"How do you know?" I blurted, and someone shushed me from behind. Claire and Jasmine both stared at me for a second, like I'd asked the question in Swahili. "I mean, how do you know when a guy likes you?" I whispered. If someone like Claire had doubts, it had to be confusing. Besides, I didn't want Jasmine to change the subject if Claire wanted to talk about this.

Jasmine chuckled. "You just . . . know. It's, like, obvious." She looked at Claire with her eyebrows raised. I knew the look. The look that said, *Tell me again why you brought your little sister?* I couldn't believe how much she changed when I didn't hold a camera.

It's not that I disliked Jasmine. She'd been hanging around since she met Claire in ninth grade. I guess I just wished she liked me.

And I wished I could talk to my sister more, now that there were important things to talk about.

I met Marcus again the next Saturday at the Arts Club, glad to be able to be myself around someone again.

Armando came up to us right away and asked, "You watch coffee all day?"

Marcus nodded, so I did too. We didn't have plans for the

rest of the day, and it wasn't like we had anywhere else to go.

Ten minutes after Armando left, a swarm of customers came through the door. I had never been in on a Saturday, and it caught me off guard. Marcus met the first couple at the counter, and within five minutes, a line up formed and he needed my help. I stood beside him taking orders, surprised at his expertise at making the specialty coffees. *Had he done this before?* He ground the espresso beans without even looking at them, and moved back and forth between machines with finesse.

Another hidden talent. Which only made me want to learn more about him. We were a pretty good team and worked without stopping until almost noon.

When the last customers had gone, Marcus pushed a silver canister in my direction. "Here. You try," he said.

I held the container under the big cappuccino machine and he talked me through making my very own latte. It was actually easier than I expected, and fun to be able to leave my milk under the spout to make it extra frothy. After that, we sat and silently drank our coffees, proud of our work. At least I was.

The next two hours passed without much activity.

"So . . . we're seniors next year," Marcus said. "I guess we should think about what comes next. After high school." He paused, but not long enough for me to comment. "I gotta get out of Alder Grove. I started working on the old man's Chevy the other day."

I wasn't quite sure what one had to do with the other, but I nodded. It was the first time Marcus had ever said a word about his dad, or ever let on that Marcus had a part of his life he was unhappy with.

"I don't know what I'm going to do," I said. "But if I'm lucky enough to get into college, believe me, I won't just throw that away." I couldn't keep the bitterness toward Claire from leaking out in my voice. We'd been off school for two weeks, and she hadn't been practicing ballet, or really doing much of anything, other than getting in my way and taking over the TV whenever I wanted it. Fortunately for her, I think our parents were too busy at work to notice.

At two in the afternoon, I glanced to the opening door and did a double-take. Shayleen strutted into the café with three guys I recognized from school. She was so busy talking, she didn't notice me at first. But I couldn't stop staring at her. Her skirt barely covered the tops of her thighs. I watched her move through the place as though she'd been here many times. When she finally noticed me, she stood too far from the door to nonchalantly make a retreat, and had been looking at the counter for too long to pretend I wasn't there.

I reached to pat down my hair, suddenly self-conscious. It

hadn't occurred to me that I might see people from school at the café, since I'd never known about the place until Marcus introduced me.

"What are you doing here?" She pulled her arms across her chest.

"I work here," I said, with as much false confidence as I could muster. It was stupid to play this up like it was a real job. She could so easily find out the truth. I just couldn't help myself. I wanted it to sound like I had more right to be here than she did. This was my and Marcus's place.

"Oh," she said, glancing at the door. I knew she wanted to leave, to tell her friends, "Let's go somewhere else." But at the same time she didn't like to be pushed around.

"Iced mocha," she finally said.

Marcus started to make the drink while I took the other orders and made change. The boy right beside Shayleen paid for her coffee, and I wondered if this was a new boyfriend. And if so, why were the other two tagging along?

"Is it hot out?" I asked the one guy who kept looking at me. Marcus and I hadn't been outside the doors since nine a.m. so I had no idea.

"Yeah," Shayleen's boyfriend said. "I can't wait to get in the pool." He was the cutest of the three, but they all had a rough-around-the-edges, uncombed look about them.

Shayleen nudged her guy with an elbow. He stopped talking and they all got quiet. Finally I turned to help Marcus while they stood staring at us.

We brought their drinks to the counter. It didn't surprise me when Shayleen directed her group to go drink them at the park. I let out a big breath after the door closed behind them. Marcus didn't seem to notice my stress over the whole ordeal. Or at least he didn't say anything about it.

Then another lull hit. Marcus walked around the café, talking more about the paintings on the walls, and I followed him. I liked his voice. It was quiet and deep for a seventeen-year-old. He rambled on about his favorite Michelangelo repro.

"And this is a van Gogh," he said, moving on to another one. *Portrait of Dr. Gachet*. The original sold for eighty-two and a half million." He nodded his approval toward it.

Then he moved on to the next one. *"The Yellow House,"* he said. "By some unknown, uh, Guy Roberts, I think." Marcus was already walking away from it. "Worth five hundred, at most."

The next painting, a new one—or at least, one I didn't remember from my last visit—was disturbing. An older man held a young boy down by his throat. With his other hand he held a knife.

"Wh—who's this by?" I asked.

Marcus swallowed so loud I could hear it. "Uh, Caravaggio,"

he said. "It's pretty . . . famous." He angled his face away from me, a hardness forming around his jaw. It was a difficult painting to look at, but looking at Marcus was almost harder. I wanted to reach for his hand. But just as I worked up enough courage to do it he headed back to our table, sat down, and started sipping his coffee.

When Armando returned, he shuffled through the door and over behind the counter. Then he came over and dropped two twenties on the table between us. Not exactly top dollar for a full day's work, but we both beamed anyway. We'd made it ourselves.

"You good kids," he said to us in his heavily accented tongue.

We thanked him as he walked away. Then he turned back and said, or asked, I couldn't tell quite which, "You work Saturdays now."

And that's how Marcus and I got our first jobs.

I told my parents as soon as I got home.

"Good for you, honey," Dad said from just outside the front closet.

Mom, pruning the plants in our living room, seemed slightly more interested. "Hmm. What kind of job?"

"It's just a Saturday thing, Mom. It'll be good experience, and it's not like I do anything else on Saturdays. It's probably just for the summer." I didn't know why I felt the need to convince her, since she didn't seem to be arguing.

Claire sat quietly on the couch. She just followed me around the room with her sad eyes while one of her favorite movies played in the background.

I wanted to say something to her, but I was afraid it would come out in a scream. *Why don't you just get a friggin' job? I mean, if you're not going to bother going to college . . .*

But before I could complete my ranting thoughts, Claire interjected, "Yeah, I got a job, too!"

"Oh?" Dad was about to reach for the front door, but stopped and looked between me and Claire. "Well, that's great, honey."

Mom jumped in, "I didn't know you'd been applying. It won't get in the way of your ballet practice, I hope?" She stopped watering her plants and turned to Claire.

What ballet practice? I wondered. Sure, she'd been going to her summer class once a week, but other than that I hadn't seen her dance bag leave its spot inside her bedroom door even once since school let out. Not like last year, when she was always dancing in her room or even booking extra time at the studio.

Claire crossed the room toward the stairs, not looking at any of us. "Oh, no, of course not, Mom. But I need to save some money for when I get into performing-arts school. It's probably more expensive than regular college."

The "probably" made it clear, at least to me, that she hadn't looked into that yet, and part of me wondered if she ever planned on it.

"What schools have you been considering?" Mom asked, possibly thinking the same thing.

"Oh, there are so many of them," Claire said. "I'll . . . have to order some brochures."

With Claire's vague answers, Mom quickly changed the subject back to Claire's new job, asking her a million questions about where it was and what she'd be doing.

Claire was halfway up the stairs before she turned back and said, "I'm just starting as a stock girl at Carmine's Clothing. In the back," she added. "It's no big deal."

But of course, it was a big deal that Claire was doing something. Because it was always a big deal whenever Claire did *anything*.

Even though it felt like everything had changed since I'd worked on the photo-set and discovered my ability with photography, standing in my house with my family, I realized that nothing had changed.

Claire would always overshadow me. My life wasn't as important as hers.

CHAPTER EIGHTEEN

Most days, Claire didn't get home in time to eat with us, or said she'd just grabbed something on the way home, but when she did, she spent most of the time moving her food from side to side. She took tiny bites—one pea, or a single grain of rice—then went back to rearranging her plate. I wondered what consumed her, since she still wouldn't talk to me about anything real. If I watched her for long enough, she started eating normally.

Tonight, though, she stole the chicken drumstick before I even had a chance. Mom always put one drumstick aside for Dad, and Claire and I usually at least discussed who would get the other one, but I'd just assumed that with her new diet, I'd get it this time.

"I thought you were a vegetable now, Claire."

She raised her eyebrows. "Very funny. Actually, Loann, I still eat a lot of vegetables. I'm just trying to be smart. I need some protein for my muscles, too."

She only called me Loann at home, when she was pissed. So, what, she couldn't take a joke now either?

Mom didn't seem to notice the way Claire ate—or didn't—so the next night, I tried to point it out to her.

"Claire," I said pointedly, "can I get you some more mashed potatoes?" I scooped a big dollop out of the bowl and moved it toward her plate. I don't know why I felt so antagonizing toward her. Maybe I was just trying to force her to pay attention to me again. To remember who I was and that we used to actually like each other.

"No. Thank you, Loann." She pulled her skimpily decorated plate closer to herself.

"How's your meal, Claire?" I pressed. "Not much there, huh?"

Claire's eyes widened, like she couldn't believe what I'd said, but it was pretty much just stating the obvious. "Well some of us watch what we eat," she snapped back. "Why don't you look at your own problems, first?"

I swallowed. She was right, of course. I never really held back from eating whatever I wanted. And because of that, I was too embarrassed to wear a bathing suit without a big T-shirt over my top every summer.

Mom, off in her own world, quietly jabbed at her own dinner, and I had to wonder, *Didn't she care about anything that happened at the dinner table anymore?*

Marcus didn't show the next Friday at the Arts Club. Even though it had only been a few days, I missed him. I headed home to check and see if he'd e-mailed me, expecting to find the house empty, but Claire sat alone on the couch. She just stared at the wall and didn't seem to even flinch when I said hi to her.

I walked around the far side of the couch to see her face. Tears streaked her cheeks. *Was she still upset over our argument about food last night? Or was it something more serious?* I went over and sat beside her.

"You're not working today," I said softly.

That's when she started to really cry. And not her normal, prim little snivels. Big, snotty, crocodile tears.

"Oh, Loey," she said. "Oh, Loey, it was awful." With a big flourish, she threw her face into her hands. I reached over and patted her back, expecting her next words to be about getting fired, but then she wailed, "We broke up!"

It took me a second to catch up. "Wait, you and Josh?"

She let out an even louder wail, so I rubbed circles on her back as it pulsed up and down. I certainly didn't expect the two of them to get married or anything, but Jaz and Laz had been dating for so long that I just assumed Josh and Claire would too.

I was also surprised at the relief I felt that they weren't together anymore. I'd always thought I was happy for Claire, getting *the* Josh. But maybe . . . I wasn't.

"What happened?" I asked.

She didn't answer right away, but draped her long, slender body over my shoulders in a hug. I moved my hands around to her back and continued circling. When we were younger and closer to the same size, we used to hug all the time or, at the very least, throw an arm over the other's shoulder. This felt so awkward now. We were such different shapes. But still, I was happy to have my sister needing me.

"It just . . . I don't even know," she finally breathed out between her sobs.

After several minutes of me soaking up her tears with my dark green T-shirt, she inched back to her place on the couch. Then she smoothed her capris and said, "You're the best, Loey."

Even though I hadn't done anything, her words made my insides flutter. They made me remember long-ago days, when we knew how to help each other. I knew this wasn't the time to talk about her weird eating, but I also wondered if this was the cause of it. Now that it was over between them, sure, she'd probably be upset for a few days, but then maybe she'd be less stressed. She's so beautiful and popular, I had no doubt that she'd find a new boyfriend in no time.

Claire stayed in her room through dinner that night, and left early the next day for work. I figured she probably needed a breather from talking about it, so I made excuses to Mom for her. A few days later, I noticed that she wasn't talking to Jasmine, either. She usually spent her evenings at the very least gabbing on the phone, but these days she just sat on the couch, watching TV with me. Mom and Dad both headed back to their jobs most evenings, if they even made it home for dinner, so Claire and I were left on our own. We didn't really talk much, and some days she didn't want anything to eat—not even a salad. I tried to keep the conversation light and happy, to let her know she didn't have to talk about Josh if she didn't want to, but she seemed to be in a cranky mood no matter what I said. She flipped TV shows, even when I was watching one. She played cell-phone games with one hand and held a death-grip on the TV remote with the other. Rather than arguing with her, I headed for my room and lay on my bed to think.

Had Josh been mean when they broke up? That didn't seem like Josh, but Claire had become such a mess.

By Saturday, Claire still hadn't said another word about the breakup. I stood behind the Arts Club counter, washing dishes and thinking about her, when who should walk through the doors but Josh and three of his buddies.

The same friends who had tormented Marcus at his locker last year. *How had they found this tiny, tucked-away café? Was I the only one who hadn't known about this place?*

Josh smiled right away when he saw me. "Loann. Hi! Your sister told me you worked here." The way he talked about Claire, it sounded like he wasn't the least bit torn up over their breakup. My thoughts went immediately to Claire—was she just being melodramatic about the whole thing? I mean, they hadn't been dating *that* long. But then my second thought—she told him I worked here? *Really?* And he remembered?

"Um, hi," I finally spit out.

Marcus moved to the back end of the counter and cleaned one of the machines that we hadn't used all morning. I glanced back at him and felt a flush to my face, having my two *favorite* guys so close to me at the same time.

Josh ordered an Americano, and I didn't bother asking Marcus for help. I made the drink and slid it over. When Josh passed me his money, I swear, he grasped my hand as he placed the bills in it.

What was that for? Was it supposed to be a message about Claire? Maybe it was his way of saying he *did* miss her, even if he was acting strong in front of his friends.

I offered him a sympathetic smile as I gave him his change.

Then one of his friends butted in front of him at the counter.

The guy, I think his name was Ron, eyed Marcus while he asked for a grandé dark roast. After filling his cup, I passed it over. I waited for Ron to pay, but he didn't reach for his pocket. Instead he leaned in a little and said, "Thanks, Loann."

He turned to leave.

What? Seriously?

"Hey, buddy!" I called out as they walked for the door. "You have to pay for that."

"Oh, sorry," Ron called back, not sounding sorry in the least. "Is it Loann, or is it Slow-ann?"

He kept walking but then Josh grabbed him by the shoulder. Ron stopped in place and went rigid, as if he couldn't believe Josh would challenge him.

The other two guys headed outside, like the stench of their friends' body odor wasn't enough to hide behind.

I could see a silent battle going on between Josh and Ron.

"Funny," I said. "I'd be more inclined to think a guy who couldn't remember to pay the cashier was the slow one." I stared at Ron and didn't relent. Who cared if he hated me? Then Marcus and I would have another thing in common. "But don't worry if you're too broke." I flicked the donation can for a charity organization that Armando kept beside the till. "We keep a fund here to help the mentally disabled."

I spun back to the coffeemaker and cleaned it as if the

boys weren't worth my attention. I heard the door open and close, but didn't turn for fear I'd start shaking.

Then footsteps sounded near the cash register. I glanced up just as Josh placed a five-dollar bill on the counter.

"Sorry about that," he said, and left without giving me a chance to reply, or offer any change.

Marcus was quiet after the café cleared out. I couldn't stop thinking about the whole scene: not only about how I'd stood up to Ron but also how awesome Josh had been. I could definitely understand why Claire was heartbroken.

"That was really cool of Josh," I said.

Marcus just *pftted* at my comment.

"What's that supposed to mean?"

He raised his eyebrows and passed me a latte he'd just made. I set it down. I knew Marcus was just insecure. I mean, the guys were way bigger than him. And more popular. Though I thought Marcus was just as cute.

"No, really. What did you mean by that? Because Josh has always been nothing but nice to you." *And to me*, I added silently in my head.

Marcus shrugged. "I just think they're all the same. Josh puts up a better front than the rest of them. That's all."

I wanted to argue, to tell Marcus that lumping Josh with the other jocks was just as bad as them picking on him. But I clamped my mouth shut.

Maybe Marcus was jealous. And maybe that meant he had the kind of feelings for me that I had for him.

Maybe.

I hadn't allowed myself to hope since that time in the genie outfit. Since the time I'd offered him three wishes, and he'd almost made one. A smile lit up my face. Let Marcus get mad about Josh.

Let him get really, really mad.

CHAPTER NINETEEN

On Monday I was so happy to see Jasmine at our house, I almost hugged her. Claire really needed a friend. Someone who knew how to talk to her and bring her out of her mopey, selfish funk. I couldn't do it. I wondered if Claire acted this way at work, too. I doubted that would fly at a brand-new job. And didn't she have to work today? I thought she'd said it was Monday to Friday.

I wandered into the kitchen at lunchtime, expecting them to be chatting and stop the moment they saw me, but they just sat there stoically, staring down at the table.

"Hey, Jasmine!" I tried to infuse the room with some cheeriness, even though I'd already said hi an hour ago when she arrived. Still, I swear, a look of relief crossed her face when she met my gaze.

"Hey, Loann. What are you up to today?"

"Working later," I said. I told her about my job at the Arts Club, where I'd started working more than just Saturdays. Jasmine sat taller and acted genuinely interested. Claire sunk lower into her chair, like I was putting her to sleep.

Whatever. I just wanted a sandwich.

As I waited for my bread to toast, I listened to them crunch at their salads. By the time my toast popped, I had the meat, cheese, and mustard out on the counter. I couldn't get out of the wordless chamber fast enough.

"Mmm. Smells good, Loann," Jasmine said. "Would you make me one, too?"

Was she serious? Her raised eyebrows looked like she was. "Sure." I dropped two more slices of bread into the toaster.

As I finished assembling my sandwich, Jasmine murmured to Claire, "I thought you said there was no other food in the house. That your mom hadn't been shopping in weeks."

Claire scoffed. "Yeah, well, if you want food like *that*." She pushed her salad away and crossed her arms. "Do you have any idea how many carbs are in a sandwich?"

Jasmine scrunched her face. "I'm just hungry. It's not like I'm scarfing down chocolate bars."

Claire looked her best friend up and down. "Okay. Whatever you say."

I couldn't believe this. I'd always thought Claire was the

amiable one. The one who won her popularity, at least in part, by her ability to get along with everyone. *Who was this girl?*

When Jasmine's toast popped, it sounded like a gunshot in the quiet. I quickly threw together her sandwich, not even knowing if she'd eat it now, then placed it on the table in front of her. I avoided Claire's glare on my way out of the room.

While I ate lunch alone at my desk, I dug through my shoe box of negatives and pictures, trying not to think of the weirdness downstairs. Each time I held up a strip of negatives toward the window, the little squares sparked so many memories.

I cringed when I came across the photos of Mom making elaborate gestures toward the camera, and the shots of Claire's dainty hand held out like a stop sign. I was surprised how many pictures had accumulated in my box. The spontaneous ones were something else. I had a great one of Claire in the bathroom, putting on her mascara. She leaned into the mirror with the most serious look. Her full lips formed a funny oval shape with her concentration. With the click of my camera, she had jumped away from the counter, getting a swipe on her cheek. She flashed me a look and pointed at me with her mascara wand, but I could tell she was fighting a smile.

The great thing about my pictures of Claire was that they all said something. It was effortless with her as my subject. She was beautiful, of course, but so many other things seemed to be going on inside her, and all of that emotion came through clearly on film. If a person had only ever heard her speak they would think she was one kind of person, but in my pictures she was quite another.

But the girl down at our kitchen table? She was another yet.

Apparently Monday's lunch with Jasmine was a one-time deal. Day after day passed with no sign of Claire's best friend, and who could blame her after the way Claire had acted? Most nights Claire just stayed in her room with her iPod docked and playing.

I'd been thinking about putting together a photography portfolio to see if there was some place to submit it for a scholarship, but by the end of the week, I could no longer concentrate with Claire next door. It was as if she radiated her agitated energy.

I wondered what had happened to the days when she never stayed home on a Friday or Saturday night. She hadn't even gone to her job all week.

She pulled my bathroom door shut, and a few seconds later I heard the water running. My photos were spread all over my desk, but I didn't have much idea of how to start putting together a portfolio. Should I pick my favorites? Or look for ones that went together?

An odd noise caught my attention from the bathroom. It

was a gurgling or choking sound. The water was running, so I wondered what Claire was doing in there.

I walked to the door, to see if she was okay. Then I heard it. Claire was vomiting.

At dinner, I'd made a point of dishing some food out on Claire's plate before she came to the table. When she tried to escape with most of it covered by her napkin, I'd called her on it, said she was wasting food when we couldn't afford it, and Mom had made her sit down and finish her plate.

So she was just going to throw it all up instead?

I had to talk to her about this. She couldn't stay this upset about her breakup with Josh forever. I knocked on the bathroom door.

"What?" Claire asked over the running water. "I'm busy!" She sounded angry and bossy.

"Busy with what?" Yeah, I felt like a tool, but I couldn't keep letting her push me away. Not now.

She didn't answer.

"Can I, uh, talk to you when you're done?"

Thirty seconds later the water stopped, then Claire jostled open the door to my room and walked back through the bathroom to hers. She didn't acknowledge me in any way.

I made the trek through the bathroom, which smelled strongly of air freshener, and into Claire's room. She sat at her desk and looked out her window, tapping her pen. I took a few uncomfortable steps across the room and sat on her bed.

I picked at the edge of her bedspread, like I used to do when we were younger. I'd sit here and listen while she talked on the phone, and she didn't seem to mind. In fact, during our middle-school years, I think she liked having an audience as she talked about the boys she was interested in.

But that was years ago, and this felt way different. I didn't even know how to start a conversation in this thorny silence.

"Are you . . . do you think you're fat or something?" I asked finally.

Claire's knuckles whitened around her pen. "No, of course not," she said in a much angrier tone that I expected. "Do *you* think I'm fat?"

I didn't know how to reply. Obviously I did not think she was fat, but somehow I didn't think that was the answer she was looking for. But what *did* she want to hear?

She glanced over at the bathroom, and a worried look crossed her face. Then Claire spoke as though she didn't really want anyone to hear her. "Don't worry, I won't do it again." She flicked her pen harder. "You should just be glad that everyone doesn't want *you* to be something you're not, Loann. You don't know what it's like. It's too hard."

I don't know what that's *like? Give me a break! The term "unmet expectations" was pretty much invented for me! But* okay. This was about her, and somehow she was struggling in a way that I didn't understand.

Claire's bottom lip trembled.

"You . . . you're so thin already. And so pretty." I started saying it to make her feel better, but by the end I was shaking my head. *Didn't she already know that?*

"He told me I was pretty," she said with a humorless laugh. It took me a second to realize she meant Josh. "That's the best part of having a boyfriend, Loey. They treat you special and tell you you're beautiful. Girls need that, you know?"

She sounded sad, wistful. And she'd called me Loey, which was a good sign.

"What about you?" she asked.

I wasn't sure what she meant, so I answered her question with a question. "Why don't boys like me, Claire?"

Immediately I felt uncomfortable for asking, but Claire seemed to think nothing of it. In fact, I think it made her brighten a bit. She tilted her head at me.

"I know I'm not pretty enough," I added, to make sure she understood I had a *few* of the family brain cells. "But is that all there is?"

"Oh, Loey," she said as she came over and draped her light arm around my shoulders. "Is that what you think? That you're not good enough?" She squeezed me as she said it. "If anything, Loey, if anything at all, you're too good for *them*. For all of them."

I felt my forehead contorting.

Claire continued, "I think maybe you intimidate boys."

How could I ever intimidate anyone? I thought back to when Josh and his friends had been in the café. But no, I hadn't intimidated Ron. Josh had come back to pay, and that was just because he's nice. I had never told Claire that he'd stopped by that day, and I wondered if I should have.

Claire sat up on her knees behind me on the bed and took the sides of my hair, pulled them away from my face, and gathered them on top of my head. Unlatching the barrette from her own hair with her free hand, she fastened it into mine. We looked across the room together into her antique mirror, our faces close.

"See how pretty you are?" she said.

My mouth twitched. I didn't know if I could see it.

But one thing I was quite certain of: I couldn't say for sure that I didn't see it.

CHAPTER TWENTY

Marcus and I both looked up from our spot behind the front hedges when Mom's car pulled into the driveway. When Marcus and I weren't at the café, we went on what we called "photography hunts" around town or just in my yard. I was excited to have so many rolls of film ready to develop when we got back to school in the fall.

Claire got out on the passenger side of the car, Mom on the other, the two of them already in midargument. I looked over at Marcus, who had gone frozen. I didn't get what the big deal was. Mom wasn't *that* scary.

Claire's words trailed behind her toward the house. "Mom, I've been dancing for practically my whole life. I just want time to concentrate on other things for a while. Like finding the right college."

My mind couldn't compute this conversation. Claire now wanted to dump ballet to go to a regular college, instead of a performing-arts school?

"You can do both, Claire. It's not fair to the other dancers if you quit in the middle of the season."

"But, Mom—"

Their voices escalated as they walked into the house, but Claire's words were cut off by the door. I handed Marcus my camera and told him I'd be right back. Then I raced around to the back door. I could hear Mom's and Claire's voices as soon as I was in the house, but peered through an inch-wide opening of the kitchen door anyway.

"This is what you asked us for." Mom marched around the living room, tidying up the couch cushions. "We paid good money for you to be a part of the summer program. Finish up the session. Then we'll talk about it."

Claire let out a melodramatic sigh and dropped her dance bag. "I knew you wouldn't understand."

Understand what?! Claire seriously wanted to drop ballet, the only real thing she was doing with her life, because she didn't have time for it? She'd hardly been working, but of course, Mom probably didn't know that. What was Claire so busy with? Soap operas?

"I understand just fine, Claire. But you committed to the summer performance." I was proud of Mom, sticking to her guns even though it went against Claire's sudden college aspi-rations.

"I'm not doing the recital," Claire said, pulling her arms across her chest like a two-year-old.

Mom straightened, but didn't reply right away. I pushed the door a little wider. Claire jutted her chin forward, waiting for her rebuttal.

Mom placed her hands firmly on her hips. "You will do exactly what we tell you while you're still living in our house."

Claire dropped her head in her hands and started to cry. "Why, Mom? Why do you care? It's just a stupid show." If this was true, I wondered why Claire cared so much.

"Claire, it is not stupid." Mom put an arm around her and stroked her back. "You and the girls have been work-ing toward this, and they'll be counting on you. Mrs. Avery's counting on you. They need you. You know that."

Claire always had a big solo right in the middle of the show, and it wouldn't be the same without her. Why was that hard for her to grasp?

But after a few seconds, she wiped away her tears, looked back at Mom, and nodded.

That was the end of that. Claire would continue ballet. I let out a breath. Even though the argument had nothing to do with me, the idea of Claire getting her way right now, when she seemed so unlike herself, scared me. For once in my life I was glad to have such a bull-headed mother.

Summer was like a fever in Alder Grove, Wisconsin: too hot and too long. Armando seemed happy enough to work in the air-conditioned café, so I asked Marcus if he'd be into heading for the bridge. I didn't know why; it wasn't like Armando ever interfered with us. The idea of being alone with Marcus just seemed more, well, exciting.

Neither of us could wait to get into the water. Marcus took off his shirt as we walked. I stopped for a second to adjust my flip-flop, which had come partway off in my surprise. Before Marcus turned to find me, I saw a large, purplish-black bruise across the middle of his back.

I opened my mouth to say something, but stopped myself. We were friends. Because I didn't pry. Marcus only talked about stuff when he wanted to. This was obviously part of the reason he didn't want to talk about his family.

But I couldn't just leave it alone, either. Never being one for subtlety, I blurted, "Ow, what happened?"

Marcus stiffened, hung his shirt over a shoulder to cover most of the bruise, and picked up his pace again.

By the time we reached the river, he still hadn't answered

me. He didn't walk toward the bridge. He rushed ahead and jumped in from the bank.

"Yeow!" he yelled, surfacing. He kept ducking underwater and floating on his back, keeping his bruise hidden. "C'mon, Curly, you're gonna like this!"

Judging by his shout, the water must be freezing. I dipped my toe in. *Brrrr.*

I looked down at my jean shorts, already imagining how gross and heavy they would feel wet. I peeled them off, taking a quick peek for Marcus's reaction, but thankfully he was underwater.

Standing in my T-shirt and underwear, I tried to cover my legs with my hands. Marcus splashed around and came up for air, still oblivious. To avoid being seen half-naked, I decided to tackle the cold in one fell swoop and just get in the water. But I worried about my white underwear, too. Would it become see-through when it was wet? When Marcus bobbed up again, I decided I couldn't stand around wondering about that.

The cold hit me like an enormous bowl of ice cubes, and I squealed as I came up out of it. Marcus laughed at me, but I didn't care. I was practically hyperventilating from the cold.

My curly hair straightened down my back and Marcus stared at my forehead. As much as I disliked my curly hair, it suited me. I tried to run my fingers through the strands plastered to my forehead but my fingers snagged. I yanked harder until the hairs pulled apart, then tried to scrunch them into curls so my face wouldn't look freakishly round.

Marcus cackled. "Hah, I guess I won't buy you a flat iron."

Although it was the same kind of remark Shayleen might have made—and probably wouldn't have bothered me at all—this hit me hard. I was tired of feeling frumpy and ugly, especially around Marcus. I pulled a few strands of hair forward to hide my face. Tears welled up in the corners of my eyes.

"Aw, c'mon, Loann. Where's your comeback?" he said, still trying to rile me. "C'mon," he said again, a little quieter.

I pushed my lips together to stop them from quivering.

"Aren't you gonna tell me about my hot bod?" He gestured to his far-from-Taylor-Lautner frame.

The slow-moving water rippled toward me as he stepped closer. Then his still-warm hand rested on my shoulder. I couldn't look up at him or I'd start crying, I knew I would.

He slid his arms around my neck and pulled me closer. My rigid body relaxed a little.

"You just look different, that's all," he murmured into my wet hair.

Marcus and I had never been this close. His whole body felt warm against mine. Or maybe my body was the warm one, it was hard to tell. Shivers that had nothing to do with the water ran up and down my spine. I put my hands on his hips, willing myself to be strong and just breathe.

"I didn't mean anything by it," he said, pulling me in tighter. "I'm sorry, Loey."

I wasn't worried about my hair anymore. It felt good being this close to Marcus and I wanted him to know I hoped he wouldn't let me go. Tentatively, I felt his waist. Then I let my hands move around to his lower back. His breath caught, which made me shiver again.

Marcus's hand stroked the back of my wet hair in a way that his fingers wouldn't catch in my curls. I closed my eyes and tried to be bold, starting to move my hands in tiny circles, exploring his wet, shirtless body.

Suddenly he jumped, then stiffened, and I remembered the purple bruise on his back. I dropped my hands to his waist and fisted them, holding my breath, hoping he could relax into me again.

But Marcus pulled away and dunked underwater, swimming off a few feet. When he popped up a moment later, he said, "Hey, can you do a handstand?"

I bit my lip in disappointment.

Marcus was a good friend, the best I'd ever had, and I didn't want to ruin our friendship.

But then, was he even that good of a friend? I mean, we didn't talk about anything really serious. If I really wanted to be his friend, I had to ask about this.

He came up out of the water and didn't react at all to the fact that I still hadn't attempted a handstand. In fact, he stayed so busy with his synchronized swimming tricks, I was sure he was trying to avoid something. Or everything.

Every time Marcus went under, I took a step toward him, and consciously or unconsciously, he moved away from me. By the time I'd taken five or six steps, he was against the grassy riverbank and didn't have room to dive down again.

"Trying to corner me?" He said it like it was a joke, but it was true and we both knew it.

"What happened to your back, Marcus?"

He stared down at me, didn't say a word, but his face hardened.

"I know you don't like to talk about it, but—"

"I thought you got it," he practically spit in my face. His suddenly loud, curt tone made me take a step back. "I thought we were friends, Loann."

"We *are* fr—look, Marcus. Friends can talk about stuff. No matter how bad."

He shook his head, looking hurt and angry.

"It's not just you. It's me, too. I need someone to talk through stuff with, and, well . . ." I trailed off because he wasn't softening, not one iota. "Listen, if we can't talk about stuff that's real, then maybe we aren't truly friends at all."

I said it to bait him, but he just nodded. Then he pulled

himself up onto the bank behind him. I was about to take it all back, to try to make things revert to the way they were before, when he said, "You're right. I don't know why I didn't see it," in a tone void of emotion.

"No, Marcus, no." I pushed through the water toward him, but it felt like the current had suddenly doubled and was pulling me in the opposite direction.

He crossed the bridge in three long strides, snapped his shirt up from the ground, and darted into the trees before I could get myself out of the water.

My stomach clenched as I thought a hundred self-deprecating remarks about my stupid mouth that I never seemed able to keep shut.

But halfway home, I picked up my pace as my anger at myself turned into just plain anger.

Why couldn't he talk to me about anything? Maybe it stung so badly because our conversation rang true. Maybe we'd never really been friends and we were just each other's default way to spend our extra time.

I headed straight for the computer at home and opened a blank e-mail. But I had no idea what to say. Finally I just typed Marcus's e-mail address and "Can we talk?" in the subject line. I hit send.

I could tell Claire was home by the sound from her iPod dock. I tiptoed by quietly, not wanting to talk to anyone. The door to the bathroom was ajar, and I nudged it closed for some privacy. I thought back to my talk with Claire the other night in her room.

I was glad I talked to her. Glad I confronted her, because things could get better for her now.

But I wasn't so sure that same thing would happen with Marcus.

CHAPTER TWENTY-ONE

I checked my e-mail later that evening. Nothing. In the morning, still, not a thing. Marcus and I needed to talk, so I headed for the Arts Club.

The day was another scorcher. The heat from yesterday hung on like sticky, wet honey. I walked as quickly as I could without drowning in my own sweat. Usually Marcus beat me to the café, and I always wondered if he and Armando had actual conversations before I arrived. But today I got there first. I felt awkward, since Armando had never said a word directly to me. I was in the mood for facing some fears, though.

I strode up to the counter and dropped my backpack on the floor. "Hi, Armando."

He smiled over at me and nodded.

"So . . . Marcus isn't here yet, huh?"

He shook his head, as he wiped off one of the counters that already looked plenty clean to me. "No. No yet," he said.

"He . . ." I had to think of how to word this. "He has some problems at home."

Armando stopped wiping and scrunched his thick eyebrows together, but didn't look at me. *Great. Was this a family trait—avoiding talking about problems?*

After a moment Armando said, "Marcus no talk about it." He started wiping again. "You talk to him."

I had to suppress a balk. "I've tried."

Armando nodded and didn't say anything else until a few minutes later. "I go now. I stop two places. I no be long."

It must have seemed obvious, even to Armando, that I'd been ditched.

Once the door shut behind him, I sat down on a stool by the counter and let out a loud sigh for no one's benefit but my own. I just wanted to go back to bed. Pretend the last twenty-four hours hadn't happened.

But as I processed that, I shook my head. That wasn't what I wanted. If Marcus couldn't talk to me, if he couldn't be bothered to return my e-mail or to show up for work, who needed him?

I'd have to think of what to tell Armando. I liked having a

job, and especially one with so little pressure. But I wouldn't work with Marcus anymore, not after the way he'd treated me. I'd have to figure out a way to tell Armando that I wanted to switch off days with his nephew. It's not like it took more than one employee to run the place, anyway.

As I finished that thought, my first customers walked in. I stood and got to work, suppressing an eye roll, but after making the fifth coffee, I noticed how time moved much faster when I wasn't alone with my thoughts. And when Armando came back, I could go home and do the head-burying thing.

My busy streak continued for more than an hour. When I looked up to my next customer, my saliva caught midswallow.

"Josh," I squeaked out.

He smiled and blinked his long eyelashes. "Hi, Loann."

"Americano?" I asked, and was instantly embarrassed for remembering his order from weeks ago.

He raised his eyebrows. "Yeah. You're pretty good at your job."

I shrugged one shoulder apprehensively. Since there were other customers waiting, I backed away to make his drink.

"How's your sister?" he asked over the loud rumble of the coffee grinder.

I waited until I finished grinding, which gave me time to pull a few tendrils of composure together. "Pretty good, I guess."

So that was why he was here. He wanted to get back together with Claire and I was his link. I forced a smile and passed over his drink.

"Um . . . two eighty-five, please."

He placed a bill in my hand, holding it there, like he'd done last time, but longer. "I was hoping we could get together and talk. Maybe tonight?"

My throat went dry. In fact, I was pretty sure every drop of liquid in my entire body had suddenly evaporated. He was still holding my hand.

I nodded, or at least I think I did, and he added, "Seven o'clock? Out by the portable classrooms behind the school?"

He must have early football practice this afternoon if he'd be at the school. All I could do was nod again. Josh glanced back to the person waiting behind him and pulled his hand away.

"Keep the change," he said, and left.

He'd given me a ten-dollar bill.

I served the next customers in a daze. I was allowed to date, but surely my sister's ex-boyfriend wasn't asking me out on a date. Was it a joke? No, Josh seemed too nice of a guy for that. He must want to talk about Claire. But truly, I didn't care why he wanted to spend time with me. I'd tell him anything he wanted to know about Claire, or anything else, for that matter.

As I served customer after customer, I came up with a few conversation starters: How Claire spent most of her time at home these days, no new boyfriend yet. Or what about photography? My camera had come from him, after all. Maybe he had suddenly realized how much we have in common.

The house was deserted when I got home, but I couldn't sit still. I had to tell somebody about seeing Josh. Of course, I couldn't very well tell Claire, even if she were home. And I couldn't tell Marcus.

I picked up the phone and hesitated for a second, then dialed Deirdre's phone number.

After three rings, I recognized her voice. "Hey, it's Loann," I said.

A pause followed, and then, "Oh, hey!" like she had to remind herself how to speak. The truth was, it did seem weird, me calling her. Neither of us had ever been phone people.

"I, um, was wondering how your summer's been?"

She went on to tell me she'd joined the swim club at the local pool and had been working a few days a week at her mom's office. "So pretty busy, really," she said.

I picked at my thumbnail. It just seemed too weird to call her up out of the blue to tell her I had a date, which wasn't even really a date. "I—got a job too," I said finally. I told her about the Arts Club and she seemed impressed. By the time

I'd finished filling her in, she had to leave for swim practice.

"Well, I guess I'll see you in school, then," I said.

"For sure," she agreed, then said good-bye and hung up.

I stared down at the phone. It's not like our conversation had gone badly, so why did it leave me feeling so alone?

After dinner, I took off my oversize LA Kings T-shirt in my room and looked at myself in my bra. Even being alone in my bedroom, I slouched forward to make my breasts look less obvious. My C-cup bra was getting too small and I bulged out of the sides and the middle. Asking Mom for a new one would be out of the question, both for money and embarrassment factors, and the thought of not being able to use my money for more film—well, maybe I'd think about that next month.

As I moved hangers back and forth in my closet looking for something to wear, I swallowed at the spark of an idea.

In my bottom dresser drawer, I dug with both hands until I felt the ribbing I was looking for. I tugged at one of the pink tank tops I'd gotten for my birthday, and studied it. It looked tiny, but it had some stretch, and I might as well make use of at least one of them. I walked over to the mirror, pulling the tank over my head and down so it almost touched my belly button. I glanced back toward the mirror.

No matter how much I slouched, my breasts looked enormous. I angled to the side and then back again. But maybe I could see myself as pretty. Not just my boobs, but the rest of me too. I wasn't so bad, was I? I wanted to believe, even for just a second, that Josh might really like *me*.

Claire's soft footsteps sounded on the stairs. I snatched a button-down denim shirt from the closet, threw it on, and pulled it closed over the tank top. I let out a breath of relief as Claire closed her bedroom door.

I did what I could to tidy my hair, swiped a lip gloss of Claire's off the bathroom counter, and headed out.

As I dashed down our driveway, my nerves came on in full force. *I was going to meet Josh Garrison!* What was I thinking? What if I couldn't think of anything to say?

I should have brought my camera, I thought, a block from the school. I couldn't seem to keep anything straight tonight.

Before long, the detached classrooms came into view. They were new last year because of a sudden increase in freshman students. They looked like two big orange-and-white trailers from the local fair—like they should house a roomful of clowns. Though considering some of the guys in my Spanish class, that might not be too far off.

I didn't see any evidence of a recent football practice, or any other signs of life, for that matter. Maybe I had the wrong place. Or maybe—more likely—I'd imagined the whole invitation this morning.

I heard a sound from within the trees beside the portable

classrooms and saw a flash of Josh's light brown hair. I had a moment of boldness and unbuttoned my denim shirt, tying it at the waist to reveal the top beneath. Holding my shoulders back, I tried to feel as beautiful as Claire looked.

When he came into full view, I wanted to run away. I was tempted to slouch forward, button my shirt back to my throat, and hope Josh hadn't seen me. But at the sound of my name, I knew it was too late.

"Loann . . . hi." He spoke just above a whisper.

"Hi." My hands started to sweat.

"I'm glad you came," he said. "I didn't know if you would. You look pretty."

I laughed a little because, I don't know, I thought he was joking. But he kept an even smile. "I, um, I was going to bring my camera," I said, just to say something.

Josh nodded. "You should have." He raised his eyebrows and the motion seemed filled with innuendo.

I didn't quite get what he meant, so I went on. "I mean, you're into photography too, right?" I wanted to get my footing before I said something stupid, like how cute he was, or how much I *loved* being here alone with him, or how much I wanted him to kiss me the same way I'd seen him kiss my sister.

"Yeah, I never could figure out how to work that old thing," he said. "It was my dad's. But I'm glad you like it."

Before my disappointment could register, he reached over

and picked up my hand in his. He led me to where there was a blanket on the ground among the trees. It all seemed so romantic. I wondered back to when he and Claire had been together. Had they done stuff like this? All I'd ever seen them do was eat lunch together at school or head up to Claire's room at home. For once I wasn't jealous of what Claire had had. I thought maybe . . . maybe this was supposed to be romantic for *me*.

I considered taking off my shoes and plunking myself down when Josh laced his fingers through mine. He pulled me toward him, and I moved like a rag doll. His other hand lifted my chin.

It was all so surreal. *Could this really be happening?* With my face tilted toward his, Josh seemed so close, and before I knew it, his lips pressed hard against mine. His tongue thrust into my mouth.

He was kissing me! Josh Garrison was kissing *me!* A real kiss, not like the little pecks from my aunts and uncles. I guess I didn't know what to expect from my first kiss, but it was odd. Not like you think when you see it on TV or even when I was watching him and Claire. It felt hard and wet and a little like a dental checkup, him exploring my mouth with his tongue. My stomach flip-flopped and I kept reminding myself not to laugh or pull away. Reminding myself that *I was kissing Josh Garrison.*

The words "You look pretty" swam in my head. Then:

Was it weird, that I was kissing Claire's ex-boyfriend?

I couldn't concentrate. It just felt so good to be wanted. That Josh wanted this too.

Both of his hands moved down and fiddled at my waist, and seconds later, my denim shirt fell in the dirt behind me. I pulled my hands over my stomach, but in one smooth motion Josh put them on *his* waist. I figured if I stayed close to him, my belly fat wouldn't be as obvious, so I latched my shaky fingers onto the belt loops of his jeans.

As if he could feel my insecurity, Josh's hands moved to the middle of my back and he drew me in so my stomach and chest were against his. He pulled at the back of my tank top, then through my tank top to my bra. The clasp released and the weight of my breasts dropped from the underwire. Josh kissed me more determinedly, with his lips and his tongue. I didn't know how to respond. I let my tongue follow his lead, but was that right? Should I have been doing something else? Suddenly I wished I'd listened more to Shayleen, back when she seemed overeager to give me advice.

Josh's hands stroked the sides of my waist. I wanted to pull his hands away and yank my tank top down, but I held strong and kept my fingers in his belt loops.

He whispered between kisses, "You're so different from your sister," and for some reason in that second, it felt like . . . a compliment.

"You're beautiful," he said next, and I kept letting the word ring through my head as his hands made their way up my front and under my bra.

Claire was right, girls needed to hear these things. Girls needed to feel this way. A dark curl fell in my face and I pushed it away, marveling over how he could think *I* was beautiful.

"I love your tits," he whispered, as he felt their shape. "They're so much nicer than your sister's."

When he said that, I couldn't help myself. My tongue thrust into his mouth, suddenly doing its own thing. I kissed him back, feeling exhilarated at each new part of his mouth mine discovered. No one had ever told me I was better than Claire. At anything.

He stroked and fondled my breasts, and I felt out of control as he kept whispering about them. I loved the word "tits" when he said it. I loved how he touched them, and I loved how his mouth felt against mine.

I hardly noticed when he lowered me down onto the blanket. He took off my tank top and bra and I was surprised that my embarrassment about my body had faded. He stopped kissing me to fiddle with the button on my jeans.

"Wha—"

"I bet there's lots of ways you're better than your sister," he said, and kissed me again. As he caressed my hips, pulling my pants down, I had a wisp of an idea: *I could really be as beautiful as Claire*. For seconds, maybe even minutes, I let myself get taken away in my beauty and in my arousal.

I let out a gust of air when his whole weight moved on top of me. "It's okay, I've got a condom," he whispered.

My eyes shot open. *Was he . . . Were we . . .* A moment later, a sudden sharpness between my legs made me cry out. It was painful, like a knife.

"Shh," Josh whispered.

I pursed my lips together to hold my sounds in. He was going inside me. *We were having sex. I was having sex with Josh Garrison.*

In a small part of my brain, I knew this was exciting, this was what I wanted. Wasn't it? If I wanted to kiss Josh, if I wanted to be his girlfriend, didn't this come with it? So why did it suddenly feel like something else?

I had no idea how I had gotten here or what I was doing.

The sound of the cars in the distance echoed in my head. Ants crawled up my arm. I didn't move. I lay there with him on top of me, not even believing what was happening. Josh had stopped kissing me and kept his face down beside mine in the blanket. I gritted my teeth, unable to process all the thoughts and emotions swarming through my mind. I did all I could not to cry. I tried to hang on to his words, the way he told me I was pretty, beautiful, even, but with him pushing inside of me, they made my stomach queasy.

Funny, what you think of in moments like these. I didn't think about Claire or about what my parents would think. I thought about Shayleen. "Romantic" and "tender" and "gentle" reverberated as though they were coming out of her bragging seventh-grade mouth. Although I could relate those words to the soap operas Claire was addicted to, I couldn't relate a single one to this moment.

When it was done, Josh pushed himself off and dropped onto his back on the blanket. An immediate chill hit me as his sweat on my bare chest made contact with the brisk evening air. A throbbing pain filled my whole lower body. I kept my eyes down while I sat up and gathered my things, feeling extremely shy again about my breasts, my belly fat, my thighs. There was a splotch of blood on the blanket and I quickly tried to cover it while pulling up my pants, but nothing was going back on right.

Josh lay there, breathing heavily. I tried to look over at him, but couldn't do it. *Why had I had sex with a guy I barely knew? A guy who used to date my sister?* I fumbled to get my bra back on, but my hands shook. I finally just left the clasp undone and wrapped my denim shirt across my front. Josh caught my hand and held it on the blanket. I wondered if he could feel the earthquake that was erupting inside me. He leaned in and kissed me at the top of my cheek, right on the bone. It was the softest kiss he'd given me all night.

I was sure I was going to fall apart right there in front of him. But then he gave me this smile. It was the same cocky and distanced smile I'd seen him give his friends in the hallways so many times at school. He lifted his hand and patted my cheek twice, then popped up to a standing position like he was ready to run a race.

I didn't know what any of it meant. I wanted to smile back, but was afraid that any movement on my face whatsoever would break the dam of emotions that I was holding back with all my might.

It wasn't until he turned away from me and started walking, leaving me and his dirty blanket behind, that I realized what had just happened.

And what I was—or wasn't—to him.

CHAPTER TWENTY-TWO

I got home at nine-thirty and went straight to my room. The bathroom door was ajar again, and oddly, *I* reached over to shut it this time. I'd never really had something to hide from my sister before. But this.

This.

My whole body trembled and shivered, and I threw on my Kings T-shirt over top my clothes. I lay on my bed and stared up at the ceiling, thoughts and feelings piling on one another like a multicar accident, and because I couldn't process anything of the evening, my thoughts kept returning to Shayleen.

I couldn't get her and everything she'd told us after the big seventh-grade sex talk out of my brain. The things I questioned were first about her: *Had she lied about her sexual experience?* Then I started to question myself. *Did I do it wrong? Is there something wrong with me?* Maybe it wasn't supposed to hurt like that.

And Josh? I couldn't even go there. I couldn't let myself wonder if something so monumental for me had meant next to nothing to him.

I had to talk to someone—and it wasn't going to be my parents. After a dozen deep breaths, I padded down the hall and knocked on Claire's door. She told me to wait, and then after what felt like forever, she opened the door with an arm outstretched, inviting me in like she was a welcoming hostess on a cruise ship. I shuffled to her bed and sat down, and the bounce of the mattress caused an M&M's wrapper to fly out from under it. Claire snatched the wrapper from the floor and threw it into the garbage can beside her desk, which was already nearly overflowing. She shoved it down the side and murmured something about Jasmine. I interrupted her blabbering.

"Does sex hurt?" My foot fluttered beneath me, but I looked at her intently when I said it. If there was any more lying or denial I wouldn't miss it like I had with Shayleen. I just wished I'd had this conversation earlier, years ago.

"I don't know, Loey, I haven't done it yet," she said, flipping through her desk calendar.

I tried not to let the shock register on my face. "What about Josh?"

"Oh, he wanted to, Loey. Boy, did he want to!" She laughed and I could tell it was true, and that she was over that whole relationship. "That's why I broke up with him. I wasn't ready, and he didn't want to wait."

She broke up with him? Since when? I'd always assumed Josh had broken up with Claire, since she'd been so upset. I'd thought Josh could have had anything he wanted, with anyone. But no, I guess just with me.

Part of me still didn't believe it, after all the time they'd spent up in her bedroom. Would anyone really pretend to be a virgin if they weren't one, though? I'd always felt so behind, so naïve. I studied her. She really wasn't lying.

I couldn't process it. She seemed so sure, while I didn't know what the hell I was doing. What I'd done.

"So you really haven't done it?" I forced out.

"No, I want to wait until I'm married, Loey. Why?"

Married? She sounded serious. Then it hit me. She was *proud* of her virtue. That would be just like Claire. She stared at me, waiting for an answer. "Uh . . ." *Why, exactly, would I be asking?* "Just wondering." I sprung up and headed for the door to hide the tears I felt welling up.

"Loey, do you have a boyfriend?" she asked in a teasing tone. "Come on, Loey. Tell me."

I shook my head. Claire tried to chase after me, but I shut her door on her. I got into my room and hooked the lock before dropping onto my bed and letting it all out.

So, what? Josh was just with me to get back at her? To prove something?

I hated him. I hated him and I hated Shayleen. I hated liars. And I even hated Claire, if nothing else, for making it all true.

All night I tossed and turned. In a groggy stupor, I heard Josh whispering, as though he was right beside me, "It's okay, I've got a condom." Over and over again, it ran in my head as if a CD was skipping. It didn't occur to me until about the twenty-fifth time, that I could be pregnant. I mean, condoms weren't a hundred percent, right?

Josh had told me he had a condom to reassure me, but I wondered if pregnancy would've even occurred to me if he hadn't. Would I have stopped him if he hadn't had one? I tried not to think about any diseases the condom may have saved me from, but I couldn't help myself. *How many girls had Josh been with before me?* I started to cry again and buried my head under my pillow to deaden the sound.

An hour later, I headed down for breakfast, hoping no one would ask about my red eyes.

Mom raced around the kitchen—not out of the ordinary

for seven-thirty on a weekday. Claire sat hunched over a magazine at the kitchen table with a large glass of water. My anger
came back in full force and I strode into the kitchen practically
begging for a fight.

Sure, Claire had stopped puking, but she still had one
fault. She was barely eating.

"Want some toast, Claire?" I asked.

"Uh . . . no thanks, Loey. You go ahead."

Funny how she never questioned what I ate the way she
did with Jasmine. Obviously she didn't care how *I* looked.

I plunked a piece of bread into the toaster, then stomped
to the other side of the kitchen.

"Apple?" I asked as I picked one up, tossed it in the air,
and then held it out toward her. Mom was now chattering
on her cell, and turned away from me as if annoyed by my
volume.

Claire glanced up and shook her head. I put the apple
down and picked up a banana.

"Banana?" I asked a little louder. She shook her head
harder, like she had flying insects in her hair. I walked over
and placed the banana on the table in front of her anyway. I
went to the pantry and yanked the door open.

"Cereal?" I asked, walking over and dropping two boxes
in front of Claire. Just then, my toast popped up. Claire kept

her eyes on her magazine and away from the spread I'd laid before her. I dropped my toast onto a plate, grabbed a knife and the butter, and went to sit down beside her.

Right beside her.

I hated her for being pretty and thin and sweet and honest and virtuous.

I spread a thick layer of butter across the toast within six inches of her face. She did everything she could to ignore me, but her face became pale, then gray, then an odd shade of green, and I wondered if she might puke right here in the kitchen. I scraped another full knife-load of butter out of the container and continued with another smear.

"You sure?" I held it directly under her nose.

She backed her chair away from the table, stared straight at me, and whispered, "I hate you."

Good. Now we're even.

Mom didn't notice a thing when Claire stood up and left the room. I was certain the production I'd put on could not have been missed, but Mom faced the wall calendar, telling Mrs. Emerson about Claire's next dance performance. To top it off, she droned on about how much Claire absolutely loved her ballet!

When Mom hung up the phone, she looked at my grease-dripping toast and said, "Loann, honey, why don't you have some fruit instead? You're never going to keep a pretty little figure if you eat like that."

I stared at her for a long moment, wondering what I could possibly say in reply. Finally I dropped the toast onto a plate and walked out the door without a word.

CHAPTER TWENTY-THREE

At first I thought maybe I'd just hang out and cry by the river. After all, Marcus had ditched me for work yesterday. If he bothered to show today, I could just ditch him right back. But it wasn't in my nature to be irresponsible, no matter how much I wanted to. At the very least, I needed to lay out a schedule of which days Marcus would work and which days I would work. Besides, I couldn't help myself. A small part of me hoped Josh would come back into the café—that maybe I'd read that last look wrong, and the night before had actually meant something to him.

I marched into the café with such purpose I didn't even notice Marcus alone on the other side of the counter until I'd crossed half the floor. Armando had apparently already left for the day.

I stopped in place. "Oh. I guess you've got it today, then." I spun for the exit.

"Wait, Loey." I didn't feel like obeying him, but then he added, "Please wait," in a quieter voice.

I turned. My venom from the breakfast table with Claire this morning still lingered in my veins. "What? It really doesn't take two of us to run this place, Marcus. And as you mentioned yesterday—no, wait, yesterday was the day you didn't bother to show up or call. As you mentioned the day *before* yesterday," I went on, "we're not really friends. You obviously have no ability to talk about your life with me, and I have no ability to keep my mouth shut, especially about something like this." I stared at him for a few seconds, thinking he'd simply nod and we'd be done. But he stepped around the counter and walked toward me.

"Don't you understand?" he said in the calmest voice. "This," he motioned between himself and me, "this is my life. My whole life." His eyes were so intense, so round and pleading, I couldn't look away. "That other stuff," he waved off to the side. "That's not me. It's not any part of who I am or who I want to be, and that's why I don't want to talk about it with you."

He was good. His words started to soften my conviction. *Started.* "But even if you don't want it to be, I need to know." My soft voice surprised me. "Somebody needs to know."

Marcus grabbed one of my hands. Then the other. They were

so warm in mine, but today I wasn't thinking about romance. After last night with Josh, I never wanted to hope for romance again. But I knew Marcus didn't have it in him to do what Josh had. He would never push me with something like that.

We stood there for a long time, and I could feel Marcus wanting me to look up at him, but I just couldn't. I couldn't pretend there was nothing wrong when I knew a major part of him was hurting. I couldn't *not* see that anymore.

"I need some time," he said finally. I was about to protest when he added, "We'll talk about everything, if that's what you need. I promise. But . . . not here. Maybe at my apartment." I tilted up to look at him. *Was he serious?* "I just need to figure out a good time."

I had so many more questions, but the door opened behind me. I looked over my shoulder to see Shayleen. Alone. I pulled my hands back from Marcus.

"Oh." She stopped in place and looked at me, then stared down at my hands. "Oh, I thought . . ." she trailed off and just stood there staring like she'd never seen fingers before. I walked for the counter.

"Iced mocha?" I asked on my way, then wanted to slap myself. I needed to stop being so obvious about remembering *certain* people's orders. To Shayleen it must be obvious how much I lacked having a life. Marcus followed me behind the counter and reached for a cup to make up her order.

"So . . . I heard something," she said in this different, almost sweet voice as I passed her the change. For a second her tone reminded me of when I'd truly liked hanging out with her. "About you and Josh Garrison," she added, looking over at Marcus.

All the oxygen in the room disappeared and I sucked in nothingness.

"Is it true?" she asked. The blender whir stopped behind me, and I could feel Marcus's stare.

It had only been last night! How fast could word have gotten around? Did Josh put all the shameful details up on Facebook or something? I grabbed the side of my T-shirt and twisted it into a ball.

"I-I don't know what you're talking about." I forced a laugh, like this was funny, even though it so was not.

Shayleen studied my face. She shook her head and let out a little snicker as she took her cup from Marcus. "I didn't think it could be true," she said scornfully. "By the way, your mochas need more chocolate."

It took everything I had not to yell after her when she went. But what would I yell? That I *had* been with Josh last night? That we'd had sex, oh, and by the way, it meant nothing to him? I didn't want to shout that any more than I wanted to shout about my frizzy hair or my fat thighs.

I remembered Marcus behind me. I wanted to say something, but I barely wanted to admit to *myself* that any of this was true. We were probably both relieved when the door opened again, this time to a steady stream of customers.

During the next lull, Marcus came up behind me while I finished making us each a latte. I felt him there, right behind me, and it made me nervous. The thought of being close to anyone right now just made my insides squirm. I didn't want to think about Josh, but I couldn't help it with Marcus's chest practically touching my back.

"You okay?" he asked, when I stopped the machine.

I nodded, but kept my back to him. I sidestepped to get out of close range and then handed him his mug. "Yeah. Fine." I led the way to our table, and after a minute he followed.

Even though silent sipping was normal for us, today it felt longer and quieter than ever before.

Claire stormed past me and up the stairs when I got home, and I had to think for a minute what it was about. I'd forgotten all about our breakfast episode.

But then I had another sickening thought: If Shayleen had heard about Josh and me, had Claire heard too?

Claire didn't sit with us at dinner, leaving me to do the dishes, even though it wasn't my turn. I padded for the kitchen without complaint, and was actually glad for the solitude.

She must *hate* me. What kind of a person sleeps with her

sister's ex-boyfriend? And only weeks after they'd broken up! I'd been so angry with her this morning, but it wasn't even her I was really angry at. I was mad at myself. And I was way too embarrassed to talk to her about what I'd done.

Dishes were the least I could do.

The next morning, when she still wouldn't look at me, I decided my only escape was the Arts Club.

Marcus and I spent the next few days practically taking over Armando's business. We learned where to call to order the coffee and syrups; we paid the heat and light bills; and we divvied up the profits according to Armando's directions. It didn't work out to much more than we'd made before. In the early mornings before we opened, we repainted the walls, still in bright yellows and oranges, but covering all the dings and dents from years past. We sanded, by hand, every piece of furniture in that place and varnished them up to look antique-brand-new. We even hand-painted an ARTS CLUB CAFÉ sign that could be seen from the main road. The place had needed a facelift, and the whole process felt cathartic.

The more I distracted myself with physical work, the less I thought about Josh. It seemed to get a bit easier each day to put him out of my mind. Josh didn't drop by the café, and as days passed I stopped wanting him to. He didn't call the house, either. At least, not that Claire had mentioned. Then again, she probably wouldn't have mentioned it. She still hadn't spoken a word to me, and I felt sick every time I had to go home and face her.

Armando's visits to the café became just that: "visits." He worked a few hours here and there to give us a break, but he never stayed long. Marcus and I each had our own sets of keys, and although Armando's phone number was pasted beside the old black rotary-dial phone, we never used it.

"I've been thinking of adding a few items to the menu," Marcus said, scanning the chalkboard above us. He had also given me his phone number. I think it was an act of reassurance, to let me know he was still working toward opening up. I stuffed the number into my book bag, but knew I'd never actually call it.

"Any specific ideas?" I prodded.

He pulled up a Saran-wrapped bundle of biscotti from under the counter. "This."

I stared at the package, which had a handwritten note about the macadamia nuts and chocolate variety. "Yum." It was almost dinnertime. My mouth watered. A lot.

"You know how cops are known for hanging out in dough-nut shops?" he said. "Uncle Armando says that in his small Italian town, they were known for scarfing back biscotti."

"Really?" I asked.

"Yeah, he always laughs about it like it's some kind of big

joke. '*Polizia*, biscotti, ha, ha, ha,'" Marcus mimicked Armando's accent, which made me burst out laughing. "So that's our first item for the menu," he said. "But we need more. Help me brainstorm and I'll go to the store tomorrow."

Marcus's enthusiasm was contagious. It reminded me of when we'd first had the idea for the photo-set. I sat down to help him make a very long list. Scanning the food items, my eyes settled on lemon squares, Claire's favorite. At least they used to be. She almost never ate meals with the family anymore, and I'd assumed that was because she was mad at me. But maybe it was still about her eating. Maybe she still *wasn't* eating.

"You okay?" Marcus asked, breaking me from my daze.

I shook my head. "Claire . . . she hardly eats at home anymore." The words spilled out of me, like they'd been waiting to be released forever.

"You worry about her a lot, huh?" he asked, and for a second I felt offended, like he was criticizing me, but when I looked over, I sensed something else: Envy.

"You don't have any brothers or sisters, do you?" I asked.

He shook his head, looking even sadder. I knew he wanted to understand. To help.

"It can be good," I said. "But it also can definitely be hard."

He nodded. "I can see that."

CHAPTER TWENTY-FOUR

I had never, in my whole life, been so happy to get my period. As I practically skipped toward the café, I tried to thank God with at least the same fervency I'd pleaded to Him to not let me be pregnant. In a way, it felt like that chapter in my life was over. I could let my mistake with Josh go, or maybe even pretend it hadn't happened.

When I turned the corner, Marcus was coming from down the block in the other direction. I waited so we could walk the rest of the way to the café together.

"C'mon," I said, not wanting to give him time to notice my giddiness so I'd have to explain it.

"Someone's in a hurry. Had an extra serving of Wheaties this morning, did we?"

"Yeah, well, forgot to comb our hair, this morning, did *we*?" I gestured at Marcus's windblown dark hair.

We both laughed as we got to the door of the café.

I still worried about Marcus, and spent much of my time at the Arts Club trying to gently get him to talk about his problems at home. I couldn't help imagining him not showing up again—or worse, showing up with something more serious than a bruise.

After another promise that Marcus would take me to his place soon, I headed home for the day. There weren't any cars in the driveway, and I looked up at the cloudless expanse of sky. It was too nice to be inside. Instead I headed around the side of the house to the backyard, pulling my camera from my bag as I walked.

To my surprise, Claire was stretched out on a towel, wearing only a bikini. I stopped in place.

Our backyard was private, not only because of the tall shrubbery separating us from our neighbors, but also because Mom had lined most of the back windows with plants, to give them as much sun as possible, so it wasn't easy to just peek outside. It must have been the privacy that enticed Claire to shed her clothes, because I hadn't seen this much of her since swimming lessons in middle school. And even then, she'd worn a one-piece.

I wasn't sure I wanted to see this much of her now.

I'd always known Claire to be skinny, but this was something different. Even from twenty feet away, I could see a net-work of veins under her skin. Her whole body had a bluish-gray hue. She lay flat on her back and her hip bones jutted out like salt and pepper shakers on an otherwise empty table. Her eyes were closed, so I stood there gawking at what appeared more like a science experiment than my hot teenage sister.

I don't know what made me do it, but I pulled my cam-era to my eye. My hand rotated the lens into focus, and for a second I thought I had seen it wrong. Maybe it wasn't so bad. With all the greenery as her backdrop and her hair swept over one shoulder, it actually made a really beautiful shot.

When I clicked the shutter, even though it was quiet, Claire's eyes shot open. She must have felt me there. She sat up and glared at me. I pulled my camera behind my back, then darted my eyes over to the shrubs.

"What are you looking at?" she said, defensively.

"Uh, nothing. I d-didn't expect anyone to be out here."

Claire threw a towel over herself, holding it tightly around her chest with one hand. With the other, she gathered her clothes and book. "I just wanted a little privacy. I guess that's not allowed around here."

"I'll go. I'm, uh, I'm sorry, Claire."

She started to cry and she folded over her knees so I couldn't see her face.

"I don't know what to say." I inched toward her. "There's

obviously something wrong, but I don't know how to help you, Claire."

When she looked up, her eyes were red—not just the whites, but even the pupils had a reddish glow. "You want to help, Loann?" It came out more like a growl than her normal Disneyland voice. "Just leave me alone." She dropped her head onto her knees again and covered it with her scrawny arms.

I watched Claire's back pulse for a minute, then stepped out of the yard feeling shaken. I turned and ran for the bridge.

I was tempted to call Marcus, but I didn't want to mess things up there, too. As my feet dangled over the edge, I questioned myself over and over again. *Why did I just run away from her? Don't I care about my sister at all?*

I balled my fists. I did. I loved my sister. It was just hard to remember that when we were fighting. But she needed help.

I walked almost all the way across town to the nursing home where Mom works. I hadn't been there since last summer, when they had an employee picnic. The administration lady didn't recognize me, and told me to wait in the lobby while they paged my mom. I paced back and forth across the lobby floor about a million times.

"Loann!" She came rushing toward me, her arm outstretched and face contorted. "What's wrong?"

"I—I just wanted to talk to you," I said, needing to calm her down. I mean, it wasn't like someone had died.

She looked between my probably red eyes and my fidgety fingers. Her worry didn't seem to lessen.

"It's Claire," I said. "There's something . . . she hasn't been eating. She looks awful, Mom."

I could feel the administration clerk's eyes on me. Mom blinked a couple of times. "Oh," she said finally, nodding. "Okay, well, I'll talk to her, honey." She put a hand on my shoulder. "Of course I'll talk to her."

I let out a breath.

Mom glanced toward the administration desk and turned her body slightly to shield our conversation. "Is that . . . why you came all the way down here?"

I swallowed. Nodded. She wouldn't understand the severity of it until she saw it herself, but I hoped she at least had some idea by the way I could barely talk.

"I'll be home for dinner," Mom said. "Do you want to wait and I'll give you a ride?"

I hesitated for a second, but then agreed. Maybe if Mom and I walked into the house together, we could be a strong front. We could talk to Claire about how much she's changed and what she's doing to herself.

Claire was making her way from the kitchen with a big casserole dish of steaming food when we walked in. She already had the rest of the dinner on the table: chicken, potatoes, rolls, and corn. She sat in her usual chair with her hair tied back, fitted cardigan zipped halfway up, makeup drawn with precision.

"Hi, Loey." She smiled.

Claire isn't mad at me anymore? I concentrated on my cutlery. *She probably will be again soon.* "Hi," I forced out.

Mom sat too and we silently helped ourselves to food. The tension at the table was palpable.

"Thank you for making dinner," Mom said. Her eyes were on Claire's plate, which was filled with food tonight.

Claire took a bite of her potato. "Sure," she said with a smile, like she did this all the time. "I didn't know if Dad would be home." She motioned to the place setting she'd put out for him, but he hadn't been home at dinnertime for at least a week.

Mom was fixated on eating her corn, not bothering to respond. I could see she was trying to figure out how to broach the subject of Claire's eating, now that she was apparently eating properly.

"So, Mom. I wanted to talk to you about something," Claire said.

We both stopped eating.

"I'm not sure if you're aware," Claire said, looking at Mom, and not at me, "but Loann has been going after Josh." She paused and I felt my face, my whole body, rush with heat. "My ex-boyfriend, Josh," she added.

I tried to swallow my bite of corn, but it wouldn't go down. Shaking my head, I tried to get some words from my brain to my mouth, but neither of them was working right. "It—it wasn't like that," I said.

"Look, Mom," Claire went on. "I'm not mad, but we both know Loann has been jealous of me for a long time."

I couldn't believe she was talking about me like I wasn't even here. From what she'd just told Mom, I wasn't sure how much Claire knew—did she just think I liked Josh, or did she know I'd actually slept with him? But when she took a glance in my direction and looked down my body, I could tell. She knew everything.

"She obviously just wants to see my faults," Claire went on. "You know, to make herself feel better."

"No!" I shouted at Claire, then Mom. "No! This is not about me!"

Claire spoke over me. "I just think maybe you should have a talk with her about Josh. I wouldn't want to see her get hurt." She finally met my eyes then, with a tilted head and smile that was anything but sympathetic.

I sat there with my mouth open, but nothing was coming out. Mom stared down at her food, avoiding both of us, and I was glad for every second that passed when she didn't ask me about Josh.

"So anyway"—Claire snapped her head from me and

switched gears instantly—"I thought maybe I'd go into fashion design. I could see myself doing something like that. Creating new styles." She barely took a breath. "To be responsible for something like that—wow, it'd be a lot of pressure, Mom, but I think I could do it. What do you think? Is it a good choice for me? I'm going to talk to the state college tomorrow about their fashion design program. What do you think Dad will say? Will he like the idea?"

I studied my food. Each kernel of corn, each roasted potato, trying to keep straight what was real and what was only illusion. She just changed the subject like it was nothing, but it felt like a warning: *Keep your mouth shut, Loann, and I'll keep mine shut.*

Dad walked in the door just then, which only added to the surreal feeling. He caught up on Claire's fashion design plans quickly, since she was, apparently, the only one with the ability to talk.

"Well, it sounds like a great major. You've got to decide soon if you want to get in for January, honey. But what about performing-arts school?"

She flipped her hair over her shoulder. "I'm really glad you'd let me try," she said, "but I just don't think it's the right direction for me. I'm just going to finish the summer ballet production . . ." She glanced at Mom. ". . . and then I'm taking a break for a while."

Mom took another bite but still wouldn't make eye contact with me. Did she really think I had been lying about Claire's eating problems? Did she think I would make that all up because I was jealous? I'd heard of siblings who fought maliciously, I'd seen them in movies, but it had always seemed so far removed from our close relationship, I could barely process this.

"What night is that production, again?" Dad asked.

Mom stopped chewing. She took her napkin off her lap and placed it beside her food carefully. "I've told you a hundred times," she said in slow, measured words. "It's this Thursday, the eighteenth." Her anger and confusion from earlier needed an outlet. She'd found one.

I took a small bite of potato, but it sat on my tongue, unchewed.

"Oh, the eighteenth," he said lightly, but I knew where this was going. Something work-related had most definitely come up on Thursday the eighteenth.

But then Claire interrupted.

"You really don't have to come. I mean, it's just another boring recital, and to be honest, it's not much different from the last one."

As if Mom hadn't heard Claire, she said, "I have a busy life too," aimed right at Dad.

He held up both hands like he was under arrest. "I didn't say . . ."

"Hey! It's okay. Please don't fight about this," Claire said louder. "I mean it, you guys," she went on. "I appreciate you wanting to be there, but I'd almost rather you not be. I'm kind of embarrassed that Mrs. Avery chose such a similar program to the last one. You'd be bored to death, I swear."

Suddenly it all made sense to me. Claire didn't want them to go because Claire didn't want them to see the way she looked.

Mom and Dad stared at each other, and I could tell Mom was still brimming for an argument, but Claire wiped her mouth, stood, and cleared her half-full plate. "It's settled, then," she said. "Nobody needs to take time off work for me."

There was silence around the table as Claire headed for the kitchen, and then came back through for the stairs. I waited for her to close her bedroom door before I said, "I think you should go. Both of you. She says she doesn't want you there, but she really does. She needs you to *see* her," I said.

If they didn't agree, I'd have to come right out and tell them everything about what I saw today. I'd have to force them to go upstairs right now and confront her. I *had* to. But then I wondered if Claire would only work harder to hide it. They needed to see this for themselves.

Mom nodded. "I'll be there."

And surprisingly, Dad did too. "Thursday night. I'll go mark it in my phone."

CHAPTER TWENTY-FIVE

When I found Claire back camped out on the couch later in the week, I said, "Oh, hi," in surprise. "Aren't you supposed to be working?" I had no idea why I asked this. I just didn't know how to talk to her after the dinner episode. Now that she'd come right out and spoken about me and Josh. Now that she'd hidden what she was doing to herself from our parents and I had secretly strategized to get them to her ballet recital.

She shifted her legs underneath her and reached for the TV remote. "They changed my schedule."

Even though I didn't completely believe her, I was relieved at her normal, non-threatening response. "I'm getting a snack," I said on my way to the kitchen. "Want anything?"

Claire shook her head, engrossed in some judge show on

TV. Just before I reached the kitchen door, she called out, "Unless you want to mix me a protein shake."

Her words had an underlying meaning. *We're not okay yet. You need to earn it, Loey.*

And I wanted to earn it. I couldn't stand feeling so guilty or worried or confused. I nodded. "Sure."

In the kitchen, I propped the blender into place and opened the fridge to grab the skim milk. Mom's coffee cream sat right beside the milk carton, and I stared at the two containers. It didn't take long to decide. Claire didn't have a single fat cell. Somebody had to stop her from wasting away.

With sudden clarity, I grabbed the cream and poured most of the container into the blender. I put the container back into the fridge, rotating it behind the skim milk, and dumped a scoop of protein powder into the running machine. After pouring it into a cup and washing the blender, I carried her drink and my chip bag back to the living room.

I set her cup on the coffee table and pulled at the top of the chip bag.

"Should you be eating those, Loey?" Claire glanced at my thighs and then reached for her shake.

I opened my mouth to say something, but then closed it again. It hurt, of course, even if I had wanted her to be as concerned about my eating as she had been about Jasmine having a sandwich. Then again, I deserved this after what I'd done with Josh. And I didn't have the strength to throw anything back at her. It didn't feel like there was any strong part left in me, and I wondered if Josh had taken that from me too.

Claire flipped channels incessantly and I wondered what had *her* so edgy.

She stopped flipping and grimaced at her drink. "What did you use, Loann?"

"What do you mean?" I felt my face flush and tried to take even breaths to hide my sudden heart palpitations.

She stood and marched for the kitchen. I thought about following, but I was also pretty petrified to be in the same room with her. How did she *know?*

Seconds later, she strode back through the kitchen door with the coffee cream container in her hand. "It's almost gone, Loann. Did you use *this* in my protein shake?"

I swallowed hard and gave my head a minuscule shake.

How would Claire have even known how much had been in there? But somehow she did. I probably couldn't skirt around this one. "Um, I don't think so," I said.

"You did!" She glared at me, her eyebrows pulling together until they were almost one. It made her look a little crazy. At first I thought she had caught on to my scheming. But then her voice softened slightly. "You can't make mistakes like that when you're making my food. Okay, Loey?"

I nodded, my throat dry. "Okay." I was so uncomfortable,

I headed for the door. "Um, I forgot some stuff at the café."

I rushed outside and back to the Arts Club, glad to see Marcus still there. Since a line had formed for coffee, I slid behind the counter and helped Marcus before he had a chance to ask. I felt like I could breathe for the first time in the two hours since I'd left.

"You missed me that much?" he asked when he passed me two coffees for customers. "You had to come back?"

A blush warmed my face. He'd made a few comments here and there that I wasn't sure were flirtatious hints, or jokes. "Couldn't stay away," I replied, meeting his eyes for just a second. But I didn't want to get flustered and mess up orders, so I turned back to the next customers and tried to concentrate.

Marcus didn't talk to me about anything other than coffee until our line of customers slowed down.

"So is this going to be a regular thing now? You taking the hum-drum out of all my evenings?"

Was he flirting? He took a step closer and raised his eyebrows.

"I—uh—didn't even know you worked nights," I said, kind of stalling, kind of prying to see what he really meant by all this.

"Whenever I can." He shifted uncomfortably. "I'll be in tomorrow night for sure," he said in a brighter voice. "You should come. We could make it like a regular date."

He gave me a little friendly nudge with his elbow to my arm. Like it had been a joke.

"Actually, my sister has this ballet thing tomorrow night," I said, letting out a big breath. "It's—pretty important that I go."

"Yeah?"

I swallowed, feeling a bit of betrayal at the thought of telling anybody about this. But how could I expect Marcus to open up to me if I didn't open up to him? "Claire, she has some pretty big problems," I said.

I told him how I'd found her suntanning in our backyard. "My mom wouldn't really listen because Claire's been telling her stuff about me being jealous." I shifted and decided to gloss over the bit about Josh. "Anyway, I'm not sure my mom believed me, so I convinced her to go see for herself at the ballet production, even though Claire doesn't want any of us to go."

Marcus nodded. "Wow. Is she going to be mad?"

"I'd been trying not to focus on that part," I said, cringing.

"Well, I'll miss you," he said, giving my hair a little ruffle.

The next night, my family got dressed up: me with my camera—at Mom's request, Dad with his smartphone, and Mom with her uppity "I'm a ballerina's mother" attitude.

Claire had been picked up by one of the other dancers a couple of hours ago, still with no idea we were coming. She'd looked so cheery, I felt even guiltier about my deception. But my parents needed to know.

Mrs. Avery's ballet troupe was more about performance than the other local school, so we'd been going to at least four productions a year for as long as I could remember. As usual, Mrs. Avery was racing around the lobby, saying hellos and finishing up last-minute details for the show when we arrived. She hurried right over when she saw Mom.

"Beth! I'm so glad you could make it. Claire didn't think you'd be able to."

Another pang of guilt stabbed at me.

"Oh, I wouldn't miss a single show." Mom gave Dad a pointed look, since we all knew he'd missed several over the years. "They really do grow up so fast, don't they?"

Mrs. Avery nodded. "I've kept the auditorium cool. I really hope Claire's skin rash won't be a problem."

I looked up. Mom's face contorted. "Her . . . what?" Mom asked.

Mrs. Avery glanced away and I sensed she had somewhere else she needed to be. "I've felt awful for her. Such a beautiful girl, and with so many skin problems at such a young age. She's been a real trooper, practicing all summer in her sweats, even though we knew she must be dying from the heat."

Mom held a curled hand in front of her mouth. Mrs. Avery went on.

"I'm sorry, Beth, but I really have to catch our music man over there." She nodded at Dad and me, then hurried away.

When Mrs. Avery was out of earshot, Mom avoided my eyes and whispered, "Have you heard anything about a rash?" to Dad.

We moved into the auditorium slowly, like none of us really wanted to.

The production started and I fiddled with my camera on my lap, glad to have something to hold on to. I wondered how my parents would take this—seeing what Claire had been doing to herself when she couldn't hide it under layers of clothing. I doubted Mrs. Avery would allow sweats in one of her shows.

I tapped nervous fingers on my camera as three large scenes went by with no sign of Claire. I wondered if she *had* dropped out without telling Mom. But no. Mrs. Avery seemed to think Claire would be dancing. When I glanced over, Mom's eyes were doing that hard-blinking thing, which meant she had questions too.

Mom gasped, which brought me back to the moment. All the other dancers wore slim, tank-style bodysuits. But Claire appeared onstage in thick tights that reached to her ballet slippers and a long-sleeve fitted top under her tank. Even through the material, Claire's bony knees and knobby joints made her look like one of those wooden puppets, the kind that wouldn't have a hope of balance without a puppet master manipulating the strings from above. I figured God must have her strings, because otherwise I didn't have a clue how she could stand.

Dad and Mom whispered beside me, though I couldn't make out what they were saying. I felt stares from other parents in the auditorium, and realized Claire's cover-up hadn't fooled anyone. I felt partly thankful, but partly embarrassed for her, almost like I was the one up there. Keeping my eyes trained ahead, I watched Claire drawl her way across the stage and back. Even though she kept up with her group, there was an unmistakable feeling that she was on the verge of falling behind the other dancers.

While everyone was taken with the prima ballerina's big scene on the other side of the stage—the scene that would have been Claire's, in any other show—I snuck my camera to my eye. I didn't attach the flash, and during the next round of applause I clicked the shutter, a shot of Claire and her entourage holding a staged pose. Feeling sick to my stomach, I packed my camera away, not wanting any more memories of what we were seeing.

Claire was soon back in the limelight, scurrying behind the other ballerinas. I thought I could actually hear her huffing and puffing from my seat in the twenty-third row.

By the end of the performance, I had given Claire my all:

every prayer, every bit of energy I could transmit through the atmosphere. I was spent.

When the lights came up, Mom didn't jump into her usual eager socializing mode. She sat in her seat with us, offering a nod and a timid wave to the other ladies who caught her eye. No one came over to talk to Mom, or to offer their praises like they usually did after one of Claire's performances. I kept my head down and pretended to adjust my camera to look busy. After the auditorium had pretty much cleared, my family silently rose and filed out.

Claire emerged alone from the dressing room in an overcoat with her head down. She didn't notice us at first. The second her eye caught us, it was as if the world had stopped.

After a long pause, she marched right out the door without saying a word. Mom strode after her, followed reluctantly by me and Dad.

"Claire," Mom said in a tone that said a million things. *You will stop and listen to me, young lady. What happened? Who have you become? What can we do about this?*

Claire didn't stop. "You weren't supposed to be here," she said, as though this was all our fault, and there wouldn't be a problem if we hadn't come.

"The car's this way, Claire," Dad said. He didn't yell. He'd never been the disciplinary parent. But when his stern tone came out, there was this instant fear that rose up. At least in me. Obviously in Claire, too, because she stopped in place. Her whole jaw trembled.

Mom and Dad and Claire all stood there like dogs at the ends of their leashes. If Claire didn't follow along to the car, my parents wouldn't know what to do with her. If Claire walked, it would be more than two miles, and I doubted she had the stamina for it. But she probably didn't have the energy for a barrage of questions from our parents, either. I wondered who was supposed to give her a ride home. Had they deserted her?

I took a step toward Claire. Then another. Without a word, I grabbed her hand and gently tugged her toward the car. She came willingly, and even though there were no tears on her cheeks, she shook like she was bawling her head off.

During the car ride home, my whole family stayed silent. Claire headed straight for her room without saying a word to any of us. I stood in the foyer while my parents sat in the living room together eyeing me, like they were waiting for me to get out of earshot. I headed for the stairs. They obviously needed to talk. But before I left, I turned back to say, "Are you going to do something about this?" Because I had to know.

Mom looked away, and I wondered if it was guilt—for not believing me. Or for letting that whole auditorium of people see her daughter's problem before she could admit to it.

Dad nodded. "Yes, Loann." He let out a long breath. "Why don't you head up to bed."

I did.

I thought I would be happy to have this off my chest. To have someone else dealing with it.

But I was anything but happy.

CHAPTER TWENTY-SIX

The next morning, Mom made an appointment for Claire to see Dr. Quinton. Apparently, Claire had regained some emotional strength overnight and walked into the kitchen with balled fists.

"But, Mom, I have to work today," she said, and took a bite of her banana, as if to prove she was fine.

I held my tongue from telling Mom that Claire hadn't been working at all lately. I wanted to keep out of this as much as possible. Claire probably didn't know that I'd been the one to make the family go to her ballet production and I didn't want that to accidentally come out.

"I took the morning off. You're going." Mom plunked the dishes in the dishwasher roughly, and I cringed with each one, waiting for one to break.

"Besides, I don't know what you're so worried about," Claire went on, as if she hadn't heard Mom. "So I lost a few pounds. I'll put it back on. You know how it is when you're a teenager." Claire tried to give Mom a knowing nod, but Mom wouldn't have it.

"Dr. Quinton can see you this morning, and so we're going this morning. I'll call your boss if you need me to," she added.

"Why can't we go tomorrow?"

"Today," Mom said firmly, not even bothering with the obvious argument: that *she* had already taken this morning off.

"I'll eat more, I will," Claire practically begged.

At least Claire was admitting she avoided food more than she avoided bad fashion. Though she said it as though it was really no big deal.

"Ten minutes." Mom headed out of the room. "Get your shoes on." Her voice gave away a slight quiver.

I don't know what happened in Dr. Quinton's office, but when they got home, Claire went straight to her room and slammed the door. Mom strode for the phone on the hutch. She hadn't noticed me, so I picked up a book and slunk into the couch to make myself invisible.

"I'd like to admit my daughter," was the first bit of conversation I caught. Mom leaned forward against the hutch while she talked, like she had a stomachache.

Mom wasn't talking to the University of Wisconsin. It was a hospital of some kind.

The more Mom went on, giving doctors' names and Claire's medical history, the more I realized it wasn't just a stupid crash diet or even an eating disorder they were talking about. Claire had some serious medical problems. From putting the pieces together of words Mom repeated, I understood that San Diego had a clinic that could treat liver and stomach disorders as part of their program. *Claire had a serious liver or stomach problem?*

"Uh, yes . . . I appreciate you making allowances with your waiting list . . ." Mom went on. I could hear her trying to force strength and calm into each of her words. "Claire Rochester. Yes, we'll be there by the end of the week."

Mom noisily fumbled the handset back into its holder. As she turned my way, I brought my book up to my face, probably a little too close, maybe a little too fast. I just didn't know what to say, and I doubted Mom did either.

Wednesday morning, Mom rushed between arranging her luggage, phone calls, and programming her GPS for the trip. She'd worked herself into a frenzy since she'd found out about Claire. "There's dinner in the fridge, Loann. Your dad won't be home until late."

No surprise there. Dad hadn't been home at a reasonable

hour since Claire's recital. It had always annoyed me the way he ran away whenever things got stressful, but this was really serious. It was his oldest daughter, and I was having a hard time believing he could try to avoid *this*.

When Mom seemed to have everything together, she kissed me on the forehead, told me she'd be back the following night, then moved like a whirlwind toward the front door. Claire inched herself in that direction, but looked back at me like she wished I'd grab her hand and pull her back. "Bye," she said in nearly a whisper.

"I hope . . ." The words stuck in my throat. What did I hope? I hoped to have my happy, normal sister back. I hoped she wouldn't ever hide something this big from me again.

"I hope it helps," I said finally.

When the door closed behind them, I stood in place and just listened to the silence. The sick feeling in my stomach intensified until it almost snaked up my throat. Claire had looked so scared and I hadn't even hugged her, hadn't even really said good-bye. All I'd been able to think about lately was how weird she'd been acting, how much she'd been hiding, but the truth was, five minutes after she left, I ached to have her back.

I'd told Marcus I probably wouldn't be in today, but I couldn't stay in the empty house. I grabbed my bag and headed out the door, just to stop thinking about her.

* * *

Armando was nowhere in sight, and Marcus sat alone at our table. He wore a long-sleeve black shirt today, which must've been stifling in the heat. He was probably covering up another bruise. I looked at him for a long time before finally pulling out a chair. Could I really find it in me to argue with him about opening up today?

"My sister has stomach problems from her eating disorder," I said, my voice empty and tired.

"Yeah," he said, but by his tone it might as well have been *Duh*, which sure didn't seem very sympathetic.

"She's going away to a clinic of some kind in California."

"Hmm, good."

"Good?" I scowled at him. "That's all you have to say?" I shook my head and stood up. He called out something as the door shut behind me, but I ignored him. I so was not in the mood for his short answers today. I picked up my pace and ran all the way to the high school.

There was a soccer practice going on in the backfield. I steered clear of that and headed toward the portable classrooms. As I walked behind the buildings, I was overcome by a flood of emotions. Tears spilled down my cheeks as I sat down between the trees. Somehow, the place where I'd been with Josh, the place where I'd been so stupid and careless and lost a piece of myself—that was the place I wanted to be.

I let myself get good and angry, and remembered every stupid thing I'd ever done. I pulled at the roots of my hair until it hurt and didn't bother to wipe my eyes or my nose.

The strange thing was, being in this spot, I felt completely different than I had the last time I had come here. Last time I'd been starry-eyed, not just about Josh, but about Claire, too. My one-night stand with Josh was only the start of my realizations. Nothing was what I'd thought it had been back then.

Two hours later, the punishment finally felt like enough. At least for the moment. I picked myself up, and headed for home.

Over the past few months, Claire had become pretty private about her room. Whenever I knocked, she usually just met me at the door, then started to close it in my face if I tried to come in.

But now all I wanted to do was sit on her bed and pretend she hadn't left.

When I walked into her room, though, the first thing that registered was the stench. All those dinners she'd brought to her room to eat—I wondered if they were still in here somewhere. *Ugh*. I scrunched up my nose as I strode to open her window, then headed for her unmade bed.

I'd heard Mom call her bulimic, but I was pretty sure there'd also been long stretches when Claire didn't eat at all.

I wondered how many kinds of disorders she really had. But then, it didn't really matter, did it? What mattered was that I hadn't figured it out sooner. I'd never paid close enough attention.

"I miss you, Claire." I lay back on her bed and murmured into the ether. But after five minutes, I couldn't wallow anymore. And I couldn't stand the thought of Claire's normally pristine bedroom looking like this.

After making her bed, and tidying up her messy clothes, I dug through her drawers, looking for anything that might be rotting. I could barely believe my eyes at the top drawer. Skittles, Milky Ways, Reese's Peanut Butter Cups—she practically had a whole candy store in her desk! I closed the drawer tentatively, wondering if it would be better to dump it all in the garbage or tell Mom first. Opening the other drawers by rote, I found a bag of rotting fruit in the back of the bottom one. That would explain the stench, which actually felt like a relief. I grabbed it, and the rest of her garbage, too, figuring I should empty it, since she probably wouldn't be back for a while. But when I reached for her garbage can and looked inside, I blinked hard, not believing my eyes.

I'd given Claire copies of the grad pictures I'd taken of her, Josh, Jaz, and Laz. And sure, it would have been expected for her to stuff them away somewhere after her breakup with Josh, at least until she got over it.

But that was more than a month ago. And the grad pictures I saw now, crumpled at the bottom of her garbage can, had nothing against Josh.

Every impression of *Claire* had been obliterated with thick black felt marker.

What did my sister think of herself? Did she hate herself that much, and I'd never even seen it?

I didn't look away from the garbage can until our doorbell rang, snapping me out of my daze. I made my way down the stairs, but I wasn't in the mood to talk to anyone. The person outside started knocking, annoying me even more.

I swung open the front door.

Marcus.

"I don't know what you want me to say," he grumbled.

"Then don't say anything. You're pretty good at that," I snapped. I didn't invite him in. If anything, I gave the door a slight push closed to give him the hint.

"Yeah, well, I just came to say I'm sorry. I meant that it was good that Claire's getting some help. I'm sure it's been really hard and confusing for you." He turned to leave.

He knew how to make me feel like crap in two sentences flat. *Crud.* He was a good guy for tracking me down, even when I'd been such a bitch. And I knew none of this was his fault. I guess it was just easier to take it out on him than on myself.

I walked outside and down the driveway in my socks, until I stood at the edge of our street. Marcus had made it across to the other side already.

"Hey, putz!" I yelled.

"What?" he asked, without making any effort to laugh or retort or come back.

"You want to make me some coffee? I could use some help." I motioned my head back toward the house.

Even with the distance, I could see him crack a grin. He started to walk toward me.

I waited for him and then led the way to the kitchen without a word. I was mentally forming my apology, because he definitely did deserve one. Marcus opened Mom's coffee-maker, looked inside it, then closed it again.

He turned to me. "I should make you dinner."

"Yeah. Sure," I said, caught off guard. "Can you cook?"

"Kinda," he said.

"Mom said she left something in the fridge, so we could just heat it up," I told him, in an attempt to let him off the hook if he hadn't really meant *cook* cook me dinner. I tried to act like I wasn't practically hyperventilating at the thought of him making dinner for me—a real date if there ever was one.

I braced myself for him to take back the offer.

But then he said, "Let's go to my place. I'll cook for you there."

CHAPTER TWENTY-SEVEN

We rode the elevator to Marcus's third-floor apartment in silence. He had explained on the way that his mom was called into work and his dad always bowled until ten on Wednesdays. It seemed like he'd really thought this through, and maybe it hadn't been a last-minute invitation. Maybe the reason he'd been short with me at the Arts Club was because he was nervous.

He pulled a key from his pocket and slipped it into the lock. We both stood there for a second, staring down at it like we had to work up the guts for whatever we might get into inside. The lock clicked open. My heart pounded hard against my chest. I could hardly believe Marcus was finally bringing me here.

I followed him into the dark hallway, and even when

he flipped on a light, the yellowy glow didn't do much to brighten the beige walls. We kicked off our shoes and he led the way down the hall. I expected to end up in the kitchen, but instead we stood in his bedroom.

It was small, more like an office. I was willing to bet the knee-high cabinet at the end of his bed was put there because his bed didn't quite fit his long legs. An old-looking computer dwarfed a small desk beside the bed. It definitely didn't look like this place suited tall and lanky Marcus, and I tried to picture him coming back here every day. Sitting in his chair. Sleeping in his bed. Thinking about being in Marcus's bedroom made my heart speed up.

"I just have to change," he said, and lifted his shirt over his head so quickly I didn't have a chance to back up and give him some privacy.

He grabbed a short-sleeve shirt, but stood there for a few seconds, looking at me. Or letting me look.

A dark red mark stretched across his chest. One of his arms was covered in bandaging.

I covered my mouth. "Oh, Marcus." I reached out my hand, but I didn't actually want to touch anywhere it might hurt. I drew back my hand.

He pulled the new shirt on, covering his injuries.

"It's exactly what you think," he said. "My dad. It's been happening for a long time."

This new intimacy between us felt scary. Fragile. And I didn't want to do anything to break it. I took a few slow breaths, then said his name again.

He cringed and turned his face away, like I'd slapped him. "Just . . . give me a minute." He blinked hard a couple of times. We'd gotten this far, and I would let him take his time with this if that's what he needed.

I scanned his room again, in an attempt to take the pressure off. I looked again at the computer desk in the corner, his bed covered with a plain navy comforter, the picture of us on his small dresser . . .

Wait. Picture of us? I picked up the frame to study it.

Marcus had taken the family print I'd given him from Claire's grad and cropped out the rest of the family and Claire's friends. I smiled at that, wishing I'd thought to do the same thing. Marcus and I looked good together, despite our height difference. I remembered what he'd said about me being his whole life, and it didn't escape my notice that there wasn't a single other picture in his room. I held the photo to my chest, wishing I could hold him close instead. Or do something to show him how I was here for him. No matter what.

Marcus cleared his throat behind me. "I'd better get started on dinner," he said, swishing past me out of the room.

By the time I put the picture back in place and caught up

to him, Marcus was bent over, pulling casserole dishes out of cupboards in the kitchen.

Was he going to avoid the subject now? He brought me here. He showed me the bruise. He must want to talk about it. I moved close to him, but he reached for a drawer on the opposite side. That's when I noticed the pinkness on his neck.

I swallowed. I'd never seen Marcus embarrassed before. Even when he'd been teased at school. Even when we'd almost kissed.

"So, uh, what are we making?" I wanted to show him somehow that I would give him all the time and space he needed.

"*We* are not making anything, Loey," he said, perfectly composed. "Sit down over there." He motioned to a bar stool by the phone.

I allowed myself a small smile at the renewed thought of him cooking me dinner. And in the next few minutes, Marcus fell into his element. He cracked eggs open single-handedly while whisking with his other hand.

"Wow, where'd you learn to cook?" I asked.

"I didn't," he replied.

"Coulda fooled me." Every sentence made the room feel lighter. "Maybe you should be a chef or something. Or start baking food for Armando's café."

He muffled a laugh, but I got the sense that he'd thought about it.

After sliding a casserole dish into the oven, he turned to me in the small kitchen and just started talking.

"For years I was too young to get out of here by myself. Then, as I got older, I started to question my mom on why we had to stay with him."

I nodded, afraid to interrupt.

"He threatens her with a lot of things." Marcus breathed out a humorless laugh. "I don't believe him anymore, but she still does. He mocks the idea of us going to the police and getting a restraining order. He tells us we could never make it without him. My mom says she's afraid for Uncle Armando. He's not really allowed to be living here. In the country," Marcus added.

A silence settled between us as I thought this over. "But if Armando knew things were this bad, or that he was the reason—"

"I know. It's just an excuse, anyway. My mom's just too afraid to be on her own after all these years." He softened. "She was only sixteen when she married him, and she's never done anything without him."

"That's no excuse!" I tried to rein in my volume, but I couldn't believe this. "How could she just sit by while her son gets the crap beaten out of him?"

Marcus stayed calm. He'd obviously been over and over this in his mind. "She doesn't know about most of what he does to me. He does it when she's not around. He thinks he has me under his thumb because of that, but what he doesn't know is that I'm only waiting for the right time, when Mom's ready. I don't get much time alone with her, but I'm trying to get her used to the idea, now that I'm older."

I shook my head, hoping he could see he was being blind. "She'll never be ready."

His jaw clenched and his eyes hardened.

"If you told her about everything he does, *maybe*," I said, "but otherwise, why would things change? I mean, how long has this been going on?"

He nodded, knowing my question was rhetorical. "I'm almost eighteen. I can leave soon."

"But *will* you leave your mom with him if he's abusive?" I knew Marcus. I knew the answer as I watched the realization settle in on him. Age had nothing to do with this and he knew it.

"Look, I'm scared too, okay? My dad makes the money, he pays the bills, and he knows how to calm my mom down. She . . . freaks out sometimes." He took a big breath. "I can't do all that, and she'll blame me for not being able to take care of us."

"She won't blame you for wanting to be safe," I said gently. "You need to tell her. You need to tell somebody what's really going on."

He balked. "I thought that's what this was."

I swallowed. "I'm not enough, Marcus. We need to actually *do* something. We need to get you help." I hesitated, and then said, "But we can do this together."

We stood there like that for a long time. There were things I could say about getting his mom into counseling, or going on financial assistance, but I sensed something had changed in Marcus. Maybe he'd just felt too alone to act on any possible solutions before.

There seemed to be a hint of hope in his eyes.

Seconds later, a key rattled in the door. I darted a look at Marcus but his eyes stayed fixed on the hallway that led to the entry. He took a step in front of me, and I knew it was a protective gesture. I slipped off my stool and inched behind him further.

The door opened, knocking against the wall with a thud.

"You home?" a gruff voice called. I tried to swallow, but my entire mouth, my entire face, had gone numb.

"I've got a friend here," Marcus called out, and his voice was surprisingly light. His tensed hands gave him away, though.

I heard his dad grunt before he came into view. "You're not entertaining on our budget, I hope."

My eyes darted to the oven, where the timer Marcus had set was ticking down. I couldn't breathe.

"Nope," Marcus said, his voice still light.

His dad was exactly what I expected in some ways—dark, growly face, big, muscular arms and hands—but not at all like I expected in others. I guess I'd assumed he'd be a drunk who forgot to shave and comb his hair, but this guy looked pretty respectable. He wore a short-sleeve button-down shirt with a tie, and his hair was trimmed right up over his ears.

He glared at Marcus and tilted his head to the side, trying to get a better view of me.

Marcus protectively took half a step sideways to continue blocking his view, but I did not want him to get in trouble over me.

"Hi," I said, ducking around Marcus. "I just stopped by to ask Marcus about some stuff . . ." I was about to say "for the Arts Club," but then remembered what Marcus had said about Armando and didn't want to say anything wrong. "For my job," I said. "At my parents' restaurant." I hoped his dad knew Marcus could cook and this might seem believable.

He nodded, but his eyes stayed squinty, like he didn't trust me.

"She just stopped by," Marcus repeated. "I thought you were bowling, so she wouldn't disturb you." It bothered me how much Marcus cowered around his dad.

His dad raised his eyebrows. "Yeah, I shoulda been bowling," he said, as if it was Marcus's fault he wasn't. He came a step closer and whacked Marcus on the chest in what I might have mistaken for a playful gesture if I hadn't known better. Marcus didn't flinch, didn't move a muscle, though I saw his knuckles whiten at his sides. "Can't bowl with a screwed-up hand, though, can I?" his dad added.

Silence filled the small kitchen. I needed to get out of this place. But I couldn't leave Marcus here, not with his dad.

"My friend was just leaving," Marcus said, as though he could hear my thoughts. I noticed how he hadn't used my name, and I decided I wouldn't volunteer it either. He reached for my hand and tugged me past his dad. I hoped we could come up with some sort of a whispered plan, but his dad grabbed a beer from the fridge and followed us all the way to the door. He watched me bend down to put on my shoes.

I tied them slowly, trying to think of something— anything—I could do to help. Marcus's dad obviously wasn't in a good mood, and I suspected the knock to his chest was just a prelude.

"Can you walk me home?" I asked Marcus. "It's getting kind of dark."

"Nope." His dad put a controlling hand on Marcus's shoulder. "He's not going anywhere tonight. He's got work to do around here."

"So give your parents my best," Marcus said, as if to hurry me out of his apartment. I was about to argue, say I wouldn't leave, even if it meant us both getting the crap beaten out of us. But then he added, "And tell your parents to get some biscotti for the restaurant. Certain people," he said, "really love *biscotti*."

The way he said the last part reminded me of something he'd said before. Like *polizia*, I thought suddenly. *He wants me to go to the police.*

Marcus's dad grunted, and Marcus opened the door to push me through.

"Biscotti," I said, barely able to breathe out the word. "Got it."

As he nudged the door closed behind me, I felt something fall into the back of my hoodie. Then the door shut and locked from the other side.

After finding Marcus's key in the back of the hood of my sweatshirt, I ran all the way down three flights of stairs and dialed 911 from my cell in the lobby.

I'd never called 911 before, and I couldn't help but think of how casually I'd taken the whole idea of an emergency number when we'd first learned about them in kindergarten. Emergency situations were not casual. In fact, my whole body shook with fear.

They asked me the nature of my emergency and patched me through to another operator. I had to look outside for Marcus's address while trying to talk slowly enough so they could understand me. When they asked if Marcus's dad has any weapons, I just about dropped my phone. "N-not that I know of," I said. "But maybe."

They promised they'd send a couple of officers right away, but I paced the lobby and couldn't stand the waiting. I'd assumed Marcus had just wanted me to call the police, but then why did he give me his key?

And what if Marcus's dad did have a weapon? What if he even just broke a beer bottle? My stomach clenched at mental images of injuries produced by a jagged piece of glass. *What if the police hadn't taken me seriously, or took too long to get here?*

I hadn't helped Claire soon enough, and I wasn't going to make that same mistake with Marcus. I headed for the stairs and took them three at a time back up to Marcus's floor. There were muffled sounds from inside, but they weren't loud enough to tell what was happening. When I put my ear to the door, I could hear Marcus's dad's voice, but not what he was saying. I didn't hear Marcus at all at first, but I figured he must be in there, must still be okay, if his dad was still lecturing at him. A sudden bang sounded from inside, like a baseball bat on a wall. Or against someone's head. I closed my eyes, said a quick prayer, and fumbled the key toward the lock.

Even though I was moving as fast as possible, I felt like everything was in slow motion. Voices sounded from the stairwell. *The police!* I backed up, leaving the key in the lock, just as two of them rushed from the stairwell door.

I waved them toward the door. The words "Go, go," came out of me in a choked whisper.

When one officer pushed the door wide open, I saw Marcus with a bandanna shoved in his mouth. His dad held him by his neck against the mishmashed blinds of the front window.

"Stop! Please stop!" I yelled, and the slow motion went into hyperdrive. Suddenly everything was happening at once.

The officers had moved in behind Marcus's dad, but he seemed to only notice me, yelling from the hallway. One officer told him calmly to release the boy, but in Marcus's dad's surprise, he whirled around and hit the cop, knocking him over.

At least he'd let go of Marcus in the process. The other cop pulled a gun on Marcus's dad while the officer who'd been hit got to his feet.

Marcus's dad clenched and unclenched his hands, like he was still deciding who to take his anger out on. Marcus yanked the bandanna from his mouth and rushed away from them, closer to me.

"Are you okay?" I whispered, now that the cops seemed to have gotten control over the rest of things. They handcuffed Marcus's dad and were reading him his rights.

Marcus kept his still-fearful eyes trained on his dad. "Yeah. But you should go," he said. "You don't want to get caught up in the middle of all of this."

I shook my head. "I'm not leaving you alone, Marcus."

He finally broke his stare and turned to me. "You didn't. You were here when I needed you, Loey. Now go home and be safe. *Please.*"

The officer who wasn't reading rights looked over at Marcus. Without giving me time to reply, Marcus nudged the door closed between us.

CHAPTER TWENTY-EIGHT

Because the Arts Club was only a couple of blocks away, I ran to see Armando. I couldn't sit at home by myself right now, no matter how much Marcus wanted me to. My whole body was abuzz and I needed to do something to calm myself down. Armando could probably get ahold of Marcus's mom to find out what was happening, and that, at least, felt useful.

I found the old man pacing the floor of his café.

"The police," I said, out of breath when he looked up at me. "I had to call them for Marcus."

Armando nodded like he already knew. "My niece call," he said, and I assumed he meant Marcus's mom. "She call back to tell me soon."

An awkward silence followed where we looked at each other, then at the art on the walls. I had to avert my eyes from the Caravaggio with the man gripping the boy—it disturbed me even more now.

When the phone finally rang, Armando picked up on the first ring and nodded for several seconds, without saying anything. Why couldn't Marcus have a slightly more animated uncle? How did I get involved with such a silent family? I paced again while I waited for him to get off the phone.

"Marcus fine," he said, with the first smile I'd ever seen on his face. "He go to *polizia* building. You go home and he call you."

I waited up most of the night, between staring at my phone, staring at my computer, and staring out my bedroom window in the far-fetched hope that Marcus might stop by at three a.m. I guess I nodded off, because when I looked at the clock, it was after nine.

I bolted out of bed and rushed for the computer. Still no e-mail. No phone call. Marcus was okay physically, but what else was happening? Was his mom blaming him? Was he blaming me?

After splashing cold water on my face and brushing my teeth, I raced out the door in the same clothes I'd worn yesterday. Dad's car was gone, and I wondered, fleetingly, if he'd come home at all last night.

Armando stood behind his counter looking about as exhausted as I felt. "You hear something?" he asked.

I shook my head.

We sat together for nearly half an hour. We were afraid to phone again, just in case Marcus's dad was back at home. There was a scuffing sound when the door opened and we both looked up.

Marcus.

He wasn't himself, I could tell that immediately. He was jittery and looked in all directions before finally walking toward us. Judging by his nervousness, I figured they must have released his dad. But how could Marcus be here, then? I walked right over to him to find out, but then hesitated, not knowing what to say. Not knowing all he had been through. "Are you . . . what happened?" I asked.

"He's gone," Marcus said, nodding, almost like he was convincing himself.

Armando seemed to recognize that we needed some time alone. He placed a hand on Marcus's shoulder, and then headed out with the excuse of going to call his niece.

"Do you . . ." I eyed him carefully. "Do you want to talk about it?"

He looked out the window, which I assumed meant no, but then he turned back to me and said, "It's . . . I know I shouldn't be scared anymore, but—"

"Is he in jail?" I blurted. Marcus was scaring me, too.

Marcus nodded. "Yeah. Turns out hitting that cop was the best thing he could have done, at least for us. He's in custody. It'll take some time for my mom to get used to things. She's freaking out a little, but they have a counselor at the police station they brought in to talk with her."

"Freaking out how?" If Marcus considered his jittery countenance even-keeled, I couldn't imagine what his mom was like right now.

"They're suggesting we move to a different apartment, which will probably cost more. The money's the thing she keeps coming back to, so I said I'd get a job." He looked around the cafe. "You know, a real job."

A small sound escaped my mouth, but I bit my lip to quiet it. This wasn't the end of the world. I knew Marcus and I could still see each other. The important thing was that he was safe. But it was still just . . . sad.

"When I was twelve," he started without any prompting, "my dad was beatin' on my mom. I came in and screamed for him to stop. 'Just stop it!' I yelled. You know what he did?" Marcus didn't wait for my answer. "He grabbed me and tied me to one of our kitchen chairs. He used his old fishing rope and it took about ten seconds of struggling for it to break through my skin."

I almost couldn't bear to hear it, but I knew Marcus had to get this out. *How many years had he been keeping it all to himself?* I gripped the sides of my chair beneath me to keep strong.

"He beat the crap out of my mom, right in front of me. She had blood coming out of her mouth and her ear. He slapped her, threw her, kicked her." Marcus said the words evenly, but I could tell how much talking about it affected him. "I swore I would get her out of there—one day. She lay on the floor and I thought she was dead, and I still have nightmares of seeing her there. But the more I cried, the more he beat her. Eventually I just shut up. I stopped crying and stayed perfectly still. When he directed his attention to me, I was glad. I was ready for my beating. I could take it. I wasn't dreading it; I was waiting."

My hands cramped from holding on so hard to the chair—at hearing his story and knowing that Marcus had kept it all to himself.

"My dad kicked my chair over. Then he walked out the door. That was all he had for me, and that almost made it worse."

Marcus doesn't like to fight back, was all I could say to myself, over and over again. *Marcus doesn't like to fight back*. I remembered when Marcus had gotten mad at me for talking back to the jocks at school, and tears rolled down my cheeks. He must have been terrified all the time. I put my hands over my mouth and blew into them. I needed the release.

Marcus reached over and grabbed my hands. He held them from across the table.

"Don't cry, Loey." I couldn't believe *he* was consoling *me*. "Now he's gone."

CHAPTER TWENTY-NINE

When Mom first got home, she didn't say much about her trip to California. We sat down for dinner that night, without Dad and Claire, and then Mom started to fill me in.

"You know Claire's only gone for a short time, right, Loey?" She never called me Loey, and it was enough to make me squirm. "She just needs a little help to get her nutrition sorted out. Then she'll be back and we'll try to get her college registration set for next fall. Maybe you girls can even go somewhere together."

Mom certainly had it all worked out. I wondered if Claire knew about Mom's plans. Or if Claire was aware she'd flown all the way to California for a bit of "nutritional counseling." Last I'd heard, she was bumped to the top of the list because of her severe health problems. Mom's plan would have sounded great if I believed a word of it.

Later in the week when the phone rang, I could tell from Mom's tone that Claire was on the other end.

"Oh, honey, is everything okay? How are you doing? Are they treating you well?"

I puttered around the living room, tidying up the magazines on the coffee table. Mom would probably talk Claire's ear off for a good twenty minutes, but I hoped to say hi for a minute. Life wasn't the same without Claire around. Our house was too quiet and felt like it was missing a limb. Or an organ.

Suddenly Mom thrust the phone in my face.

"Honey, it's Claire. She wants to talk to you."

I grasped the phone and put it to my ear before Mom had even let go.

"Uh . . . hi," I said into the receiver, turning my back to Mom. I couldn't believe Claire had asked for me after how cold I'd been when she left.

"Oh, Loey, I just needed to hear your voice."

It was exactly how I felt, but I couldn't bring myself to say it. I still hadn't thought of *what* I should say, so Claire continued, "It's not so bad here, Loey. They're teaching me so much about my habits and my body image."

I nodded, even though she couldn't see me, and said,

"Oh yeah?" in as peppy a voice as I could muster. But Claire seemed willing to carry the conversation all on her own.

"You looked worried when I left, and I just wanted to make sure you knew I was okay. They say that if I gain a proper body image and learn how to think in terms of a healthy lifestyle, I won't need to be here too long."

I wondered about her stomach problems, but she hadn't talked to me this nicely and openly in so long, I didn't want to say anything that might change that. Besides, if they were talking about sending her home, she must be physically healthy enough.

"That's great, Claire." A smile spread across my face. Mom was following me around trying to figure out what we were talking about. I'm sure Claire said the words "body image" thirty times in our short conversation, and soon, because someone else wanted the phone on her end, it was time to go.

Mom's shoulders slumped when I said good-bye and hung up. "Oh, um . . ." I motioned to the handset. "She had to go." To try to brighten her mood, I added, "It sounds like she's doing really well, though."

Mom changed the subject, I suspected because she felt jilted. "I'm off this weekend, Loann. Why don't we go shopping for school clothes." It sounded like more of a decision than a question.

"I'm working with Marcus."

"Can't Marcus hold down the fort for one day, honey?"

Who knew how many shifts I'd have left working with Marcus? Every day for the past week, he had been applying for different jobs around town. We didn't talk about it much, and I sure wasn't about to talk about it with Mom, who already seemed to have a problem with him. "It's really busy on weekends, Mom," I said. "This is my job." And besides, *shopping?* She didn't even try to pick an art gallery, or a restaurant, or something I would like.

She sighed loudly. I felt bad for her, I really did. But she'd never acted chummy with me before, and I wasn't about to play fill-in for her favorite offspring.

I skirted up the stairs before she could try to make me feel guilty.

After Marcus had opened up about his dad, he and I talked a lot more at the Arts Club. Never around other people, but the moment we were alone, it was as if that one incident had been a lump he had cleared from his throat.

"I can trade a guy down the street: some lawn mowing and odd jobs for his old Camaro." Marcus still didn't talk about his parents very often, but he liked to talk about cars. That subject he could utter two or even three sentences in a row about. I wasn't into cars, but I let him go on because I liked the sound of his deep voice, and his face lit up when he talked about them, as though he'd brought in half of the sunshine from outside.

He kept on about this Camaro. Apparently it didn't run, so I thought he was crazy to use up all his extra time on it. I tried to keep my mouth buttoned shut, but the arguments came tumbling out anyway. "Why waste your time? Don't you think you're going to be busy enough with another job?"

Of course, what I was really thinking was: *Do you think you'll still have any time left for me?*

"I can fix it, Loey. I know I can."

"Whatever." I shrugged. "Suit yourself."

At least I could be honest with Marcus. He knew I didn't agree, but if he really wanted to do this, he would. And we'd still be friends.

We always would.

Marcus told me a little about his new job, a graveyard shift stocking shelves in a local supermarket. The good news was, if he felt like missing out on sleep, we'd still be able to see each other sometimes.

"What do you think you're going to do after graduation?" I asked. I'd honed my skill at finding nontouchy subjects to talk about, but when he hesitated I realized I hadn't really thought about school. Could he go back to school while working graveyard shifts?

"Well, work on cars, I guess."

"Yeah? What kinda cars?" I asked a little too quickly. *Was he going to fix up cars because he wouldn't have a diploma?* My anger rose up toward his mom again for letting him make these choices. He was only seventeen!

"Classic cars, if I had a choice. Rebuild some old Chevys to blow away anything you see around nowadays . . . but most likely I'll work on cars that people can't afford to take to a real mechanic."

"Why don't you just become a real mechanic?" I knew I was pushing him, but if no one else was around to do it, I kind of had to, didn't I? A guy walked through the door but stood several feet away, perusing the menu.

Marcus scoffed, apparently not noticing our customer. "Oh, come on, Loey, can you see me down at Alec's Automotive? If you think I get teased a lot now . . ." he trailed off.

It was the first time he'd acknowledged the ribbing he'd gotten at school. I knew Marcus was probably right and I looked toward the guy at the counter to avoid admitting it.

I recognized the guy waiting. His name was Ethan, and we'd been in the same art class last year. He'd sat in the back with the other jocks, whom I suspected only took art as an easy elective.

"Hi," I said when I made it over to the other side of the counter. "Can I help you?"

"Hi." He smiled. "Loann, right?"

I felt a little shy that he knew my name. It wasn't like I'd ever talked to him. Or most guys at school, for that matter. Marcus hadn't come over to help take his order—not that I needed help with only one customer—but it still seemed odd and made me wonder: *Had Ethan ever teased Marcus?* He *was* part of that popular jock crowd.

I took Ethan's order, then headed back toward the coffee urn to fill a cup for him.

"So what've you been up to this summer?" Ethan asked.

"Not much." I tried to sound more casual than I felt, talking to a popular guy. "Working lots," I said, motioning around me.

He nodded. "Yeah, I probably should've gotten a summer job." There was a pause, but he didn't add why he hadn't or what he had been doing with his time. "So I heard some of the grads are having a party this weekend."

"Huh." I didn't know what kind of a reaction he was looking for. *Did he want me to be impressed?* "Are you going?"

He nodded. "Yeah, yeah. I just stopped in . . . I thought . . . you . . . might want to go."

He stopped by here for *me*? Was he serious? How did he even know I worked here? Claire had been invited to lots of parties during high school, and I was certain she'd have been invited to this one had she not been out of town. But this was so whacked. He was inviting *me*?

I glanced over at Marcus and wondered if he'd heard our conversation.

"Um, thanks, but I'm busy this weekend," I said.

Ethan shrugged. Smiled. He *was* kind of cute, with his reddish hair and a ton of freckles. And he'd just invited me to a party. A party put on by last year's grads!

"Well, maybe another time, then," Ethan said.

I watched him go, still not quite believing what had happened.

"You're not going?" Marcus said, now beside me, breaking me from my daze.

I shook my head. *Was he suggesting I should?* "I, uh, thought we'd do something this weekend."

He looked away, his lips pursed. "I have to work at the grocery store this weekend, Loey. It's training." He practically gritted the words out.

It took me a second to understand. He was jealous. And he was afraid that if he wasn't around, I might start hanging with someone else. Another guy.

"I don't want to go to a stupid party." I scoffed. It was part truth. Even if I went with Ethan, I knew I'd be way uncomfortable.

My words were enough to make Marcus's lip twitch up a bit.

But mine twitched down. Because I didn't want to be alone all weekend either.

CHAPTER THIRTY

On my way to the café the next day, I stopped at the Walgreens drugstore on the corner. As I was about to walk inside, I stopped and stared down at my roll of film. I had several that I wanted to develop so I could have something to show Mr. Dewdney when school started, but the ballet photo was on this roll. And the one of Claire suntanning in our backyard. I suddenly couldn't imagine offering those negatives of Claire to the local photo workers for them to gawk at. I shoved the film back in my pocket and dropped down onto the curb, feeling embarrassed, like I was concealing a full roll of porn.

Should I just throw the whole container in the garbage? Someone could still find and develop it. Why had I bothered to snap those pictures, anyway? And how could I destroy just the two shots?

I was at odds with myself. I still wanted to see the pictures, even if it was kind of sadistic. I needed to remember the hurting Claire, the messed-up Claire, but also the beautiful Claire. Because you couldn't always see all of her intricacies without a frame to hold her still.

"So I have some pictures I'd like to develop myself," I said to Marcus before even saying hello when I arrived at the Arts Club.

"Yeah?"

"I just don't know . . . um, where to get any more chemicals."

Marcus stared out into the alleyway. "Beats me," he said. And that was all he said.

He wasn't much help.

Then again, I wasn't that truthful.

Between Marcus's new job and his car repairs, I spent most of the next week alone at the Arts Club. And worse, when Marcus made it in, he was either too tired to talk or we seemed to have nothing to say. Grocery stocking didn't exactly make for riveting conversation.

On my next day off, I figured he'd be sleeping, but my doorbell rang and there he was.

"What are you doing here?" I asked, trying to subdue my joy. He should've been sleeping. I knew that.

He put down a big box on the floor of our foyer and I saw the gallon jugs sticking out. The developing supplies, from the art room. "How did you get those?" I asked, incredulous.

He shrugged. "I had to track Mr. Dewdney down through the school," he said. "I asked if we could borrow them until school starts."

As if Marcus didn't have enough to do these days. Without even thinking about what I was doing, I threw my arms around him. He stiffened. Hesitated. And I almost pulled away.

But then he wrapped his arms around me and relaxed a little. It had been a long time since we'd touched. I wanted to let him know that I liked this. That I didn't want to push him away.

We stood there for a long time without moving a muscle. I think we were both afraid of where this might go. Even though I knew Marcus would never hurt me the way Josh had, I still had a push/pull going on inside of me. I'd stopped thinking about Josh completely until I saw him downtown at a distance last week, but the hurt—the paranoid self protectiveness—still rose up at the thought of being close to anyone.

Marcus was so much taller than me, but somehow it felt like we fit. I kept reminding myself it was him. He was safe.

"It was the least I could do," he whispered, and his voice was enough to make my insides settle.

The phone rang, feeling like a fire alarm in the quiet. Before I could think of what I was doing, I pulled away and rushed to check the display on the handset. It wasn't Claire, so I let it ring.

"It's probably for my parents," I said. When Marcus looked around, I added, "Who are both working today." I could tell by our sudden discomfort, it wouldn't be easy to get close again.

He bent down, and it wasn't until then that I saw what else was in his box. A folded-up sheet of black plastic, some rubber trim, and a red lightbulb.

"What's all this for?" I asked.

He looked up at me with a smirk. "We're building a dark-room, of course."

It hadn't occurred to me when I first saw the solutions that there wasn't much I could do without a darkroom. But Marcus, the brains of this operation, led the way through the house, checking each room until we ended up in our base-ment bathroom.

When I first walked in and saw the Glade air freshener on the back of the toilet, a new thought hit me about Claire: *Had she been throwing up down here?*

But I quickly cleared that thought. She was away getting better now. I didn't have to keep thinking about the past.

Marcus and I covered the bathroom window with black

plastic, dug an electric heater out of the garage, attached the rubber trim for the bottom of the door, and screwed in the red lightbulb.

He hadn't been over for a while, but with no one home, he seemed comfortable enough. It felt good to be working at something with him, and the more relaxed things became, the more hope I had that we might hug again. If not today, one day.

"It'll be nice to be able to work at this again," I said quietly in the dark to him as we developed my first roll. "I've missed you."

"I know." His hand fumbled onto my arm. It was a sweet moment, until he added, "I'd probably miss me too."

I elbowed him in the ribs until he squawked. As much as I felt disappointed by him breaking the moment, it came with a certain amount of relief. We were such good friends, and the thought of changing our relationship didn't quite feel safe, but in a way that had nothing to do with Josh or what I'd been through. Maybe we just weren't ready for that. I wondered if Marcus felt the same way.

He switched to the regular lightbulb and pulled a magnifying glass from his box of supplies. "I couldn't haul the enlarger all the way over here to make prints," he said.

"No, this is awesome," I said. But my mouth snapped shut when I saw the negative of Claire on the side of the stage.

Now I couldn't blame it on the lighting, or my blurry eyes, or my oversensitivity to what anyone else in the crowd might have been thinking. The sharp edges on the negative only emphasized *her* sharp edges. Her bones sticking out, her ribs, her gaunt figure staring back at me.

"Wow," Marcus said, and it was the first time I could recall anyone saying "Wow" about my sister in that tone. I was tempted to throw my hand over the negative, but it was too late. Besides, if I could let anyone see this, it would be Marcus.

"Yeah. I, uh, kind of didn't want anyone at Walgreens to see this," I said finally.

Marcus nodded. "You're a good sister."

I stared at him. "No." I blinked to clear my eyes. "I'm not."

Marcus put a hand on my shoulder, probably to try to reassure me, but I couldn't concentrate. I studied the picture, looking for a clue as to what had happened to my beautiful sister.

"Do you think the clinic will help?" Marcus rubbed a slow circle on my back.

"It has to," I replied too fast. "She'll see a doctor and a counselor regularly when she gets back." I hoped it would be enough, but how would I, or anyone else, tell if it wasn't? She'd been so good at hiding her problems before. The thought sickened me and I couldn't concentrate on developing.

After Marcus left, I trekked up to my bedroom to grab my shoe box full of photos.

I dug out one from the spring, of Claire finishing her homework on the living room floor. Then I pulled out a grad print of Claire and Jasmine in the backyard. I added the sun-tanning negative. I laid the shots out on my bed and stared down at the three very different girls in front of me. I felt like I was seeing my sister as a stranger for the first time.

It wasn't just the skinny arms and legs. Her ribs. Her now-frizzy hair. Deeper, in her eyes, it was as though she'd lost something of who she used to be.

Or maybe she'd lost everything.

CHAPTER THIRTY-ONE

The next time Claire called, I picked up the phone right away. In fact, since finding the air freshener downstairs and studying her pictures, I'd kept the phone beside me, waiting for her call.

"Loey!" she said in her usual bright tone.

"How are you?" I asked right away, and after she'd raced on a bit with her peppy reply, I interrupted. "Are you really okay now? Really?"

She paused and then her voice dropped to a deeper, more somber octave. "I'm getting better. But it takes time, Loey."

I had to know more. "Th-That time . . ." I stuttered a bit on my words, but she waited. "That time you were throwing up in our bathroom . . ." Part of me was afraid she'd deny it, so I raced on. "Was that the only time, Claire?"

She hesitated again. "No, it wasn't, Loey." I waited for her to tell me about the downstairs bathroom. It would at least make it easier to believe she was being honest now. But instead she said, "I started when I was thirteen. But I've only been doing it daily for the last year or so."

I gulped. *Thirteen? Daily?* I blinked hard. "Oh, Claire." *How? When? Why didn't I know?* All my questions caught in my throat.

When I didn't say anything else, Claire filled the uncomfortable silence. "Things are going really well here, Loey. They're teaching me a lot, and I get to come home really soon!" By the end of her sentence her voice had regained its chipper tone.

I couldn't smile. I could hardly breathe.

I purposed to stay home more and talk to Claire each time she called, and soon I realized I was happier when she didn't talk about the past. Instead we discussed our futures: school, college, jobs. Each time I spoke with her, she sounded better, like her old self. Healthy. Happy. I lay on her bed most times when we were on the phone, and it helped to bring back some of the better memories of the two of us, even of our family when we used to be more of a tight unit, rather than all of us going our own directions. I thought about family vacations, Claire and I laughing ourselves silly in a game of hide-and-seek. What Claire had gone through was an unfortunate route to get my old sister back, but I was happy she was back just the same.

Claire had been gone for almost three weeks, and I had dwelled almost solely on when she would be home again so we could work together to get our family and ourselves back to normal, but at the end of August, I suddenly had something more urgent to think about.

Senior year.

On our first day back, Marcus and I met at the Arts Club so we could walk together. Dark circles rimmed his eyes like a boxer. He looked awful.

"Did you have to work all night?" I reached up and ran my fingers through his hair to try to straighten it a bit. I'd never felt his hair before, and it was so soft and silky. He bent over so I could reach better and I lifted my left hand to fix the other side.

I didn't want to stop, and when I noticed his eyes were closed, I suspected he didn't want me to either. I wanted to run my hands down onto his face. His neck. I was trying to work up the courage when he stumbled toward me.

He straightened abruptly and I pulled my hands away.

"Tired, huh?" I asked, feeling more than a little embarrassed. I'd been thinking about being closer to him and he'd probably only been thinking about being closer to his bed.

He nodded, and we walked in silence for a few minutes.

I don't know if I was feeling superjilted by Marcus, or maybe it was the fact that I'd have to face Josh today, but the more I walked, the more agitated I became. I finally couldn't hold back my thoughts any longer. "It's just not fair," I said, "that your mom makes you work full time during your senior year."

"My mom's not making me do anything," he said. "She's just having a hard time. It's only been a few weeks." Marcus, always the one to give people more credit than they deserved. Though considering I had been on the receiving end of that trait, I swallowed down my rebuttal.

When we opened the school doors, the jocks stood across the lobby as if they were there screening everyone coming in. It was a new group, and included only one of the guys who I'd seen bugging Marcus before. But Josh was with them. He was turned away, talking to another of the guys, but I would recognize his straight, confident posture anywhere.

Even the thought of Josh made my insides weak. Why had I let him do whatever he wanted, when he obviously didn't give a crap about me? I'd done so well, putting him out of my mind when I didn't have to see him, but now it was unavoidable. When other people from Josh's group eyed me, I wondered how many of them knew.

Marcus noticeably stiffened beside me, too.

I hadn't heard from Ethan after he'd invited me to that

party. But he was with the group and broke away when he saw me.

I swallowed. Seeing Ethan with Josh, I couldn't help but wonder . . . had he only invited me to a party because of something he'd heard about me? Something he'd heard from Josh?

He joined Marcus and me in step.

"Hi, Loann. How's it going?"

I forced a smile, wanting to give Ethan the benefit of the doubt. "I'm pretty good. All ready for senior year?"

Ethan nodded and started jabbering on about his electives. Marcus didn't even glance in Ethan's direction.

When we reached our lockers, Ethan was just coming to the end of his story about rearranging his schedule.

"Well I'm glad it worked out," I said. "I guess I'll see you around?"

Ethan nodded, taking the hint and backing away. "Yeah, see you at lunch."

Marcus didn't say a word to me as we arranged our new notebooks in our lockers. I didn't know if he was jealous, or what, but it felt almost impossible to break the silence.

I decided to just address the issue head-on. "So it's kinda weird, that Ethan guy following me around, huh?"

"No, Loann." He sighed. "It's not weird at all."

I wasn't sure exactly what he meant, but it felt like a compliment. "Well, he's totally not my type."

Marcus had such a complete nonreaction, I regretted trying to make him feel better. *Why bother, if he was barely going to notice?*

When the warning bell rang, I silently walked Marcus to his first class to make sure he didn't nod off on the way. We didn't meet up again until drama, which was right before lunch.

Everything looked exactly as it had last year: Shayleen at the front, with Deirdre a few seats behind now that they weren't friends. Marcus in the back.

Deirdre gave me a wave when she spotted me, but she seemed involved conversing with another girl. I waved back and headed straight for the seat beside Marcus.

He was dozing on one arm. With nothing else to do, Ethan's mention of lunch kept coming back to me. I'd avoided the cafeteria most of last year, and it sounded kind of nice to be wanted in there during my senior year.

The more I thought about it, were Ethan and Josh really even friends? Maybe Ethan really did like me. And even if I didn't *really* like him, not in that way, I kind of wanted to know his motives.

"What do you think about eating in the cafeteria today?" I whispered to Marcus.

"Hmm?" His eyelashes fluttered, but he didn't fully open his eyes. "I think I need to take a nap somewhere during lunch."

So it was settled. I was on my own.

* * *

The first face I saw when I walked into the cafeteria was Deirdre's. Her table looked like the safest option, since I couldn't imagine myself just plunking down with a group of senior guys. Then Ethan appeared in front of me, intercepting my path.

"Hey, Loann. We're over here." He pointed to a table near the windows, a table I always remembered the popular seniors—my sister's crowd—sitting at last year. I sized it up. Not only was Josh nowhere in sight, the table was not all guys. In fact, it was a mix of seniors, including some girls I recognized from last year's art class. It really didn't seem so bad.

Most of the people had bought their lunches already, and I followed Ethan toward them and sat down with my brown bag, feeling slightly embarrassed by it.

"Want to share my fries?" Ethan asked, pushing the carton toward me.

I let out my breath. Just when I started to relax, though, I heard a familiar voice behind me. Ethan and I had sat facing the windows, with our backs to the rest of the cafeteria, so I didn't notice Josh's approach until I heard him.

"Hey, Ethan," Josh said, passing behind us and heading to the opposite end of the table. "I wanted to talk to you about something. Why don't you slide down here?" Josh didn't acknowledge me at all.

I swallowed. I didn't want anything to do with Josh anymore, but it hurt to feel so completely unimportant. A small part of me had held out hope that somehow I'd had it wrong—Josh hadn't just used me and never called again. It had to have been something bigger than that—he'd had a family tragedy, or he'd had to leave the country, or something that I didn't know the details of.

But clearly I couldn't believe that now.

Ethan, to my surprise, didn't say a word back to Josh. In fact, he didn't respond at all, and I wondered what was going on here. There was obviously some kind of tension between them.

Before I finished that thought, someone sat down on my opposite side. I glanced over and saw Ron, the guy who hadn't paid for his coffee at the Arts Club during the summer.

I reached for a French fry to be doing something with my hands, but I knocked Ethan's hand in the process.

"So how's it going, Loann?" Ron asked. His face was close—too close—and I could smell his onion-y breath. His hand dropped under the table and onto my knee. I shut my eyes for a second, not wanting to believe that this was exactly what I thought it had been.

Josh had told all his friends what we had done. And now *everyone* wanted to help themselves to the easy girl who gives it all up on the first date.

When I opened my eyes, Josh's jaw looked hardened, and he just stared at the three of us.

Ron's hand slid up from my knee to my thigh. I jumped and then stood in one quick motion. The whole table looked over at my abrupt move.

"I, uh, remembered I have to see a teacher," I said, stepping over the bench and nearly toppling over in an attempt to get my other leg out quickly. Ethan murmured for me to wait up, and when I turned to go, there was Shayleen, right in my face.

"Oh. I was just coming to sit with you," she said, her voice all sweet, like it had been in the Arts Club that day over a month ago. There was a demand in her eyes, like she was daring me to leave. I was her "in" at this table.

But I couldn't do it. Not for Shayleen, who'd been so incredibly mean to me last year; not for Ron, who I couldn't stand the sight of; not even for Ethan, because I hated guys who seemed deceptively nice, and I had a strong feeling his intentions weren't pure, either.

Without a word, I darted to the side of Shayleen and made a beeline for the cafeteria doors. As soon as I pushed through them, there on the other side stood Marcus.

"I was just coming to find you," he said, but I was willing to bet he had been at least five minutes from actually working up the nerve to open the doors.

Still, I was so happy to see him. And he was willing to miss out on sleep to make sure I was okay, which made me want to hug him and tell him how awesome he was. But I wasn't about to get in the way of any more of his sleeping time. "Don't worry," I said, leading the way down the hall. "It sucks in there just as much as it did last year." *Even more*, I added silently. "Come on. Let's find you a place to get some rest."

CHAPTER THIRTY-TWO

We ended up back in the school theater, but today, rather than wandering around backstage, we headed for the cushy auditorium seats, with only twenty minutes left of the lunch period.

"Mrs. Andersen caught me nodding off during English," he told me as we leaned back and put our feet up. Our only light was from the safety lights on the stage. "I've got to get some rest or they're going to start calling my mom."

"Are you sure that's such a bad thing?"

He turned his head slightly away from me. He didn't want to talk about it and I figured I should change the subject. I tried to think of a way to talk about what had happened in the cafeteria. I also wanted to tell Marcus about Josh, or at least give him some idea of what had happened, but when I started to say something, his eyes were closed and his mouth hung half-open.

He needed the sleep, so I quieted myself and leaned my head back. Closing my eyes, I attempted to have my own little nap, if nothing else to avoid thinking about all the things that had gone wrong already this year.

The bell woke us both with a start. I could barely make it to class before the second bell at the best of times, but being groggy, both of us stumbled between the seats toward the doors.

When I rushed into art class, I told Mr. Dewdney that I'd return the developing chemicals tomorrow, when I got a ride from my mom. He didn't seem worried. And he even remembered my name!

Actually, he seemed so relaxed this year that I suspected he'd had a really great summer. Or he had a new lady in his life. He'd even dropped a few pounds.

For nearly five minutes after the bell, Mr. Dewdney just gazed from the front with a smile as people got reacquainted after the summer. Since I didn't want to talk to Ethan again—or the girls who had been at our lunch table—I took a seat near the door and flipped through the portfolio I'd started working on. So far it was just a book, really, with a few of my favorite photos laid out haphazardly on each page. Now that I was flipping through, I was amazed at how many of the photos were of Claire. She was just so photogenic.

"All right, class," Mr. Dewdney finally said. Everyone

quieted down quickly, as if showing their gratitude for the catch-up time. "As you know, senior year will have more of a focus on preparing portfolios. With this in mind, you can expect the year to be less structured."

Who was this man, and what had he done with my art teacher?

"We're working on themes this year, people, and you may use any medium you like."

My hand shot up.

Without looking over at me, he said, "Yes, Loann. You may work with photography."

I grinned. Not only could I work on a portfolio to go with my college applications, I could use class hours and get teacher feedback on it.

I left class with an extra spring in my step. Marcus had three hours before his shift started, and I couldn't wait to tell him all about my portfolio ideas. We were at the Arts Club before I realized I'd been doing all the talking and he hadn't said a word. I quickly came to the grudging conclusion that hanging out was not what he needed most. I stopped and pointed him in the direction of his apartment.

"You need to get some sleep," I told him.

He shook his head. "I've got calc homework. I can't believe they assigned homework on the first day." He sounded resigned. Like he expected to never sleep again.

I grabbed his backpack from his arm. He let it go without a fight. "Seriously, Marcus. Go home. I'll figure something out for your homework."

He didn't argue, and a moment later I found myself in the café alone, having no idea why I offered to do his homework. Math wasn't exactly my strong suit. *School* wasn't exactly my strong suit. I'd taken precalc last year, and was able to take an extra year of Spanish instead of math this year, but Marcus, he was good with numbers. I flipped open his book, hoping some of it might be review from last year.

It wasn't. I didn't understand it at all.

By the time Armando returned to relieve me, I rushed home with an idea. Claire kept almost everything she'd ever owned. I wondered if she might have kept her school books, too.

As soon as I walked in the door, Mom caught me midstep between the foyer and the stairs. It was like she knew exactly what I had planned. And somehow I didn't think she'd understand why doing Marcus's homework for him was okay.

"What?" I asked, defensively.

"Claire comes into O'Hare Saturday," she said, surprising me. "Want to ride in with me to pick her up?"

"Of course. Yeah," I said, but part of me had trouble believing it. At first the weeks without her had seemed so long, and it felt like her absence might go on forever. But now, I don't know, it seemed like too short a time for her to be completely better. The clinic must know best, though, right?

As I headed for Claire's room, I felt guilty about how much time I'd been spending in there. After that first time, it just got more and more comfortable. But would she even want me in there once she got back?

Sure enough, Claire still had her calculus binder in her closet, with all her other schoolbooks. She'd had the same teacher as Marcus, and apparently she'd used the same textbook.

I swiped the whole binder and tiptoed back to my room with it. When I was done with Marcus's homework I shoved Claire's notes under my bed, just in case I needed to help him out again.

The next morning, Mom drove me to school with the darkroom solutions. Two senior guys I didn't even know followed me down the hall, and I felt defenseless with my arms full.

"Look, what do you guys want?" I finally spun and confronted the two guys who were right on my heels. "Contrary to what you may have heard, I'm not looking for a date."

The guys looked at each other, then back at me, and my face heated to three hundred degrees. I totally had it wrong. They burst out laughing and walked right on by me.

There weren't too many people within earshot, but unfortunately Shayleen was one of them. She whisked past me going the opposite direction.

"You really screwed things up, you know." She said it without even looking at me. "You were at *their* table. You could have been someone."

I watched her walk down the hall, wondering if I was supposed to feel some regret from her words. Instead I just felt sad for her.

I ended up bringing Claire's binder to school, since Marcus couldn't keep up with anything for the rest of the week. He napped while I worked on homework—his and mine—through the lunch hours. We barely spoke during the day.

"You can't keep this up, Marcus. Seriously," I said on Friday.

"It's the weekend," he said, like that made it all better. "And I have Sunday off."

It didn't excite me at all that he had a day off like I thought it would. He would have to spend the whole day sleeping. He had no choice.

"Well I can't keep doing your homework for you. I really think you'd get better marks, at least in English, by yourself, even if you are tired." I said it as a joke, but he didn't take it that way.

"I never asked you to do my homework, Loann." He sounded grumpy, and I took immediate offense.

"I can't believe you! Fine, do it yourself, then." I knew he had to go straight to work, so I spun toward the Arts Club. When I got through the doors, I glanced out the window and he was still standing in the place where I'd left him, his backpack at his feet. I could tell he was sorry, but he didn't even seem to have the energy to come in and say it.

As much as I wanted to run back out and forgive him, I felt terribly conflicted. He couldn't go on like this, and if his mom wasn't going to think about what was best for him, someone had to.

Something needed to change with him. And soon.

Saturday morning on the three-hour drive to Chicago, Mom drove and I stared out the window, first at the miles of lonely, grassy farmland, and later at the complicated highway over-passes and crammed-in buildings of the city. I had to admit, something about the big city attracted me. Growing up, I had always assumed I would go to a small Wisconsin college, but my mind started to veer as we made our way from one high-way interchange to the next. Chicago looked, well, exciting. I thought about Marcus. I'd miss him if I went off to college, but what difference did it make? I missed him now.

We waited in the arrivals terminal for half an hour before we saw Claire. Or should I say, before we *recognized* Claire. I wasn't sure how long she'd been standing there by the time we noticed her and her extra twenty-five pounds. I didn't remember ever seeing her face so filled out. Mom had warned me repeatedly that the counselors instructed us not to make her feel self-conscious. I didn't know where to look—not at her face, not at her body. Discreet wasn't exactly my middle name, so I zoomed in on her bag.

"Wow, Claire, did you get a new suitcase? This is *really* nice!"

"Loey!" She threw her arms around me and gave me a big bear hug. It felt good to hug her now, not so bony. Just comfortable. Just Claire.

Before we could ask her any questions, she picked up her bags and started chattering, leading the way to the parking garage. "The campus . . ." she described in no fewer than five hundred words, then a full outline of the beaches, the ocean, and her new friends. I had to wonder why she bothered coming home.

Even though I felt a little hurt, I couldn't help smiling. It was great to have her home and, more important, back to her cheery, confident self.

"It was kind of like one big slumber party," she went on. "The girls and I, we'd tell our secrets until late at night. And the food, it really wasn't that bad. Lots of fresh veggies. They keep a hired chef and everything."

Mom and I had yet to add a word to anything she said. Claire kept interjecting with the phrase "I'm okay now" every couple of sentences, and if it wasn't for that, I might have actually believed that she was.

She brought back booklets galore with lists of foods and their caloric equivalents, macronutrient pyramids, and the healthy diet plan that she was supposed to adhere to. Mom went nuts in the kitchen. We ate so much chicken, I thought I might hatch something.

"Your sister has some permanent liver damage," Mom told me one morning in the kitchen before Claire was up. "She'll have to be on a special diet for the rest of her life. We'll have to be careful with what kinds of foods we give her."

I hadn't realized the extent of how much her life would be different. How much *our* lives would be different. I guess I thought she'd just come home and eat normally again.

Something else irked me about Mom's statement, though. Not because I didn't care about my sister, but because of all she'd kept hidden from us before. What foods we "gave her" didn't seem to have much bearing on what she had eaten before. One thing had changed since she left: I didn't trust my sister anymore.

Claire went to regular doctor's appointments because of her liver damage, and everyone was glad for that. I should have had confidence, like my parents, that with a doctor keeping up on her, Claire wouldn't starve herself into oblivion again.

But I just didn't completely believe it.

One afternoon I sat in the kitchen and watched her slice carrots into slats the width of paper. As she sheared, she told me more of her stories about her new friends, whom she kept up with through G-chat.

"Some of the girls have their own websites. And the chat

rooms are really fun. Kind of like we never left."

As glad as I was to see Claire happy, her enthusiasm seemed a bit much. "So why did you?" I murmured under my breath.

"Did you know, since I'm over eighteen, I'm legally an adult. Mom and Dad can't tell me what to do, pry into my private stuff. You know, like medical records and stuff."

Why was she telling me this? Claire had been away for her eighteenth birthday. We'd sent her gifts and called, and she'd reassured us that they celebrated with her in California. She'd even said it had been the best birthday ever, which felt a bit off at the time. The same way her last sentence felt off.

"Claire, don't you *want* to get better?"

She cocked her head and stared at me, her gray eyes glazing over. "Of course I do, Loey."

Her whole attitude, her weirdness, made me angry. And driven. I cleaned every inch of the café in an effort to be the best employee in the history of the world. I stayed up late doing homework, right at the dining room table so Claire wouldn't miss it. I left my college brochures on the coffee table, right under the TV remote.

I wanted to remind her of all we'd talked about on the phone while she was away. Of all she'd looked forward to coming home to and becoming.

CHAPTER THIRTY-THREE

On Monday at lunchtime, there was an edge to Marcus's voice. "You don't have to sit in the auditorium and watch me sleep." His eyes were on Ethan, just down the hall.

I'd steered clear of Ethan and Ron since the cafeteria episode, plus avoided any of the gazes of other guys I thought could be friends with Josh, but Marcus was wide-awake enough today to realize something was up.

"Look . . ." I searched for the words that would make sense without having to spell it all out, here in the middle of the hallway. "It's just really not like that."

"What is it like?" he asked, flipping open his math binder and thumbing through all the homework I'd done for him. "This was really cool of you, Loey. But seriously, I can't have you doing stuff like this for me. First of all, I'm not that smart, and the teacher is bound to catch on. But also? You just shouldn't have to cheat for me. You're not a cheater."

Then Josh appeared, leaning against a locker to talk to Ethan. *Not a cheater?* No. I just sleep with my sister's boyfriend when they were barely broken up. Claire seemed to have forgiven me, but I still just couldn't forgive myself.

"So do you have a plan?" I asked Marcus, as a distraction. I hoped he was finally ready to talk to his mom, tell her he couldn't keep up with two jobs and school.

"I'm working on it," he said. "I've found this online-schooling program—"

"Um, what?"

He kept flipping calc pages like he hadn't heard me.

"You're not seriously thinking of dropping out of school."

By the look on his face, he was.

I shook my head and shut my locker. "I can't watch you do this to yourself," I said, and headed off to class.

I made a point of avoiding Marcus for the rest of the day. I had to show him I was serious—*this* was serious—before he did something stupid.

When Marcus didn't show up at school the next day, I was livid. I called his house and e-mailed him, but got no response from either.

I spent the whole day stewing about it. At the Arts Club later that afternoon, I demanded an answer from Armando. "Did Marcus quit school?"

Armando's eyes widened. "No. Marcus good boy. He no quit school."

"Well, do you know if he's sick? Because he wasn't there today."

Armando didn't have any answers for me. He looked almost as tired as his nephew, since he'd been filling all the daytime shifts since school started up.

At home, Claire followed me up the stairs and into my bedroom, not seeming to take the hint about my grumpy mood or my desire to be alone. I couldn't exactly ask her to leave, when I knew she was still trying to adjust to being back.

"Body image" was still a major player in her vocabulary, as were "self-control," "support," and "encouragement." I tried to be positive, but then Claire seemed positive enough for the whole family. She spoke as though every experience had been full of perfect beauty and wonder. Today I just wasn't in the mood for it.

I stared down at my art portfolio as she chattered on. The project was frustrating me to no end. Some of my pictures were good. Maybe even most of them. But they didn't have a theme, like Mr. Dewdney had wanted.

"You should have seen the campus, Loey. You would've loved it! Sometimes we took long walks under the palm trees. Or we packed a picnic lunch and went out as a group. And of course the weather was nothing like this dreary mess." She paraded around my room waving her arms as though if we both tried really hard, we could see the palm trees growing in our front yard.

I was sick of her bragging. It was like she was trying to cover something up all the time.

"Now that you're home, I guess you'll be looking for a job, huh?" In the past week, I had decided that too much free time had been a big part of Claire's problem. I, for one, didn't eat nearly as much junk now that I kept myself so busy between work, school, and college prep, and I was convinced that busyness would help any kind of food issue.

She studied her nails. "Actually, Dad got me a job over at Marvin's."

"Marvin's Gas?" I asked, incredulous. "What about, like, the mall or something?"

She looked away. "Uh, no. I didn't try there." She went to her room and came back moments later with an armful of brown polyester. "This is my uniform?" She spread it out on my bed. Her voice rose at the end, like it was a question. "I've never worn a uniform before."

I didn't know what to say, what she wanted me to say.

Was I supposed to rescue her from this? But that would be pretty difficult if she wasn't at least trying to find something better herself.

"Don't you want more than this?" I asked.

That dazed look came over her again. "No. This'll be fine." Then her face brightened. "I met the manager already. His name's Ray. He's kinda quiet, but *really* cute."

At first, I was surprised to hear her opening up to me about boys, but then I remembered: She had no one else.

Our role reversal took me by surprise. Where was Jasmine? Or her other friends? I was used to being the one left alone to figure things out on my own. I didn't know how to be the advice-giver. Besides, I really needed to get to my homework. I opened a textbook to give her the hint.

"Do you know what was funny about the campus in San Diego?" she asked.

I gave my head a quick shake as I buried it in my English binder. I knew what was coming . . . the wonderful ambiance, the support, and the love. I flipped pages of my textbook loudly, nearly tearing one.

"Most of the girls didn't want to get better."

I held my page midflip. It was the first negative thing I'd heard out of Claire's mouth since she'd been home.

She went on. "Maybe in short spurts they did. But then it always ended the same."

When she said, "always ended the same," part of me knew she was talking about herself, too. I stayed as still as the chair beneath me, thinking maybe if I didn't move a muscle, she would continue.

"Sometimes," she added, "the girls would even try to outdo each other."

After several seconds of silence, I had to ask. "Outdo each other how?"

Claire laughed. "Oh, nothing, Loey. It wasn't so bad." She shook her head like she was just being silly.

I stared down at my homework, not reading a single word on the page. *Pressing her to talk about her experience at the clinic may hinder her from moving on,* the counselor from San Diego had told Mom.

Claire looked out my window. "Sophie used to tell us how she would binge and purge through the days, because her parents worked all the time and with five brothers and sisters, the house was always full of food. She couldn't wait to get back home so she could slide back into her routine."

I kept my eyes averted, thinking that maybe if I didn't look at Claire, she would tell me more. More of the truth.

"Brianne said she'd usually spend her entire evenings on the elliptical. The girls said these things as if that's what they were good at, what they were proud of."

"And what did you say?" I asked before I could stop myself.

After a long pause, long enough that I didn't think she was going to answer, Claire said, "I told them I didn't do much. That I wasn't that bad." She looked out my window, but something had changed. Something had faltered within her. "They told me, 'Don't worry, you will be.'"

The reflection of her tears gleamed in my window. I could see how afraid she was.

"It's not true," I said, but had to swallow my misgivings. My sister had barely been home for a few weeks, and there had already been times I didn't trust that she wasn't falling back into it. "Look at you, Claire, you've got so much going for you. You're beautiful and talented, and so smart. You can do anything you want with your life." I felt like I was trying to convince myself as much as her.

"You're probably right," she said in a dull tone, and I knew I had it wrong.

All wrong.

The next day at school, I thought about Claire. Why couldn't she see the amazing person she was?

In art class, I had an idea: *What if I designed my composite around Claire so I could show her how beautiful she is?* I could blow up photos of her features, like her eyes in that image with the mascara wand, and set them on just the right angles. She would *have* to see it then.

I'd put one single word, "Beauty," right in the middle with her photos around it.

To make my day even better, Marcus called back. He hadn't been in school again, but at least he wasn't avoiding me.

"Hi, Loey," he said, sounding as tired as last week. "I've thought of another way," he said.

"Without quitting school?" I asked, not allowing my hopes to rise just yet.

Even though we were on the phone, I could sense him shaking his head. "I'm cutting the job to two nights per week. I might be tired on Mondays, but it'll be bearable." Before I had a chance to worry about where he'd make up the difference in money, he explained that, too. "If I can fix up the Camaro, I can get some good money for it. I'll have to work on it in the afternoons, but at least it's not graveyard shifts at the supermarket."

"That's great," I said. And I meant it, even if I still couldn't quite picture Marcus as a mechanic.

As I put down the phone, Claire walked through the front door, followed by a cute guy. They both wore matching brown polyester. Claire gave a shy wave in my direction, but didn't make any effort to introduce her friend. I figured he must be Ray from the gas station.

He *was* cute. She wasn't lying about that. But in kind of a nonconformist way, which seemed an odd match for Claire.

His dark brown hair was brushed straight down all around, as though he'd gotten out of the shower and left it that way.

Claire told him she was going upstairs to change, and then before I knew it, Ray stood in the doorway all alone.

"You like *Seinfeld*?" I asked in his direction. In the late afternoon, comedy reruns were all that seemed to be on.

"Yeah," he said, louder than I expected. I gestured my head to the side to invite him over to watch. He sat on the far side of the couch. As Kramer came on, sporting an unusually funny, three-sizes-too-small suit, we both started to laugh. I snorted a little.

I looked at him, "Sorry," I said through my laughter. "Sometimes I do that."

"You're as funny as Kramer."

"Yeah, well, you should see me when I back-comb my hair."

He chuckled again. Claire came down the stairs in an over-size white cotton T-shirt and loose pants—not exactly much of an improvement over the polyester. I felt bad for her. She was probably still so self-conscious. I couldn't wait to finish my art project so I could show her.

Ray quieted when Claire came in and took a seat across from us, but I continued.

"I don't know, maybe after high school I should go into acting. Get my own sitcom?" I laughed.

Ray grinned, then asked, "You're still in high school?"

"Yeah, senior year. Could be worse."

We talked a bit more, about school, about Marvin's Gas Station, about college—which Ray had no intention of attending. When pressed, Claire offered a few vague, softly worded answers, but basically it seemed up to me to entertain her date.

When Mom called us for dinner, we assembled around the dining room table. I sat between Mom and Ray, shoveling in bite after bite to give Claire a chance to communicate with him, but she kept her face in her chicken breast, her shoulders hunched forward as though she were ducking for shelter.

"Great dinner, Mrs. Rochester," Ray said.

"Thank you, Ray." She wiped her mouth with her napkin. "So you work with Claire at the gas station?" she asked.

He indicated his agreement.

And then it was quiet. Too quiet.

After what felt like a lifetime of silence, I couldn't stand it any longer. "So if you don't want to go to college, Ray, what do you want to do?"

"You don't want to go to college?" Mom stiffened, sitting up straighter and looking over at Claire's down-turned head.

"I want to travel," he said, not reacting to any tension. "See the world while I'm young, then I'll decide if I want a career of some kind." He took a bite of his broccoli salad and looked over at me as he chewed. "You seem pretty sure you're going to college. What's your big *dream job*?" He accentuated the words, as if anything I said would be ridiculous.

With the challenge in his voice, I felt a little unsure about being honest. I wasn't ready for anyone to smash my dream of being a photographer. "Hmm. I don't know. I guess whatever it takes to work as a comedienne for NBC."

Ray sniffed out a laugh. I caught Claire's eye, just for a second. The way she squinted at me made me feel like I'd done something wrong.

I immediately thought of Josh. Did she think I was trying to *flirt* with Ray?

I clamped my mouth shut through the rest of dinner, heading straight to my room after. A part of me felt guilty all over again—about Josh, about Ray, I didn't know. But then the more I thought about it, the more I realized I *hadn't* done anything wrong tonight. I'd only made conversation with Ray because nobody else would.

Claire stormed into the kitchen the next morning. She glared at me as I poured my cereal. At first I was stunned by her out-of-character actions, but then I thought she must be kidding around. Her steely eyes drilled into me, though. She grabbed a banana and spun to head into the living room. I followed her, trying to come to terms that she was serious.

"Okay, Claire, it's obvious you're mad at me. Why, I have no idea, but you're not hiding it very well."

"You have no idea?" she asked, in the meanest tone I'd ever heard from her. Like sandpaper against a cheese grater. "You really don't know, Loann?"

"No, I don't, unless this is about Josh." It nearly made my lungs collapse to even say his name. "Believe me, I wish more than anything else in the world that none of that had happened—"

"This is *not* about Josh!"

Was she seriously this angry over last night? "I was just trying to help with the conversation," I said. "I would never . . ." I trailed off, not able to say the words about what Josh and I had done.

"I would've talked if you had just shut up, even for a minute!" she yelled.

Okay, now she was talking crazy. "I could see you were just itching to get a word in edgewise, Claire." I shook my head as I turned away to head back to the kitchen.

From behind me, she said, "I just . . ."

The room became so quiet I could hear the refrigerator's buzz through the door. Then came her quiet sobbing, and she whispered, "I wish I could be funny or smart, or say something worthwhile."

She was jealous . . . of me? I'd never had a guy really like me for me. Aside from Marcus, I'd never really had *friends* who liked me. Claire seemed to make friends or boyfriends everywhere she went. And yeah, I'd screwed up with Josh. Big-time. But seriously, I was the one who would never be the same, who was afraid to even be touched, and who was still trying to repair my tattered self-esteem.

For someone she thought had so many worthwhile things to say, I couldn't think of a single one.

I'd spent so much of my life admiring everything about Claire, I didn't know how to grasp the concept of any of this.

CHAPTER THIRTY-FOUR

This was the new rule: Mom would divvy up specific portions for Claire at mealtimes and Claire would eat it all without nitpicking or complaining. Dad made it home more often for dinner, too, which must have also been part of the New Rochester Mealtime Manifesto.

Claire wouldn't meet my eyes all through dinner. She didn't talk to Mom or Dad, either. I'd tried all day at school to convince myself that she'd been having a bad day, but her words about Ray and how easily I talked with him, I just couldn't get them out of my mind. But when I really thought about it, when was the last time I'd seen her acting chatty with anyone other than me? She seemed happy enough heading off to work each day, and I'd assumed she was making friends there, but maybe not. Maybe Ray was her only glimmer of socialization at the moment.

Mom set the timer after dinner—another new rule. Claire had to stay out of the bathroom or leave the door open for at least an hour. She headed for the kitchen with her plate, while I sat and listened to Mom and Dad banter back and forth about the phone bill.

"Oh, save your breath," Mom said. "I've heard that one before. You work so much harder than the rest of us. Meanwhile our daughter is incapable of getting back to a normal life, because she doesn't have a father!"

So maybe Mom had noticed something was still wrong with Claire.

"Doesn't have a father?" Dad huffed loudly. "Yes, that's right. This is all my fault." He cleared his throat. "I've been home every night this week, and with no appreciation, I might add. I don't have to take this." He stood up, grabbed his overcoat, and headed out the door, letting it slam hard behind him.

I quickly stacked the remaining plates and headed for the kitchen.

Claire ignored me completely, not even taking a plate as I passed it to her to put into the dishwasher. *Did she hear our parents fighting about her?*

I put the plate on the counter. "I'm worried about you, Claire." There, I said it. If Mom and Dad were too consumed to do anything about the fact that Claire came back from the clinic more insecure than when she'd left, I had to say something about it.

"I'm fine," she said with raised eyebrows, like it was a challenge.

"You're not fine," I said. "You're not doing anything to make your life better. You're not trying to get a better job or seeing your friends, you think I—"

"I'm fine," she said again, so loudly it shocked me. She pasted a smile on her face, as if to validate her point.

At school, I spoke with Marcus about it.

"My sister, I just don't know how to talk to her. I feel like she spends her whole time at home just hating herself. It's like the only time she's happy is when she goes to work at a gas station." I knew it was more about Ray than the gas station, but I felt like making a point.

Marcus snickered. "Not exactly the kind of place most girls go for a good time."

The more we talked, the more I wanted to see if the old Claire was still around at work, when she didn't think any of her family could see her. If I was doing something to hurt her self-esteem, I had to find out how to fix that. Besides, I didn't trust the idea of her having secrets, I wanted her to be happy. Maybe I was prying too much, but I didn't really care.

"I need to see what's going on," I said to Marcus. "I have a bad feeling about this."

I turned to go, ready to tell Marcus I'd see him later, but he was already walking in front of me toward the school doors. I knew I should tell Marcus to stay at school. That he couldn't afford to miss any more classes. But I was just so glad not to be alone, I didn't say a word all the way to my house.

As expected, Claire was just leaving. Marcus and I stayed down the street, behind a tree so she wouldn't see us. "I can't believe I'm spying on my own sister," I whispered.

Claire walked in the opposite direction of our hideout, with her backpack bouncing against her.

Marcus and I held back and stayed at least half a block behind her, but when we got close to downtown, rather than turning for the outskirts, where the gas station was, Claire turned the other way.

"Where is she going?" I whispered more to myself than to Marcus.

We kept following her until we were in downtown Alder Grove, and she went through the double doors into the brand-new fitness center. There were signs plastered on all the windows about a free two-week trial.

But what about her job? I knew for a fact she was scheduled for Monday through Friday hours. I was sure my parents had no idea, and the last thing I wanted was to have to go back, especially when they were already so stressed, and tell them Claire was hiding stuff again. I had to talk to her myself.

"I'm going in," I said to Marcus. "You should head back to school." He started to interrupt, but I wouldn't let him. "If there are two of us, she'll think we're ganging up on her. Besides, it's senior year. No need for both of us to put our grades in jeopardy."

Marcus paused, thinking things over. "I'll stop in at the office and tell them you're really sick. Whenever you make it in, just make sure you look . . ." A hint of a smirk crossed his face as he looked me over. "Never mind. You look the part."

I reached out to swat him, but he grabbed my arm and pulled me into a hug.

"Let me know how it goes," he murmured into my hair.

I wanted to melt into him. I wanted him to tell me this was a bad idea and drag me back to school. Because really? I had no idea how many secrets Claire was keeping but I had the feeling this was just the first of many.

Before I could resign myself to any of those thoughts, Marcus pulled away and turned me toward the front doors of the fitness center, as though he knew I needed the push.

I had to speak to two trainers and fill out paperwork galore in order to get my free trial membership. If I were really in the market for a gym, I think the paperwork alone would have turned me off. Since I was skipping school, I lied about my birthdate on the form, pretending I was a very-young-looking eighteen. They didn't question it, and soon the female trainer described the layout and led me toward the changing rooms.

The gym staff must have assumed my backpack was filled with gym gear and not school textbooks. I dropped the heavy bag in the locker room and stared down at my jeans. Oh well. It's not like I had any other options.

I hadn't seen Claire, but I had a pretty good idea of where I'd find her: On an elliptical machine.

I walked into the gym and scanned the cardio area, feeling immediately out of place. Not only was I wearing inappropriate workout gear, but everyone went about their business on their own piece of equipment and seemed to know exactly what they were doing.

There was my sister, among the seasoned gym rats, looking like Malibu Barbie in her matching hoodie, running shoes, and headband. Her loose sweatpants were the only thing that didn't quite look the part.

Moving along the side wall, I tried to stay invisible. But Claire's attention wasn't on me, anyway. Most of the gym patrons were average-looking, but one girl stood out, walking back and forth in a sports bra and short shorts. Her abs were so chiseled, I wondered if they'd been painted on. She didn't seem to be working out, just strolling back and forth through the gym as if she was offering a fashion show.

Claire's legs moved in circles faster and faster, seemingly transfixed by the fashion-show girl. Claire's towel hung over the handrail in front of her, and she kept mopping her face with it. I wondered why she didn't take off her hoodie if she was so warm.

As I got closer, I could see Claire speeding up her machine. Sweat dripped down her face and she took a long, hard gulp of water.

I'd just reached the back of the empty elliptical machine beside hers when she unzipped her hoodie. She took it off and hung it with her towel.

I nearly tripped over my own feet doing a double-take at her wiry arms. Her elbows jutted out like big, knobby meatballs on single strings of spaghetti.

I averted my eyes and blinked hard to clear the image. *How had she dropped the weight so quickly? And more important, did she think she looked okay?*

She hadn't looked my way yet, so I hopped up and started pedaling my feet.

Claire's eyes remained on the model-like girl in front of us as she ran harder and harder. I couldn't help remembering what Claire had said about the girls in San Diego trying to outdo each other.

How could I talk to her? What could I possibly say that could make a difference?

"I . . . why are you doing this, Claire?"

Claire's eyes bulged, startled, and she quickly looked down at her hoodie, then away. "I don't know what you're talking about." But I could hear in her voice—she did know. "The fitness center's pretty nice, huh? A good way to stay healthy," she added, her voice too light. "I'm going to see if Mom and Dad will get me a year membership while they're on sale." She looked over at me for the first time, a pleading in her eyes—*Please just let this go*. "You should ask for one too," she said. "We could come together!"

A tug-of-war started in my gut. My whole life I'd wanted to be included in my sister's life. To be wanted by her and feel important. But I knew that doing this, agreeing to this, would be helping her cover up her problem.

And she *had* a problem. Even if she tried to deny it, I couldn't.

Claire didn't look away, her face pale and streaked with sweat. *She really shouldn't be working out so hard.* I glanced down just in time to see her foot slide off the pedal. She tripped, nearly falling sideways off the machine.

I was still moving at a snail's pace, so I jumped off and caught her arm before she fell, but she came toppling onto me. We both fell down and one of my pedals dug into my back.

My elbow burned. I must have scraped it on something, too. "What are you doing?" I snapped at her. "You're obviously in no condition to do this!" It took Claire what seemed like forever to maneuver herself off of me and into a standing position.

It took even longer to calm my breathing.

"Whew, that was embarrassing," Claire said, looking around. And then she actually *giggled*. "I'm glad you caught me, Loey."

Rage boiled within me. "You can't do this!" I spit out, trying to untangle myself from the machine as she looked down at me, obviously too weak to give me a hand up. "Why are you doing this, Claire? What do you want, to kill yourself?" I was so angry at her, so scared for what she was becoming, I couldn't hold back. "Don't be so friggin' selfish!"

I knew she could come up with a thousand rebuttals. *It was an accident, Loey. People make mistakes. Sheesh, you've made enough stupid mistakes.*

But she didn't say any of those things. She simply said, "I don't know what you're talking about, Loann."

I stomped back to the locker room, tears streaming down my face, but I didn't know why. I wasn't sad. I was angry. So angry.

What was wrong with her?

CHAPTER THIRTY-FIVE

After the last bell, Marcus and I walked to a small garage under Armando's apartment, where Marcus had been working on fixing up the used Camaro. I was supposed to relieve Armando at the café, but I'd been a wreck all afternoon. I had been too emotional to talk in the hallway at school. Part of me needed to talk about Claire, but part of me just couldn't.

"I'm thinking of applying to Kettleton in Chicago. You'd come visit me, right?" I didn't expect an answer. I figured he probably couldn't even hear me from where he was working under his car. "Claire's really messed up, and all I want to do is escape from it all. I can't get through to her, and I just wish I wasn't even here."

Sitting and watching Marcus's feet wiggle as he maneuvered

himself into different positions gave me something to focus on. "I don't know what she wants to hear or what'll make any difference. I mean, I tell her how beautiful and talented she is, how much she could do with her life, but she just doesn't get it." I ran my foot around an oil spot on the floor.

Every so often Marcus asked me to pass him some kind of tool, which I spent far more time trying to locate than if he'd just come out and gotten it himself. An hour later, I was all talked out about Claire, and apparently Marcus had finished changing the U-joints, whatever that meant.

After sliding out from under the car, he said, "We can't always be what other people need us to be." I knew he was talking about Claire. And maybe even his mom. "You can sit around and blame yourself about it . . ." He finished putting his tools away, and then met my eyes. "Or you can get on with it."

Get on with what? But somewhere inside I knew what he meant. I obviously had to tell my parents. I just really didn't feel like I had the strength to oppose Claire. She was so good at lying now.

"Will you come home with me? I . . ." I didn't know how else to say it. "I need you, Marcus."

I felt bad for Armando, but I just couldn't go to the café today. I had to talk to Mom about this. And I probably needed to do it in front of Claire.

Marcus grabbed my hand. "Let's go."

* * *

The house was empty when we got there. It shouldn't have surprised me, I suppose. As if Claire would just wait around for me to come home and yell at her some more.

We headed upstairs for the computer room, but kept the door open in case anyone came home. I took the side seat, leaving the one in front of the computer for Marcus.

"You want to help me find a free graphics program I can use to work on some of my pictures?" My heart wasn't in it today, but it was a good distraction and I'd wanted Marcus's help with this for a while. He just hadn't had time.

We didn't have any photo software on our computer, so Marcus maximized the browser and typed something into the address bar. His hands, as usual, flew over the keys at the speed of light and I watched in amazement.

"Oops," he said. "That's the problem with typing so fast. Too many mistakes." He hit the back key several times, but our old computer took its sweet time catching up. "Hmm, one too far," he said, going for the forward button.

"Wait. Stop," I said.

A picture of a pretty girl with a long, narrow face came up on the screen. It must have been one of Claire's new cyber-friends' websites. A star flashed right in the middle.

I knew we should just click out, but I reached past Marcus for the mouse and clicked on the star.

"Come to my party!" appeared at the top of the page with a sidebar at the left. I glanced over the contents: Favorite Foods, Tips and Tricks, E-mail Me, Shana's Blog, and then that star again. I swallowed and clicked it.

The pretty girl appeared in a full head-to-toe shot. She wore thigh-high boots and a miniskirt, and couldn't have weighed even ninety pounds. Her ribs showed through her fitted T-shirt and her boots left large gaps around her thighs. I read the words beside her gaunt frame. "Come to my binge party in Columbus, Ohio!"

The next paragraph went on to say in big, bold letters: **BYOF**. And then: "But don't worry, there'll be lots here. All my favorites," which had a link. "Three bathrooms on-site. Take your turn. A party you won't want to miss. E-mail for directions."

"Oh my God," Marcus said. "What is this?"

But I could barely hear him. I clicked through all the side tabs, mostly more information about the party, until I got to the Tips and Tricks page. It was a list of bullet points. The first one said:

People will want to believe you are eating right. It's easier than you think!

I stared over the list of highest calorie-burning exercises and lowest-carb foods. At the bottom of the page there were tips on puking. I could not believe my eyes.

You don't need a toilet or even a garbage can. If you practice, a Coke can will be enough.

How many times had Mom told Claire to lay off the diet soda lately? I pushed the mouse up to the right corner, but missed the X because my hand was shaking so badly. On my second try, I hit it, and then stared at the empty desktop. I sat there in stunned disbelief.

Marcus put his hand over mine, but thankfully he didn't say a word. I couldn't speak. Couldn't answer questions about this sick life of my sister's.

I shook my head. "I've been trying to talk to her. The clinic only made her worse!" I was practically choking on my words. "I don't know what to do. What can *I* possibly do?"

I felt like I was going to be sick, and ran to my and Claire's shared bathroom. Bending over the toilet, I couldn't even dry-heave. It took about twenty deep breaths to calm myself down enough to stand up. As I went back to see Marcus, I heard Mom and Claire downstairs.

"I've saved a little money," Claire was saying, "and I was thinking of going to visit a friend in Ohio."

"I don't know, honey. You've been away a lot this year." I could tell Mom was distracted.

I walked over to the top of the stairs and watched them. They were still near the front closet, and hadn't seen me yet.

"Yeah, but that was for, well, you know. I just want to

have a fun trip, Mom." She smiled, and then even laughed a little. *Laughed.*

How could I care so much when Claire didn't even care? I didn't know her anymore. Didn't know that smile, didn't know what tomorrow would bring from my so-called predictable sister. I missed that. Even when she was popular in school, I understood her. And growing up, she'd always been on my side. Now she was just on her own side.

I turned to head for my room, but Marcus stood right behind me, like a big blockade to my sanity. He motioned his head down the stairs. *Did he really not see how good of a liar my sister was? Did he honestly think I could say or do anything that would make a difference?*

"Fine," I said, and Claire and Mom both looked up, realizing I was there. I marched down the stairs. "Do you know what's in Ohio?" I asked Mom, but looked at Claire.

Claire looked past me to the computer room, where the light was still on. "You don't know what you're doing, Loann. Keeping me here won't help."

"What will help, then, Claire, huh?" I'd never spoken to my sister this way. I took a step back as if I'd even scared myself, but bumped into Marcus, who was behind me again. Neither Claire nor Mom had even looked in his direction.

Mom glanced between Claire and me. "What's going on? What about this trip, Claire?"

"It's nothing!" she screamed so loudly that Mom's eyes widened. And then, as if the words had taken everything out of Claire, she doubled over.

"Well then I'm sure it can't be that big of a deal whether you go or not," Mom said in her usual patronizing tone.

But Claire didn't argue. In fact, she let out a small whimper.

"I don't know if you girls think we're made of money," Mom went on.

I ignored the fact that Mom made it sound like I wanted to go to Ohio too, and took a step toward Claire. "Are you . . . okay?"

Her hair fell in her face. She shook her head and clutched her stomach.

"I think she's hurt," I told Mom. "She's really sick."

Claire tried to stand up, but doubled over again. She took a shaky step toward the stairs and reached for the handrail to steady herself.

Mom stared, not doing or saying a thing, so finally I said, "Mom, I think you need to get Claire to the hospital."

Mom nodded, and without hesitation Marcus took one of Claire's arms and I took the other. Mom's whole body shook as she locked the front door behind us. After Marcus bent to help Claire into the backseat, Mom reached for his arm. I stared down at her hand, praying she wasn't going to do this now.

But then she said, "Thank you."

Marcus nodded, and an understanding seemed to pass between them.

I backed away, then moved around to the other side of the car and took my place beside Claire.

CHAPTER THIRTY-SIX

Dad met us at the administration desk of the hospital.

After Claire was brought into the ER, refusing to let my parents go with her, we all sat in the waiting room in stunned silence. At least for the first minute.

Mom had started going to counseling sessions in an attempt to understand Claire, and she chose then to try to convince Dad that it was his responsibility to go with her, like this was obviously the cog in her system of raising healthy kids. Which, of course, segued into another brawl over money. Right in the middle of the hospital waiting room.

"She could die, Darren." Mom spit his name like it was a cuss, then lowered her voice. "The clinic already told us her liver's congested and her stomach's a mess. What if her heart gives out?"

"I don't know what you want me to do about it, Beth. You want me at home. You want me at the counselor's. I'm working all the hours I can to hold this family together."

Marcus looked out the window, trying to avoid the whole thing. I felt bad for bringing him here. Putting him in the middle of all this. But I needed him more now than ever.

"Well, it's not working," Mom gritted out.

"These clinics don't come cheap, Beth. You're going to have to deal with Claire."

"Oh, okay. I'll deal with Claire." She shook her head. "Why should I be surprised? Let's leave this all on Beth's lap again."

Thankfully there were only two other people in the waiting room with us, but they looked as uncomfortable as Marcus. My parents continued to seethe blame messages back and forth until the doctor finally came and took them aside.

"Are you okay?" Marcus asked.

I nodded, even though I felt anything but okay. "I'm sorry you had to come here."

"I'm not." He laced his fingers through mine and squeezed my hand reassuringly. "There's no place I'd rather be." I attempted a smile, but I just felt like I had nothing left in me.

* * *

The hospital wanted to keep Claire for a few days to monitor her. We all went to visit her the next evening, but she just lay there, arms crossed, not looking at any of us. It was as if she thought it was *our* fault she'd ended up in the hospital.

The nurses kept her on an IV, so at least something was going into her that she couldn't throw up. The doctor took my parents aside, which left me uncomfortably alone with silent Claire. I stared at her for a long time, hardly believing how scraggly her hair looked. It was the first time in my life that I would have actually said I preferred my hair over hers.

"We didn't do this to you, you know," I finally murmured, annoyed by the silence.

She huffed but didn't reply.

"Do you think if Mom had said yes to Ohio, your stomach would have been fine? Is that really what you think?"

When she didn't answer, I stood to leave. I hated her for what she was doing to herself. To all of us.

On the car ride home, I lay my face against the back window and tried to tune out my parents' arguing, but it was useless.

"The doctor suggested the same clinic in San Diego, but we could find a different place," Mom said in a pleading tone.

"They're not going to release her until we have her registered somewhere. Do you have time to look into hundreds of places around the country?"

"I'll make time," Mom practically growled. She reminded me of a mama bear protecting her cubs on one of those nature shows.

The next night I kept my shift at the Arts Club. There seemed to be no reason to go to the hospital if Claire wouldn't speak to any of us. Apparently Claire *did* talk with my parents that night. To tell them she refused to go to another clinic. My parents were still arguing about it when I got home.

"We can't afford to keep her in the hospital indefinitely," Dad practically shouted.

Mom marched for the computer room, ranting something unintelligible, but I was sure she'd be researching other clinics through the night.

No official decisions about clinics had been made by the time Claire came back home, but as I understood through my parents' constant bickering, they had assured the doctor they'd get her checked in somewhere for help.

My mouth dropped open when Claire walked through our front door. She'd chopped her hair short, and looked like a boy. Besides that, her skin looked saggy and yellow and her gut stuck out above her sweatpants like she was pregnant. I wondered if this was from her stomach problems or from the hospital trying to get her weight up quickly.

330

She didn't even look in my direction.

"We'll figure out somewhere you'll like," Mom said to her from behind. "We'll figure it out together."

"Forget it. I'm not going to one of those places again," she said in a monotone from halfway up the stairs.

Dad stood in the foyer with his jaw tightening, watching Claire retreat. Without even saying a word, he stepped back outside the door and slammed it behind him. Mom's whole body reverberated from the slam.

Dad didn't come home for the next two days. He'd never, in my whole life, done that, and it freaked me out. Mom took her frustrations out on anyone in her path. I had my usual excuse of having to work, but now I saw it as that—an excuse. An escape from the tension. Just like Dad. And that only made me feel like more of a failure.

When I did come home, I could tell immediately that Claire had been Mom's only target, and if Mom couldn't fix her with love, she'd fix her somehow.

"You will eat what I made you!" Mom shouted from the bottom of the stairs.

"I'm not eating another chicken breast, Mother," came Claire's reply from the computer room.

"Claire, you get down here this minute!"

"I'll eat when I want to eat. What are you going to do,

shove it down my throat?" Claire's door slammed.

I thought for certain that the whole hospital incident would have been a dose of reality for Claire, but it was like she was driven now to *not* get better. She puked in our bathroom with my door ajar. She wasn't even bothering to try to hide it.

"Stop it!" I yelled toward the bathroom in a voice so loud it made my throat raw. "Just stop it!"

Seconds later the toilet flushed and she went into her room. I lay in bed shaking, crying, hating that I couldn't go talk to her. Because all she would say was, "What are you talking about, Loey?" and I was sure I'd feel like killing her myself.

On Friday when I got home, there was a tray of untouched food outside Claire's bedroom door. The door was open and I could hear Mom inside, pleading with Claire.

"Honey, I don't know what to do. Tell me what to do. I'll cook you anything you want. I'll drive you to any clinic in the country."

Claire didn't respond. At least nothing I heard.

"I'm going to go squeeze you some fresh orange juice. That'll be good for you." The way Mom said it, it sounded like she had finally found the solution. Orange juice would solve *everything*.

When she glanced over at me as she left Claire's room, though, I realized Mom's assurance was an act. She didn't look like my confident mother. She looked like a scared little girl. It was the first time I'd ever really seen her as a person who hurt and tried and failed. She was trying—she had always been trying—but her best wasn't good enough anymore.

Dad got home just as I headed to bed that night. The truth was, I didn't trust him anymore either. If he could so easily walk out the door once, would he do it again?

Without even saying good night, I headed up the stairs.

"Loann," Dad said, and he sounded exasperated, even though it had been the first time he'd spoken to me in days. I stood in place waiting for more, but I couldn't turn to face him.

"Loann, honey. I was talking to Bill at the office today, and his daughter went to Kettleton College. Great school," Dad said, his tone suddenly much softer. "So is that still the plan? Because I'll need to figure out the due date for the deposit and see if we can swing it."

I'd inched my way to the top of the stairs. "Uh, I'll let you know soon." But what I wondered was this: *How did he suddenly have money for college, but not to go to counseling or to send Claire for help?* At the same time, it didn't seem like Claire *wanted* the money, or the help, and I *did* want to go to college.

"What about Claire?" I asked from the staircase, a hurricane of indecision brewing in my chest. "Don't you need the money to send her to another clinic?" My voice was lifeless, like I wasn't really trying to convince anyone.

"She says she won't go," Mom said, now at the bottom of the stairs too. "And your dad says we haven't got the money, and I just don't know what to do anymore." Mom's voice broke on every second word.

"I'm not just *saying* we don't have the money, Beth. And what did the last clinic do for her?"

This arguing wasn't going anywhere. Claire could wither away to nothing in her bedroom before my parents came to an agreement on anything.

I stormed down the stairs. "I don't want your money for college!" I yelled before I reached the landing. "Use the money for Claire. She needs it and I don't. There have to be better clinics, and I'll make the money to go to college. I'll get a scholarship. I'll take care of it."

Mom and Dad both stared at me, open-mouthed.

"I mean it," I said.

Dad tilted his head and pulled on his tie. "Well, that's really sweet of you, Loann, but your mother says that Claire won't go anyway. She's eighteen. She has to make this decision." Even though Dad's words sounded soft and caring, they made my blood boil. At him, not at Claire. *Why should Claire think she's worth anything if her own father didn't think so?*

"Please," I said. "Why didn't you let the doctor make her go?" I couldn't believe my desperation to get my sister out of the house. She was wrecking us—all of us.

I knew his next statement would be about student loans and why it's not that easy to give my college money to Claire. I didn't care if it was true. It wasn't a good enough reason. I left Mom and Dad standing at the base of the stairs and marched back up to my bedroom. Maybe, *maybe*, left to their own resources, they'd think of some way they could make an effort here.

But thirty seconds later, I heard the front door slam.

Dad was gone. And I wondered if this time it would be for good.

CHAPTER THIRTY-SEVEN

In art class the next day, I stared down at the composite I'd been working on. I wanted to rip it up, throw it against the wall.

I had centered all the pictures around my one-word ornate title in the middle. But I could barely look at the pictures of Claire. This girl, this beautiful sister of mine, she didn't seem real to me anymore.

And I couldn't base my entire grade—my entire possibility of a scholarship—on some fabrication.

I sat in the darkroom with my head in my hands, staring down at my useless work. Moving a few pictures aside, I tried to replace them with some of Mom, one of Marcus's Camaro, but the whole thing was garbage.

I left it in the art room, since it was too big to cart around.

But I needed to come up with a new idea, and fast. Something I could complete quickly so I didn't miss getting graded on it, and hopefully I would still have time to submit it for a scholarship.

Leaving the school that afternoon, I saw a familiar car across the parking lot, standing out from all the newer cars surrounding it.

It honked.

I bit my lip, reining in my emotion. Marcus seemed to have impeccable timing for knowing when I needed him most.

As I walked toward his car, I could see he was wearing what I suspected was his favorite yellow shirt, since I'd seen him wear it at least once a week since his dad had been gone. "Hi, sunshine," I said. "So you got it running, huh?"

He motioned his head to the passenger side. "Get in."

It was still covered in rust patches, but the engine idled smoothly. I moved around to the other side. The door stuck a little, and I had to give it a good pull to get it open.

"I've still got a few kinks to work out." He motioned to the sticky door.

"But it runs!" I said again, my enthusiasm bubbling over.

Marcus smiled at me.

"Wait, you don't have your license." I quickly scanned the parking lot, as though there might be cops lining the place.

"Yup. I got it last week."

My heart sank that I hadn't been around to celebrate with Marcus. I had my learner's permit, but I didn't have any money for lessons. "Wow, things change, I guess, huh?"

"Yeah." He nodded. "And some things don't." He reached over and put his hand on top of mine.

My heart skipped a beat. I had so much to tell him, but at the moment all I wanted to do was sink into him. It felt like forever since I'd been able to breathe this easily.

"I'm glad you're here," I said.

"Me too."

We sat like that, his hand on mine, looking at each other, for a long time. I wondered if he remembered he still had three wishes. I wondered if he still wanted to kiss me, or if we'd just been through too much together now and he didn't think of me that way. There was such a thing as being *too* close of friends, right?

Marcus pulled his hand away and grasped the steering wheel at ten and two.

I sighed inwardly. But at least we were driving off together.

On our way off the school grounds, several students pointed at Marcus's car in appreciation, and Marcus's eyes lit up. I could tell it meant a lot to him. At the first intersection, he turned away from my house, and the Arts Club. Then we missed the turn we'd have taken to his apartment.

"So where are we going?"

"For a drive. Armando gave us the afternoon off." Marcus took one hand off the wheel and adjusted the rearview mirror. "I want to show you what this thing can do."

I laughed. I'm sure he knew whatever his eight-banger engine had in it, I was the last person who would be impressed, but for some reason I was excited right along with him.

When we got onto the north highway, a road that could barely be called a highway because it was almost always deserted, Marcus slowed the car down until it was almost stopped. Then, after glancing around to make certain there were no other cars around, he dropped his foot to the metal.

I grasped for the armrest beside me. We must have sped up to at least eighty miles per hour, though I couldn't take my eyes off the road to check. I sat rigidly, fear-struck in my seat. He didn't keep it up for more than thirty seconds, then took his foot off the gas and coasted down to a normal speed.

"Could you *not* do that again?"

"Come on, Loey, you're not the tough chick I thought you were."

"Maybe I'll start wearing a skirt," I said with annoyance.

He snickered, pulling to the side of the road and slowly bringing the car to a stop. "Actually, I didn't bring you out here to put your heart in your throat."

I gritted my teeth. "Why, then?"

"You ever heard of a Chinese Fire Drill?"

"Yeah," I said, tentatively.

He gave the horn two quick honks. "Ready, set, go!" he said, louder than I'd ever heard him. The sheer volume of his voice shocked me into obedience. Marcus opened his door and hopped out. I did the same and he raced around the back of the car, while I took the front. We slid into opposite seats and slammed our doors.

"One problem," I said. "I don't know how to drive."

"My point exactly." He dangled the keys in my face.

Marcus took the next hour to show me not only how to drive, but how to drive a *standard*. At first I spent more time laughing than driving. Or trying to control my heart rate when he put his hand over mine to help me shift gears.

"My mom would kill me if she knew I was driving with another teenager." I started the stalled vehicle and practiced shifting again, trying to coordinate the clutch with the gears. It was all very entertaining. Or at least it must have been for Marcus.

"You're pretty good, for a beginner," he said.

"Right. You being the professional, having had your license for what? A whole week?" The car stalled and I cranked the engine again. I looked down the road both ways, but it was still empty.

"You should've seen me my first time," he said. "I didn't

have the help of an expert instructor or anything." He glanced my way with a smirk and stroked the dash. "I'm surprised my poor baby here didn't choke to death."

I never did understand guys who treated their cars like real people. When I tried again, I had a better handle on it. I got my bearings, and soon we were sailing down the straight highway at nearly twenty miles per hour.

"You know, you can go faster if you want."

I'm sure he didn't mean to sound patronizing. "Yeah, I know that," I said, and stepped on the gas. It jutted us forward and the engine revved noticeably louder.

"Third," he said, cringing.

I backed my foot off of the gas.

"Don't go slower, just put it in third."

I didn't want to look away from the road to find out where third was. I backed my foot off the gas pedal again.

"Well, I guess you'll have no problem driving around Alder Grove," he said. "But I'm thinking road trips to Chicago are out for you. It'd take you two weeks just to get there."

I hit the brakes. Hard. Marcus jolted against his seat belt, and now it was my turn to laugh. I, however, was in no mood for laughing. "Just cut me some slack, Mr. Mario Andretti. I'm doing the best that I can here."

"No, you're not." Marcus raised his eyebrows and leaned back into his seat, not even giving me the courtesy of looking my way. "You're just scared. You've got to relax and learn that the car isn't going to freak out if you have to look down at the gearshift for a second."

Sometimes it pissed me off that he knew me so well. I put the gearshift back in first and started to edge away from the shoulder. But this time I kept my eyes on Marcus as I did it.

Marcus laughed and said, "Yeah, okay, Loey." Then, as I sped up, his laugh wavered. I kept my eyes on him, very happy about how I had turned this situation around.

"Faster?" I asked. I don't know what had come over me. Maybe it was the way Claire was so reckless with her life and I was tired of being the safe, sensible one. I gripped the wheel harder. I couldn't sit back and be Claire's audience anymore.

"Come on, Loann. Watch the road."

I pressed the gas pedal farther down, feeling a rush of . . . something. Exhilaration? No, it was more than that. Panic, fear, release—all of it. Marcus kept watching the road and glancing back at me every three seconds. I hit the gravel shoulder and overcompensated back onto the far side of the road.

"Okay, that's it. Pull over!"

"Oh, I'd better put it in third," I said, and made a big deal of looking down at the gear shift. "Is this one third?" I asked. My voice came out angry.

Marcus reached over and grabbed the steering wheel. "You know it is, Loann, now just watch the road."

Something snapped me back and I turned my eyes straight ahead. Even though I was still pretty close to where I should be on the road, I felt bad. It wasn't Marcus I was mad at. By the time I slowed down, my breathing had returned to normal.

"Sorry," I said once we were stopped. I turned off the engine and handed Marcus's keys back to him. "I . . . needed that."

"For what? I should be thanking you for making me reevaluate my mortality."

I didn't have the words to explain it. Marcus reached over and touched my arm and I sensed he understood, at least a little.

On our way back to civilization, Marcus took the driver's seat again. "I'll have to sell it soon, but I'll give you lessons first, until you get your license."

I didn't put up a fight. I was happy Marcus was finding time for me. And when we got back to town, he didn't have to rush off for work, so we went straight for the Arts Club. I wasn't sure what had changed, but at the moment, I didn't much care.

CHAPTER THIRTY-EIGHT

That evening, I skipped most of the way home, feeling like a little kid again. Mom was out at a counseling session and dinner was on the stove. Dad had still not come home, which brought me back to my sober thinking. It would be my fault if he didn't come home at all. As if there wasn't enough stress flying around the house without me arguing with him about my college money.

Well, Claire's fault, really. Her fault and my fault.

After knocking back a bowl of Hungarian goulash, I trekked up the stairs in search of Claire. I felt so much stronger after hanging out with Marcus and didn't have any fear of Claire bringing me down. In fact, maybe my positive energy would be contagious.

I knocked on her door and didn't hear anything at first.

A picture flashed in my head of her passed out by the toilet. I knocked again, louder, and called her name. A faint "Come in," came from the other side.

I cracked open the door and peered through. Claire was in bed, the covers up around her throat, and even from across the room, I could tell she was shivering.

"Are you okay?" I walked closer.

"Yeah," she said, as if convulsions were a normal part of life.

"You're shaking. Are you cold?" I grabbed the blanket from the foot of her bed. Her skin had a greenish hue and she looked worse than the normal frailty and paleness that not-eating brought on. *Was this from the problems with her liver?*

"No," she whispered. "Just thirsty." The water bottle beside her bed was empty.

I took it to the bathroom to refill it.

She whispered from behind me, "No, Loey, could you go get the filtered?"

I dumped the water in the bathroom sink and headed down the stairs, muttering to myself the whole way. "She'll abuse her body, puke I don't know how many times a day, but water . . . has to be filtered!" That was when I knew she had lost it.

I brought the water back upstairs, trying to recapture my positive attitude. Claire had stopped shaking and had pulled the blankets down. Sweat covered her forehead and seeped into her cropped hair. The long-sleeve white T-shirt she wore was the same one I'd seen on her yesterday. She looked like she'd fallen back asleep, but when I stood at her bedside, her eyes opened slightly.

"Have you been up today?" I asked.

"Oh, Loey, I'm just so tired."

"I should call Dr. Quinton." I stepped toward the door.

"I'm okay." She forced a bit more volume "Hey, Loey?"

She was trying to change the subject again. I took a deep breath and sighed it out. "Yeah?"

"Will you take my picture?"

I thought she was kidding, but I didn't laugh. There was nothing funny about it. Her hair was matted and frizzy. Her face was gaunt and pale without makeup. But looking in her eyes, somehow I knew she was serious.

The old Claire was back. At least for the moment.

"For real?" I asked, probably sounding callous, but I couldn't help myself. I was still me.

"You know," she said, and I wondered if she was changing the subject again, "the only time I think I've ever felt worthwhile was when you were taking my picture." She let out a little sad-sounding laugh.

I couldn't stop hearing her words over and over again in my mind. "I'll be right back," I said finally, my voice rising at the end.

"Take her picture. Picture, picture, picture," I murmured,

trying to keep my mind busy as I went to get my camera. "Photo, film. Tripod. Let's take some pictures."

Back beside her bed, I asked Claire, "Do you . . . Do you just want me to take it here?"

She lay still, her eyelet bedspread pulled back to her shoulders again.

"You tell me," she said quietly. "You're the photographer."

"Can you get up?" I felt like I had to ask, since she looked so weak.

Claire pulled the blanket back and I looked away from her legs, only partially covered by shorts. They looked like those bone charts in the science classroom.

She placed her spindly legs over the edge of the bed and tried to push herself up to a seated position. I swallowed, not believing what had happened to my sister in mere days. I put my tripod on the floor so I could help her.

"Sitting's good," I said, once she was upright. I set up my tripod and camera, desperately running words through my head. *Picture, picture, picture.* Anything to avoid the moment.

Claire smiled meekly, one of her hands brushing her hair behind her ear.

Picture, picture, picture. Just take the stupid picture. "Okay," I said, but my voice seemed to have no volume. "Why don't you look over at the window?"

She did as I directed.

"Tilt a little to the left," I said. "Not so much. There. Perfect. Stay there." I made sure the film had forwarded, then brought my eye to the viewfinder.

My breath caught. Through the camera I saw something other than my withering and frail sister. Claire's eyes lit up and seemed to take over the whole frame. She was every bit as beautiful as I'd ever known her to be. I didn't pull away to see the lifeless frame of a girl who was sitting on the bed. I was mesmerized.

"Don't move," I whispered, "That's it." I snapped a picture. "That's it, Claire. Don't move a muscle." I snapped two more. "Okay, now, head a little to the right. Uh-huh." I snapped again. "Beautiful, Claire, just beautiful." My voice trilled louder. "Okay, now bring your hand up to your hair." She did, and I snapped three more. Tears started spilling down my face. I couldn't stop them. Didn't want to. "Now straight at the camera, Claire. That's it, that's perfect. Wow, stunning." Her smile became bigger and my tears fiercer. I kept my face pressed to the camera.

I snapped a whole roll of pictures, knowing with the last one, it would be the end of our photo shoot. I wouldn't go back to my room and get another roll of film. This reprieve, with one more click, would be over.

After the last snap, I stared through the viewfinder for a long time. I don't know how long, but eventually Claire asked, "Are we done?"

"Yeah, I think so." I nodded against the camera. "That's the end of the film."

Claire lay back down and I quickly swiped the tears from my eyes. I packed my camera into its case.

"Thank you, Loey." Claire's voice was louder, stronger than it had been all evening.

"I—I didn't do anything," was all I could reply.

But for the first time in ages, I felt like I had.

After the night I took Claire's pictures, she only left her bedroom when Mom was out. When I first saw her descend the stairs, I could understand why. She looked like a flamingo trying to climb down Mt. Everest. When she finally reached the bottom, she came over and sat beside me on the couch. I couldn't help but stare.

"*Star Trek?*" she asked in an obvious attempt to divert my attention to the TV.

"Yeah, you want me to turn it?" Claire hated Star Trek. I had the remote up, poised and ready when she said, "No, no . . . *Star Trek*'s fine."

I let it play and kept my eyes on the screen, but I couldn't concentrate on anything. The actors moved across the TV, but their words seemed muted. All I could hear was Claire breathing beside me.

In a whisper, I asked, "When will it be enough, Claire?"

She didn't say anything for a long time. "You don't understand, Loey."

"You keep saying that." I looked at her. "Okay, so make me understand."

Her eyes fell to her lap. "I can't stop. That's it. It sounds so simple, doesn't it?" She laughed a halfhearted laugh. "I always thought I could stop, you know? I always thought I was strong and I knew what I was doing. Sometimes I actually believed this made me stronger than everyone. I'd start again . . . to toughen up. But now, I don't know. It's not what I thought it would be. Not at all." She stopped and took a long breath.

I stared at her, watched her mouth tremble, and remembered when she had seemed so strong. The illusion had been pretty believable.

"It all seemed so easy once." A mock tinged her laugh. "I was better than everyone." The way she said this made it sound like being better had never been a good thing. "But once the snowball starts down the hill, I don't know that there's any way to stop it. At least, there isn't for me."

What was she saying? That she was just giving up? She was going to let this kill her? We both turned back to the TV. This subject was too big not to have something trivial to balance it out.

"You have to try, Claire. You *have* to," I finally said.

"I'm so tired, Loey. I'm tired of being sick, but I think

more than that, I'm tired of the cycle. I'm tired of what I see in the mirror, but that seems to be the least of it now. There's no way out—when I went away, I learned so many new ways to hide my problems. Myself. I don't know how to pretend that I'm okay even if I'm not. Because the thing is, I don't know how to live without it. The clinic was the only place I fit in, but I hated who I became there."

It was the first time I'd heard her use the word "clinic" instead of a "campus." I grabbed her hand and held it. It was bony and limp and cold. We both stared at the screen.

"Please," I whispered, but I didn't even really know what I was asking.

After several minutes, she spoke again. "I'll go away again. I'll do it for now because I don't know what else to do, but I don't know what will change. And in some ways I'm scared of how *I'll* change."

I was scared of that, too. "I wish I could help you." It felt like I had a hunk of lead in my throat. "I wish I could go with you, or there was something—anything—I could do."

"You said you'd give up college for me," she said in a quiet voice. She must have heard my fight with our parents. "I know you'd do anything for me, Loey, and that's why I'm going to go." She smiled and a tear slid down her cheek. "I'll try to find another way. I'll—"

Just then, Mom's car rattled on the driveway. Claire

abruptly stopped what she was saying and her voice changed. The sweetness and emotion were gone. "I'll tell her tomorrow. I will," she added, knowing I needed the reassurance. "Would you . . . help me up the stairs?"

I knew what she was asking—anything not to face Mom right now. In one swoop, I picked her up in my arms and headed up the stairs, feeling like I was carrying little more than air.

CHAPTER THIRTY-NINE

Most of the time, one day is like the next when you're in high school. There are moments and events that stick out, but entire days have seldom stuck with me.

I walked to school one day in the middle of October.

One day.

Claire had been to see Dr. Quinton and decided on another clinic, this one only a few hours away in Chicago. She was set to leave the next week.

I strolled along, feeling the weight of it all falling away from me. It was peaceful, blue skies all around, the crisp air brushing my skin.

A sparrow glided along in tranquil flight. When it hit the windshield of the sedan driving beside me on Hawthorne

Street, the thud made me jump. I think it shocked me as much as the driver of the car.

The bird tumbled off the windshield and onto the road. The car drove off, but I stayed in place, waiting for I don't know what. Slowly I inched from the sidewalk into the street. The little sparrow lay still.

It wasn't until I got to school, half an hour late, that I realized how long I'd stood there transfixed by the poor sparrow. My first period teacher reprimanded me for my tardiness, but I could only stare back blankly. Even when I saw Marcus at lunch, I was still dazed. *It's just a stupid bird*, I kept telling myself.

I stared out the window during my last class, wondering if Marcus and I might practice driving after school, when suddenly there he was, leaning up against his Camaro in the parking lot. My stomach fluttered a little, and I was glad I was finally returning to my normal self.

Even though I was sure Marcus couldn't place which classroom I was in, he started leaning on the car at different angles and striking poses with his non-existent muscles and I knew it was just for me. I slapped a hand over my mouth to suppress a laugh.

One of the teacher's assistants poked her head into my history class, distracting me.

"Loann Rochester, you're wanted in the office." She

looked so serious. As I pulled my hand from my mouth, my smile went with it.

People get called to the office all the time. I, however, had never been sent to the office in the middle of class. My pencil clattered to the floor when I tried to slide it into the front pouch of my backpack.

On the walk down the hallway, I could barely focus on the TA leading the way. I rattled my brain for a viable reason for my summons. *Was it because I was late? Did someone find out I'd been doing Marcus's homework? Would they really pull me out of class because of that?*

I slowed my pace when the school office came into view. The wind was sucked out of me like I'd stepped into an airless chamber. It felt like I was watching a movie where the waiting room was on one side of a big hospital window and the cameras on the other. I could envision a scene where a doctor gives a family bad news.

In those made-for-TV movies, there's always music, but no real sound. No crying, gasping, screaming. You see all the mouths moving and all of the tears, but you don't really hear any of it. I always loved the ingenious way moviemakers could make a scene so powerful and yet so surreal. So not like real life, and yet enveloping so much of the deep emotion of real life.

Ms. Remmers, the school counselor, saw me through the office window and started toward me. She had tears in her eyes, and when she stood before me, her mouth moved, but I couldn't hear a word she was saying. I tilted my head. Even though I didn't know what was happening, I felt a knot in the pit of my stomach. My whole world became hazy. I figured I must have been crying, because a Kleenex was pressed into my hand.

There was only silence.

Nothing else was tangible about that moment, that gap in time, however long it might have been. Just that I knew in my heart that Claire was gone.

The next thing I remember was yellow. It was bright and it was right in my face. It was Marcus in his sunshine shirt.

He hugged me and patted my back methodically. His voice leaked in from far off in the distance. "Tell me what to do, Loey," he said. "Tell me how to help you."

One of his hands ran over my hair. He drew my head to his chest and it was then, I think, that I stopped holding my breath.

When I eventually pulled away, I realized we were behind the school, between the two portable classrooms.

Marcus's eyes were red. I wiped mine with my tattered Kleenex.

"My camera," I mumbled. I didn't even know why I said it, but it was like the word made my brain shutter into action. "Oh no, the pictures!" I cried.

"What? What is it, Loey?"

"I can't look at them. I can't . . . I can't . . . get any more."
I knew I wasn't making any sense, but all I could think of
were those last pictures I'd taken of Claire. They were her
last pictures. I gasped out a cry. She really, really wasn't coming back. Those pictures were all I had left of her.

Suddenly I felt desperate to get away from the school,
away from this realization, away from my camera in my locker
and my project in the art room. "I have to go home," I said,
surprised that home was the place I wanted to go for comfort,
and even more surprised by the sureness of my voice.

"I know." He stroked my hair again. "Do you want me to
go with you?"

I could barely imagine what it would be like to go home
and not find Claire in her room, but as much as I wanted
Marcus to come with me, wanted to hold on to his arms and
never let go, I couldn't. I had to get away from everything.
Right now. "No. I need to go alone."

He opened his mouth to argue, but I held up a hand and
backed away.

CHAPTER FORTY

Each day it felt a little more real. Life quickly became busy and exhausting, with a million decisions to make for Claire's funeral. Mom spent many hours on the phone, on e-mail, or running between the funeral home, the church, and the florist. It seemed like there was no time to stop, no time to eat together, just barely enough time and energy to respond to messages of either disbelief or sympathy. The morning of Claire's funeral, when things were finally on track, Mom spoke to me for the first time in what felt like ages.

"Tell me where I failed, Loann," she said from the living room couch, staring across at a blank patch of wall. Her voice was as flat as the wall in front of her.

I fiddled with the buttons on my jacket, hoping the question would disappear. But it didn't. It just hung there, unavoidably stuck in midair between us like the Goodyear Blimp. I'd hoped for things to slow down enough for us to have a conversation, but this, this was too hard. I wanted to shrug my shoulders and grumble, "I don't know," like a normal teenager might answer a question about their weekend plans. But the truth was, I had a million questions of my own for her.

Why didn't you listen to me? Or to her? Why did you have to fight with Dad all the time and demand so much from everybody?

But would any of it have made a difference anyway?

"Where did I go wrong?" she asked, not willing to let it go. I could sense the wetness around her eyes, and suddenly I realized how much *she* was hurting about this. How much she had *always* been hurting over Claire, over me, over not feeling like a good enough Mom or wife or person.

It shocked me. My whole life Mom'd been confident. Able. Strong.

Dad appeared in a dark suit, mumbling something about starting the car. Even though he had been around the house every day for the last week, I barely noticed him. He didn't return phone calls or talk to pastors. I caught him staring at the wall or the washing machine or the flowers that had been delivered, but other than that, he never seemed to actually be *doing* anything. Both my parents were like walking outlines, moving through our house. No shades of gray or dimension to either of them.

I watched Dad go and was about to follow when Mom pushed again. "Loann, where did I go wrong?"

"Wrong?" It came out of my mouth as though I was too daft to grasp the English language. Mom didn't react, just kept shaking her head, then staring into space with tears rolling down her face.

"What's right or wrong anyway?" I said, not really knowing what I meant. "Can there even be right or wrong in this?" Nothing I could say would make her feel any better, but there really wasn't any way to feel better now anyway, was there?

Mom rubbed small circles on her forehead. I faced the window and went on, maybe for my own benefit.

"Were you supposed to tell her to eat? Was I supposed to yell and scream and follow her around all day long? Would she have listened to either of us? Maybe you're not a good mother, maybe I'm not a good sister, but exactly what part of this mess should Claire have been responsible for?" I choked on the last part. It felt like such blasphemy to say these things now. But they were true. And I, for one, needed to hear them.

The funeral was a big haze.

With the nice weather, my parents had opted for a graveside service. The first person I registered seeing was Shayleen.

"I'm so sorry," she said, coming right up to me with tears streaking her face. I accepted her expression of condolence. Friends or not friends, I believed she was sorry.

I couldn't concentrate on Shayleen, though, who was still saying something to me. My eyes went to the mounds of bright blossoms. To the open casket in the middle of them.

I couldn't see inside the casket from where I stood a few feet away, thank God, and I tried to focus on Shayleen, then Deirdre, who had appeared beside her.

Were they friends again? Had Claire's death done that? I knew these weren't big questions—I had so, so many bigger ones—but I couldn't help tilting my head and staring between the two girls.

I felt Marcus behind me before he touched my shoulder. I felt his strength. He'd wanted to come over every day of the past week, but I'd told him no over and over again. It just didn't seem like there was room in our house for anyone from the outside. My parents and I seemed to need all the space we could get. But now, looking up at Marcus, I realized how wrong I'd been.

I stared at him, feeling stronger by the second.

As if Shayleen and Deirdre could sense our need to be alone, they cleared away. Marcus led me back toward a tree, away from the casket and all the people, and suddenly my chest felt lighter.

He was wearing dark pants and a blue button-down shirt. He looked so handsome, and I found myself gazing absent-mindedly again, as I had with Shayleen and Deirdre.

Marcus cleared his throat. "Um, I brought this." He held up my camera.

I blinked hard. *He thought I wanted my camera? Now? Here? He thought I wanted to remember this?*

"Those pictures, I developed them, and you were right. They were . . ." He shook his head like he didn't have the words. I didn't know what he was talking about. He motioned over his shoulder toward the parking lot. "I tried to add them to your composite, but . . ." He shook his head again. "You'll be much better at placing them, I'm sure."

I looked down at my camera like it was covered in nuclear waste and took a step away from him. "You . . . developed those pictures? The ones in my camera?" My voice squeaked on the last word.

"Yeah, you wanted me to, right?"

I shook my head, but my throat had gone dry. I didn't know how I'd ever look at any pictures of Claire again, but just knowing *those* were in existence . . . I couldn't breathe. I grabbed my stomach. Marcus reached for my hand and started tugging me toward the parking lot. His eyebrows pulled together, so I could tell he had some sense that I was losing it, but I doubted he knew how much.

I yanked my hand away. "I can't—I can't see that right now!" How could I ever look at Claire's eyes crying out for help? It would be like driving a dull knife deep into my heart. "I need to get back." I pointed to where people were milling around, waiting for the service.

"It's not starting for a few minutes yet." Marcus looked at me even more confused. "Loann, it's . . . you'll see. I promise."

I shook my head again, but he held my hand and wouldn't let it go this time. I wanted to throw a tantrum like a two-year-old, anything to not have to face those pictures, but Marcus was so slow, so gentle, and his grip was so hard that, just for a second, I wanted to be led somewhere else. Somewhere away from my sister's casket.

Marcus let go of my hand when we arrived at his car and I thought I might collapse to the ground. Strangely, my legs held out. He opened his car door and leaned in. I felt frozen in place. I just wanted to dive into the passenger seat and tell him to get me out of here.

When he emerged from the car, Marcus was holding my art project. My montage. He laid it out on the hood of his car and motioned for me to come over.

"I can't . . ." Tears streamed down my face. "I can't see her right now. You don't understand. She . . . she needed me."

Marcus moved back to me and held both my hands in his. "You still need to see this, Loey." He nudged me forward a step, but stayed behind, a hand on each of my shoulders as though he had to hold me up. And he probably did.

The first thing I saw were Claire's eyes. It was a close-up from our last photo shoot. My mouth opened in shock. They weren't pleading, like I expected. They were deep, intricate, telling eyes. They had this vivid quality, and I expected them to blink, or to water.

I looked to another photo, her hand in her hair. Even though she'd been so sick, so weak, she looked like a super-model in the shot. There was no fear or insecurity.

In another, her mouth was pursed like she had an exciting secret.

A small cry escaped me and Marcus squeezed my shoulders. I reached forward and adjusted one of the pictures he had added so the *Y* in the word "Beauty" was visible.

"You captured so much of her," Marcus whispered.

I nodded. There was so much here—so much of her depth and her thoughts and her beauty, her complicated world. But everything I had, it still wasn't all of her. It still wasn't enough.

I moved another picture over, and then another, as if by moving them I might find more underneath. But only the cardboard backing showed through.

Marcus had set my camera down beside the montage. I reached for it and checked to make sure there was film inside. Backing up, I accidentally knocked into Marcus but he quickly moved out of my way. As I turned and strode for the service, he murmured something about taking care of the composite, but I couldn't hear him. I needed to find more of my sister before it was too late.

There was a line of people paying their respects at Claire's casket, but I didn't care. I looped around the other side and avoided people's eyes as they questioned me. They didn't understand. They couldn't. But I didn't care about anyone else today. I cared about Claire.

And there she was. I'd always heard that you could tell a person's spirit was gone when they were dead, that the reason an open casket brought so much peace was because you could truly tell they'd moved on.

I didn't believe that. Claire looked like she was sleeping. I felt like I needed to see her eyes to know what was in there or what wasn't. Her face looked pudgy, like it had when she'd come back from the clinic in California. Her lips were a dry, chalky pink and I wanted so badly to give her a swipe of lip gloss. She wore her favorite white capris, and even her ankles looked thick.

It was funny, but that's what finally did it. What gave me peace. Her ankles. Claire's ankles had never, ever been thick. I pulled my camera to my eye and zoomed in on them, ignoring the quiet gasps around me. I took several shots of her ankles, one of the back of her hand, scarred from sticking her finger down her throat, a close-up of her hairline, which, despite her scraggly, boyish cut, had always stayed the same. Then just one of her pudgy face.

I had backed fully away from the casket, ready to let other people take their turn, when my stomach started to clench inside me again. It still wasn't enough. A franticness rose within me and I scanned the crowd, which was now nearly a hundred people. I searched for familiarity, and took a shot of Deirdre, with her arms now around Shayleen. That was Claire. Claire had done that. Josh stood off to the side, alone, and he looked right at me when I took a shot of him. He reached up and squeezed his forehead. The look of torment on his face might have given me a moment of happiness two weeks ago. But not today. I took another shot, just to make sure I'd captured it.

I took a shot of Mom, holding the back of a chair so she wouldn't collapse, and Dad, looking toward his car. I wanted to yell at him to just go, leave, but even as I thought the words, I could feel his pain for the first time. He'd never been enough for any of us, and he knew it.

But I didn't have time to think about him.

I needed more of Claire before there wasn't any more to find.

I found Jasmine in the crowd and thought I might be done. But the second I pulled my camera from my face, I needed more.

I started to snap pictures of the flowers by the casket, of people in the crowd I didn't even know. It still wasn't enough.

I recognized the hands on my shoulders, but pulled away. I didn't want Marcus right now. I needed to do this.

My eyes roamed more frantically. "Did you bring more film?" I asked him, my tone all-business.

"Loann." He didn't speak again for several seconds. I didn't look over at him. The pastor was preparing to start the service, and I didn't have time for this. "Loann, there's no rush," Marcus said.

I snapped to him. "What do you mean, there's no rush? All there is now is rush. All of it's over, it's practically over, and I have nothing left!"

People looked over at us, and Marcus tugged me away from the crowd.

"I need to . . ." I scanned the crowd again, pulling back, but my eyes were teary and I couldn't see properly.

Marcus slid his arms around me, enveloping my shoulders, my arms, my hands, my camera. He held me tightly, and at first I squirmed to get away, but he just kept holding me tighter and tighter, and repeating my name, "Loey . . . Loey . . . Loey."

And then I stopped. I let out a big burst of a cry.

"I know," he said into my hair. "But you'll find more of her, I promise."

"Will I?" I needed him to tell me again. To keep telling me.

He nodded and I sank a little more into him. "Look how much you have already. And think of how many other boxes of photos are at home that you haven't even used, Loey."

My breathing slowed. I did have a lot of photos at home. A lot of different images of her that I hadn't looked at in a long time.

He motioned toward his car again. "And that alone will make an amazing scholarship project."

Marcus's words filled me with a sudden new pain. It didn't seem fair of me to go on to college when my sister couldn't. I couldn't do something she had never done. Would never be able to do. That's not the way it worked with us.

"It's going to be brilliant, Loey," he whispered in my ear. "So honest."

My back became warm against him, and suddenly I just wanted him closer, so much closer. I wanted to forget about everything else except him.

"And that's just one of the things I love about you," he whispered into my neck.

Suddenly I was too warm, and besides, I couldn't be thinking about him this way. Not right now. I cleared my throat and pulled away. "It's really cool of you to bring the camera and stuff," I said in a more composed tone, like I hadn't heard him.

Marcus stood there, blinking down at me, like what I was

saying wasn't quite registering. Finally he crossed his arms. "So." He paused. "We're friends."

I nodded. In the distance I heard the pastor inviting guests to take their seats for the start of the service. I fought between my responsible side, needing to be there, and the side of me that wanted to escape.

"Let's be honest, here." Marcus met my eyes again and I fought the urge to squirm. "Where do you see this going?" He motioned between me and him.

"When?" I blurted, barely believing he would push to talk about *this* now.

He squinted his eyes a little. "I don't know. Anytime. In a month. In a year. Ten years?" After a long pause, he added quietly, "Today."

When I didn't answer, he said, "Today, here, it just . . . it makes me realize I don't want to waste any more time."

"I'm just . . . I'm not ready," I said. But even as I said it, it felt like a lie.

Marcus thought about this for a long time. "I'm not Josh, you know," he said finally.

"I know that," I whispered. "It's . . . it's not him."

He took a step closer and lifted my hand. "So what is it?"

I loved the feel of his soft, warm hand, but the rest of my body went rigid. I didn't even know why until I opened my mouth and I said, loud and angry, "How can I be happy, how can I think about this, when my sister just died? When Claire won't *ever* get married or go to college or ever even love anybody the way I love you?" For the first time, I realized I already had something Claire did not. Would never have. The thought made me sick.

Marcus tugged me closer and rested his chin against my forehead. "Loann, you deserve to be happy." He sniffed and I realized he was crying too. I wanted so badly for him to crack a joke or mock me about something. But he just went on, in all seriousness. "Look, it doesn't have to be now. Not for me. But at some point, you will need to move forward without her. You're right. She's never going to go to college. She's never going to fall in love." Even though his voice was gentle, his words hit hard, like a hammer to my skull. "But you will. And you should." He swallowed loudly. "And now you have to do everything enough for both of you." His eyes bore into mine. "That's what Claire would have wanted."

Tears spilled down my face. Marcus reached up and wiped them away with his thumbs.

"It's not going to be as hard with us as you think. I promise, Curly."

He smirked a little, and I exploded in one single, breathy laugh. I was sure people in the service could hear me, but I didn't care. It felt good to release the tension. I nodded, still not pulling my eyes away. "Okay."

"Okay?" He raised his eyebrows.

I nodded. "Okay."

Marcus took a tiny step closer. It looked like he was fighting a smile, which made me struggle not to giggle, even though there was nothing remotely funny about the moment. It was just so strange, thinking about kissing my best friend for the first time.

But then it wasn't strange at all.

Marcus leaned in a little closer, and touched a feather-light kiss to my lips. Then another. I kissed him back, just as lightly, like we were afraid of breaking each other. Or afraid of something, anyway.

But the more he kissed me, the less scary or strange it felt. The more it felt like, *Of course this would happen.*

"I think we need a picture of this," Marcus said between kisses. "Of you and me. Like this."

He wanted a picture of this? Of kissing my best friend at my sister's funeral? What could be more perfectly morbid? What could be more appallingly inappropriate? But even as I asked myself these questions, the answer came to me.

Nothing is ever perfect. Not this. Not Claire. Certainly not any of the rest of my life.

Beauty isn't perfect. It's something to be felt and something to be breathed. Claire did that every day, whether she knew it or not.

And what I had with Marcus? It was more than just friendship or even a relationship. We were becoming two people who could really see each other. The way I wished Claire could have been seen. Somehow, what we had, it was going to be enough.

It had to be.

Because Marcus was right. Claire would have wanted this for me.

And now I had to live it all enough for both of us.

AUTHOR'S NOTE

Many of us have suffered from a food issue of some kind, whether it's cutting calories on a regular basis or trying to "make up" for a junk food binge. These are simple solutions, ones that don't seem dangerous or hard to control. I've personally struggled with my perception of healthy eating on and off for years. For me, conquering this has come only by way of self-acceptance, but even still, it seems more than possible that I might fall back into destructive patterns at any time.

When it comes to severe eating disorders, often we can't understand why some people won't just make better choices when it comes to food. I have known women who have suffered severely from eating disorders, and yes, it can be easy to judge. But our lack of understanding and compassion is one reason that so many people suffer alone, only letting their disorder become worse. An eating disorder gives a false sense of control, while in reality it's an all-consuming monster that wants to take over every bit of a person's life.

My first inspiration for writing this book was a close friend of mine who has suffered for many years from a combination of severe eating disorders. I didn't write this book to show or teach her anything. I wrote it because I wanted to understand her and connect with her in a way that would be helpful rather than hurtful.

My friend can't avoid food like she'd avoid cigarettes if she were quitting smoking. She has to face her addiction every day. Sure, it gets easier. But then sometimes it gets harder again. Above all, I'm glad I made a deeper connection with her and with others. Honesty among true friends can be a hard thing to come by, but it's worth the effort not to have to endure a lifelong battle alone. You may be surprised how accepting others can be. And then maybe you'll start accepting yourself.

It's estimated that more than eight million Americans suffer from an eating disorder, and eating disorders have the highest death rate among mental illnesses. The statistics are scary—don't try to battle it by yourself. And if you're not the one suffering, and someone comes to you admitting they have a problem, be a supportive friend. Encourage him or her to seek help, and then walk through it with them. Making the first move to be honest is hard, but I guarantee there's somebody in your life who really needs you.

And who knows? Maybe you need them too.

For more information on eating disorders, where to get help, or how to be a support to someone with an eating disorder, visit the National Eating Disorders Association at www.nationaleatingdisorders.org

ACKNOWLEDGMENTS

Maybe one day I'll be able to write a book with the help of only one or two people. Today is not that day.

Never Enough had been a work in progress since 2004. It has been through so many drafts and titles and characters that I've lost count, so you can only imagine how difficult it is to name every person who had a hand in helping with various versions of this manuscript. I apologize to those I miss. I am truly thankful to all of you that Loann finally has her place in this world. First of all, a humongous thank-you to anyone who has taken the time to pick up this book or my debut novel, *Losing Faith*. I know there are mounds of wonderful new books coming out every year, and it means more to me than I can say that you've given my book a chance. You people are what dreams are made of. Thank you.

Heartfelt thanks also:

To Annette Pollert for finding my vision in my mess of pages, and for helping me bring it to life. Thank you so much for your time and unending energy on this book.

To Anica Rissi for always being such a strong supporter

and champion of my work and, really, for being such a darn cool person.

To the amazing Pulse team. I still have yet to meet many of you, but I'm so thankful for everything you do to bring my books into the world.

To Michelle Humphrey, agent extraordinaire, who leads me and protects me and offers me stellar editorial advice. She also advises on such important matters as which particular sweets we will celebrate each happy milestone with. (I'm waiting to hear from you on this one, Michelle. . . .)

To my incredibly talented writer friends, whose advice can be seen in these pages: Shana Silver (who deserves an extra-special shout-out for her insight, many hours of close examination, and last-minute saves—this girl needs to become an editor!), Elle Strauss, Caroline Starr Rose, Craig Pirrall, Tara Kelly, Amy Brecount-White, Margie Gelbwasser, Pendred Noyce, Jennifer Hoffine, Shari Green, Sharon Knauer, Pam, Katie, Lorrie, Maria, Angela, Lucie, Bonnie, Don, Joel, Stacey, James, and the whole Critique Circle gang.

To my writing community friends, the Class of 2k10, the Tenners, the Blueboarders, my Blogger friends, my Twitter friends, the Teenlitauthors, and my LiveJournal friends. You make my life fun and teach me so much.

To the awe-inspiring book blogger community, as well as teachers, librarians, and booksellers: Thank you for all you do to spread the word about YA books, especially the books of new and up-and-coming authors. Thank you, thank you, thank you!

To my high school drama teacher, Terry McLellan, for making my high school years bearable, and for being the coolest teacher ever.

Thanks always to my family: Ted, Teddy, Mom, Brent, Jody, Harry, Shelly, Kim, Duane, Bruce, and Lynda—your support means the world to me (and special thanks to Lynda and Jody, whose babysitting efforts helped me complete my revisions on time).

During the editing of this book, my dad passed away in a sudden accident. He was one of the biggest influences in every part of my life, and so, of course, he needs to be included here. But a simple thank-you is not enough. There's a special book coming for you, Dad. Just letting that one brew . . .

A terrible secret.
A terrible fate.

DON'T MISS
denise jaden's
LOSING FAITH

*t*he statue has got to go.

That's my first thought as I prep the living room for Dustin's visit later tonight. I know I'm the only one who would notice the discriminating eyes of Mom's four-inch Jesus staring down from the mantel. Dustin probably wouldn't look away from my breasts if the room were two feet deep in holy water. Still, I reach for it.

When my hand fumbles and the statue topples sideways, I pick the thing up and scan the hearth for any other too-holy housewares.

"What are you doing?" My older sister rushes in from the kitchen, scuffles across the carpet, and ignites a spark when she snatches the statue out of my hand. She settles it back into its ring of dust, adjusting it to its all-seeing viewpoint, and then eases her hand away like she's afraid the thing might fly right up to heaven. Turning, she glares at me.

Great. Caught in the act of abducting a religious icon. Not exactly the act I feared being caught in tonight.

"Actually, Faith"—I stare into her eyes so she won't miss this—"I was wondering if you could give me a lift to the church."

As expected, her whole face lights up, and I'm tempted to let her believe she's finally fished her heathen sister out of the sea of despair. It's better than telling her the truth.

"Amy's going to meet me at a coffee shop near there," I add. Not complete honesty, but close enough.

"Oh." Her face falls. "I'm not sure, Brie. I mean, I wasn't going to—" She flicks her fingernail against her thumb a few times and looks away.

She wasn't going to what? Wasn't going to youth group like she has every single Friday night since she was born? I glance at the clock above her head. Good thing Dustin's not waiting down the street somewhere, which was my initial idea. But me staying home alone on a Friday night would be far from ordinary and I don't want to raise anyone's suspicions. I stare back at Faith until she goes on.

"Celeste doesn't want to go, my car's out of gas, and I can't find my Bible." She starts for the kitchen. "Sorry, Brie, I'm not going tonight."

Usually, I strategize about as well as a fly caught in a screen door. But tonight I had taken the initiative to plan something nice—really nice—for Dustin, and tonight, of all nights, Faith's turning into someone I don't even know. What happened to her Big Salvation Plan, the one that wraps around her life in giant, multicolored jawbreaker layers of certainty?

I can't do anything about Celeste cutting out on her. They argued on the phone earlier and I learned a long time ago that I don't understand their friendship well enough to get involved. But I can fix other problems. I reach for my purse. "I have gas money."

She stops in the kitchen doorway.

I dig out the only bill I can find, walk toward her, and push it at her chest. She looks down at my hand like it's covered in warts.

"I know it's only five bucks, but that'll at least get your car to the church and back, right?" Heading to the bookshelves in the living room, I scrunch my nose because the dog, curled up on the couch, must have farted. I pull off a Bible with *Brie Jenkins* inscribed in the bottom corner of its black leather cover. "Here," I say, coughing from the flutters of dust. "Take mine."

"That's a King James Version," Faith says. "I really need my N.I.V."

Faith and her New International Version. Like it matters. And here I thought getting my parents out of the house would be the hard part, but they left before six, barely taking time to say good-bye. When I don't move my outstretched hand, Faith lets out a sigh and takes my Bible from me.

She opens it, apparently figuring this is the perfect time for her daily devotional, and I call the dog to get him and his raunchy smell out of here. "Nuisance, here, boy."

Our overweight golden retriever has selective hearing. It's probably too late anyway; Dustin will certainly end up with blond dog hair all over his pants, but I want to at least try to give the cushions a once-over with the lint roller.

I pry my fingers under the dog's mass, using all my weight to lug him off. He takes my gesture as an attempt to play and jumps up, frothing all over my freshly made-up face. I fall on my butt and let out a giggly yelp. When I look up, expecting to see Faith laughing, she just stares into the open Bible, and nibbles on her lip.

She shakes her head, and at first I think it's at me and my stupid predicament, but then she flips the page and scowls hard down at the words. I'm baffled, since I can't imagine her disagreeing with anything in The Good Book.

The loops of her blond hair mimic the paisley wallpaper behind her. It's hard to remember when my hair used to be even curlier, before Amy permanently lent me her straightening iron. It takes me a second to notice Faith's whole body trembling.

"Faith, what's—"

"Nothing." She snaps the book shut, and heads for the foyer. Her renewed determination makes me wonder if it had been my eyes that were trembling. "You wanted a ride, right? Let's go."

I follow her, but she picks up the hall phone and dials while she slips on her shoes.

"Oh, good, you're still there," she says into the handset. "I'm driving my sister to the church, so I think I am going to go. That's my sign." Her forehead creases as she stares at the floor listening.

At least she doesn't sound angry with Celeste anymore. Though she doesn't exactly sound cheery either.

"Nothing dangerous, but I need you, Celeste," Faith prods.

I wonder what kind of crazy, shake-in-your-shoes idea the church has planned for them tonight. Perhaps they'll play tag in the parking lot in bare feet.

When she glances up from her call and notices I'm still there, she whispers, "Hold on," into the receiver and moves down the hall with the phone pressed to her chest.

Fine. Not like I wanted to listen in on *that* conversation anyway. I open the door, calling, "Don't worry about me. I'll just be in the car," loud enough so they can both hear me.

Whatever. So what if they don't want me in their stupid inner circle. My own circle's coming together and it'll be much better than their little saintly one.

I collapse into the front seat of her Toyota and decide once again that I'll have to try harder to get Dad to take me driving so I can finally get my license. Then I won't have to ask Faith for anything, won't have to concern myself with what she and her friends are up to. Swiping the chip bags from around my feet, I shove them into her already full garbage bag. As I reach for one more wrapper on the dash, a new sticker above the stereo catches my eye. Or at least it wasn't here the last time I was in this traveling garbage dump. The round yellow sticker has an artsy cross on it. Almost scribbled-looking, but pre-printed on there.

Faith slides into the driver's seat and I'm about to reprimand her for defacing her vehicle—I mean, at least she has one—but I stop myself when I see the tense look on her face.

"All worked out?" I ask, even though I know Faith almost always gets her way with Celeste.

"You need a ride home, too?" she asks, backing out and then driving down the street with her eyes straight ahead. Her fingers grip the steering wheel at ten and two like it's a life preserver.

"No. Amy'll drop me." I haven't thought of a reason why *Amy* couldn't pick me up, and I hope Faith won't think to ask.

Her hands loosen and drop to the lower half of the wheel. She nods, apparently relieved that I'm not going to be any more of a burden. For a second I wonder why things had to change between us. Why aren't we still friends, or at least siblings who can have a normal conversation? But the thought is gone as soon as it enters my head.

After stopping at the corner gas station, she reaches to turn on the radio, confirming there'll be no sisterly chatter on the car ride over. Once she starts singing along, I decide I much prefer listening to her singing voice over arguing with her anyway. I nudge the radio volume down. Faith is used to this move of mine, and keeps singing without any reaction. And this is the way I like her voice—not tied to her church worship group or up on stage with everyone staring in amazement. Just her singing and me listening.

We pull into the large church parking lot, and Faith backs into a spot near the perimeter. She turns off the engine and we sit there, both staring ahead at the looming steeple.

"You okay, then?" Faith asks after several seconds.

I take that as my cue to reach for the door handle. "Sure." Something in me wonders if I should ask her the same question. "Are you—"

But a dark-haired girl with a ponytail scurries over to the driver's side and interrupts us. "Faith, oh my gosh, it's so good to see you!"

Faith and I get out on either side, and I raise my eyebrows. Only at church can people get so excited to see each other after only a day or two apart.

"Oh, you brought your sister." The girl nods approvingly.

I pull my arms across my chest and feel the scratchy condom wrapper I'd stashed in my bra. More teens move in toward Faith, toward us, and I get a mental picture of them grabbing my hands and singing "Kumbaya."

And just then, Faith's dark-haired friend makes her way around the car with a hand outstretched. I stare down at it.

"I'm not staying," I say, tucking my hands behind my back. "I mean, I'm meeting someone . . . over there." I point over my shoulder. "Thanks for the ride," I call out, but Faith waves me off, since she's now surrounded by several of her elated youth-group buddies.

I dash across the street and make a show of ducking into the Rio Café. After waiting a few minutes to make sure it's safe, I slip out into the dark alley alongside the coffee shop and race through to the next street over. The street is deserted and I hug my purse to my chest. I wish Dustin could pick me up in front of the coffee shop, but I can't chance Faith catching sight of me heading back to the house with my boyfriend.

I slink into the shadow of the art supplies store so I won't be obvious to any stray, lonely men driving past, and pull out my cell phone. After checking the street sign, I text Dustin with the coordinates.

I snap my phone shut and blow on my sweaty palms. *What if I'm not ready?* Dustin's been patient—too patient,

Amy says. And now that I've given him so many hints, how could I say no?

I won't, I decide only a second later. Even though I'm not completely at ease with this, who is, their first time?

I look up just in time to see a familiar red Toyota sail by. The smiley antenna ball catches my attention, and I squint at the back of a blond curly head in the driver's seat. It's Faith.

Worse, she's headed back in the direction of our house. There goes my special night with Dustin. Though the thought does make my racing heart slow a little.

When Dustin's lights gleam around the corner and onto the deserted street where I wait, I put Faith out of my mind. I paste on a smile, smooth down my straightened hair with both hands, and step out of the shadows into the bright lights.

ABOUT THE AUTHOR

Denise Jaden spent her high school lunch hours trying to tame her frizzy/curly hair in the bathroom or playing freeze tag in the drama room. She attended the theater program at college, and then enjoyed a variety of occupations, including stage production, mushroom farming, and Polynesian dancing. The first draft of her debut novel, *Losing Faith*, was written in twenty-one days during National Novel Writing Month. This is her second novel. She lives just outside Vancouver, Canada, with her husband, son, and an overweight shih tzu. Find out more online at www.denisejaden.com or follow her on Twitter at @denisejaden.

simonTeen

Simon & Schuster's **Simon Teen**
e-newsletter delivers current updates on
the hottest titles, exciting sweepstakes, and
exclusive content from your favorite authors.

Visit **TEEN.SimonandSchuster.com** to
sign up, post your thoughts, and find out what
every avid reader is talking about!